THE GHOST
AND WEDNESDAY'S CHILD

HAUNTING DANIELLE

THE GHOST OF MARLOW HOUSE

THE GHOST WHO LOVED DIAMONDS

THE GHOST WHO WASN'T

THE GHOST WHO WANTED REVENGE

THE GHOST OF HALLOWEEN PAST

THE GHOST WHO CAME FOR CHRISTMAS

THE GHOST OF VALENTINE PAST

THE GHOST FROM THE SEA

THE GHOST AND THE MYSTERY WRITER

THE GHOST AND THE MUSE

THE GHOST WHO STAYED HOME

THE GHOST AND THE LEPRECHAUN

THE GHOST WHO LIED

THE GHOST AND THE BRIDE

THE GHOST AND LITTLE MARIE

THE GHOST AND THE DOPPELGANGER

THE GHOST OF SECOND CHANCES

THE GHOST WHO DREAM HOPPED

THE GHOST OF CHRISTMAS SECRETS

THE GHOST WHO WAS SAY I DO

THE GHOST AND THE BABY

THE GHOST AND THE HALLOWEEN HAUNT

THE GHOST AND THE CHRISTMAS SPIRIT

THE GHOST AND THE SILVER SCREAM

THE GHOST OF A MEMORY

THE GHOST AND THE WITCHES' COVEN

THE GHOST AND THE MOUNTAIN MAN

THE GHOST AND THE BIRTHDAY BOY

THE GHOST AND THE CHURCH LADY

THE GHOST AND THE MEDIUM

THE GHOST AND THE NEW NEIGHBOR

THE GHOST AND THE WEDDING CRASHER

THE GHOST AND THE TWINS

THE GHOST AND THE POLTERGEIST

THE GHOST WHO SOUGHT REDEMPTION

THE GHOST AND WEDNESDAY'S CHILD

THE GHOST AND CHRISTMAS MAGIC

HAUNTING DANIELLE - BOOK 36

THE GHOST
AND WEDNESDAY'S CHILD

USA TODAY BESTSELLING AUTHOR
BOBBI HOLMES

The Ghost and Wednesday's Child
(Haunting Danielle, Book 36)
A Novel
By Bobbi Holmes
USA TODAY BESTSELLING AUTHOR
Cover Design: Elizabeth Mackey

ROBETH
PUBLISHING, LLC

ISBN: 978-1-949977-82-0
A

Dedicated to Mom…gee, Mom, I dedicated two books in a row to you. You were standing at the door to your next adventure, waiting to move on, when I wrote the last dedication. That long goodbye. It's been six months since you went through that door. I miss our visits and holding your hand. While I missed you back then, I miss you more now. Love you. Please visit me in a dream hop.

ONE

Traci Lind glanced in the rearview mirror to Christopher in the back seat as she turned onto Beach Drive. She had expected him to wake up by now; they had been driving for hours. As they passed the pier, she noticed the sign for Pier Café. She was hungry.

But before they could eat, she wanted to find Marlow House. From what she'd read online, it wasn't far from the pier. Slowing her car, she continued down the street, her attention on the row of west-facing houses. Then she saw it. Stopping in front of the distinctive Second Empire mansard house, she noticed the sign out front confirming the house's identity.

"I got to go to the bathroom," a small voice from the back seat said.

Traci looked in the mirror; she saw Christopher squirming in his car seat, his little hands attempting to unbuckle himself from its confines. She glanced from the rearview mirror back to Marlow House and realized she couldn't knock on their front door and start the conversation with *we need to use your bathroom*. She then remembered the sign for Pier Café.

"Hold on, Christopher." Traci pulled back into the street while turning around, heading her car toward the pier. "We're stopping to get something to eat, and you can go to the bathroom there."

TWENTY MINUTES LATER, Traci sat in the booth of Pier Café, looking over the menu, while Christopher sat next to her in the booster seat, eating the oyster crackers a purple-haired server had given them when they first sat down. They had made two stops since leaving California on Thursday, staying overnight in inexpensive motels, their sole sustenance being the peanut butter sandwiches Traci had prepared before leaving for Oregon.

But Traci couldn't stomach one more peanut butter sandwich, and by the way Christopher picked at the sandwich she'd given him for lunch earlier that day, she suspected he felt the same way.

Traci folded the menu and placed it on the table. She looked at the young boy next to her. Large for his age, most people assumed he was several years older than his four years. His vocabulary and manner of speech was also mature for his age. Mrs. Brown said it was because he spent most of his time with adults.

"Would you like a grilled cheese sandwich for dinner? And some french fries?" Traci asked him.

Christopher smiled up at Traci. "I don't have to have peanut butter again?"

Traci laughed. "No. You certainly don't. It will be a long time before either of us wants another peanut butter sandwich."

The next moment, the server who had given Christopher the crackers showed up at their table. Traci looked up at the young woman with the purple hair, order pad and pen in hand.

"Are you ready to order yet?" the server asked while flashing Christopher a grin before looking back to Traci.

"Yes, I—" Traci began only to stop mid-sentence when the server joined her in the booth. She sat across from Traci on the bench, facing her.

"I hope you don't mind if I sit down while I take your order. My feet are killing me. I swear, this place has been packed all day. My name is Carla, by the way. Now, what can I get you?"

Startled by Carla's introduction, Traci stared for a moment but then blinked several times and told Carla what she and Christopher wanted for dinner.

After scribbling down the order, Carla set the pad on the table with the pen atop it. She looked up to Traci, obviously in no hurry to get up and put in the order. "Are you visiting Frederickport? I've never seen you in here before."

Traci smiled at Carla, wondering if this might be a perfect opportunity to get the information she needed. "Yes. We're traveling through Frederickport on our way to visit family. I need someplace to stop for the night, and a friend told me about Marlow House; I hoped we could stay there. We've been moteling it, and frankly, a B and B sounded nice. But we drove by. It doesn't seem to be open."

Carla shrugged. "Yeah, I can't keep up with when they're open or not. When Danielle and Walt, that's who owns Marlow House, got married, they closed it down for a while. Was some issue with zoning. But then they reopened, yet now it's closed again, I'm pretty sure. Danielle had twins not long ago, and I doubt they want to deal with B and B guests right now. And it's not like they need the money."

"Oh, well, that's too bad. I was also hoping to ask them about one of their guests. He's the friend who told me about Marlow House in the first place. We sort of lost track, and the last time we spoke, he was coming up here. Of course, they may not remember him."

"Really? I might know him. I've probably met everyone who's stayed at Marlow House. They all come in here." Carla smiled.

"His name is Chris Johnson and—"

"Chris!"

"You know him?" Traci asked, thinking this was too good to be true. However, not surprising, she reminded herself, considering women always seemed to remember Chris.

"Why, sure. He's a friend of mine. In fact, he lives on Beach Drive, right down the street."

Traci sat up straighter. "He lives down the street? At Marlow House?"

Carla shook her head. "No. He has his own house. Although, he has sort of lived at Marlow House off and on."

"I'd love to see him. Not today, but when I come back through." Traci didn't want to sound too eager to see him. People often clammed up when strangers started asking too many questions about friends, especially concerning the friend's whereabouts.

"You could always contact his work," Carla suggested.

"Where does he work?"

"At the Glandon Foundation."

Traci shrugged. "I don't know what that is."

"It's a philanthropic organization in Frederickport. Basically, they give away money."

"Interesting," Traci muttered.

"Or surprise him and drop by his house. It's close to here, on the opposite side of the street from Marlow House. It's the newest house on Beach Drive."

TRACI PULLED her car up in front of Marlow House, made a U-turn, and parked in front of the house across the street. From what Carla had told her, Chris's was the newest house on the opposite side of the street from Marlow House. This house was definitely newer than all the others she had passed since leaving the pier.

"Are we going to a motel now?" Christopher asked from the back seat. "I want to watch TV."

"We have to stop and see someone first," Traci told him as she got out of the car, slamming the door behind her. She opened a back passenger door and helped Christopher out of his car seat. After closing his car door, she took Christopher's hand and walked with him to the front door.

By the cars in the driveway, Traci assumed someone was home. After she reached the front porch, she rang the doorbell. A few moments later, a petite redhead opened the door.

"Can I help you with something?" the woman asked.

Traci hadn't considered Chris might live with a woman now. But that didn't matter; she had to do this. After glancing around briefly, she looked back to the woman at the door and said, "I'm looking for Chris Johnson's house. I was told he lived along this section of Beach Drive. They said his house was one of the newer ones and faced the ocean."

"Umm, we recently remodeled our house, so I guess it looks newer than some of the other houses in the neighborhood. And you are?"

"So this is Chris Johnson's house?"

"No."

"Can you tell me which house is his?"

"And you are?" the woman asked again.

Traci stared at the woman for a moment and didn't answer. Instead, she said, "Come on, Christopher; this is the wrong house."

———

LILY ALMOST CALLED out to the young woman who rushed away, child in hand. But then she heard her sister, Laura, call out to her. Lily's parents had arrived that afternoon to meet their new granddaughter, and minutes earlier her sister-in-law, Kelly, had showed up with a surprise, the surprise being Lily's sister, Laura, who had just returned from Europe.

Lily closed the front door and returned to her houseguests, yet she was still curious about the woman looking for Chris, and wondered if she should call him. Laura asked who was at the door.

"I'm not sure," Lily muttered while walking to the living room window and looking outside. In the background, noisy chatter continued among her family members—with some talking about Laura's surprise return from Europe, others asking who had been at the door.

———

TRACI HAD FASTENED Christopher back into his car seat and was already sitting in the driver's seat, ready to put her key in the ignition, when she looked in the rearview mirror and spied a man walking up Beach Drive. She froze. *It can't be this simple,* she told herself. Silently she watched as a man who looked exactly like the Chris Johnson she had known crossed the street and headed to Marlow House.

UPSTAIRS in the nursery of Marlow House, Danielle had just finished breastfeeding the twins. Marie Nichols's ghost, an unlikely nanny, helped Danielle by changing Jack's diaper while Danielle attended to Addison's.

"Are you sure you'll be okay up here with them?" Danielle asked Marie before picking up a freshly diapered and dressed Addison and kissing her brow.

"Of course, dear. Lily certainly doesn't need my help; she has her mother over there. And you should go down and have some adult time with your friends."

Mediums Chris Johnson, aka Chris Glandon, and Heather Donovan, along with Heather's boyfriend, Brian Henderson, were coming over this evening to have dinner with Walt and Danielle. Brian had insisted on treating this evening and would bring takeout from a new Thai food restaurant in town.

"Thanks, Marie." Danielle gave each baby a final kiss before grabbing her cellphone off the dresser and heading into the hallway. The moment she stepped outside the nursery, the phone rang. She looked at it. Lily was calling.

"Hey, Lily," Danielle answered while walking down the hall toward the staircase.

"Hey, Dani. Something weird happened."

"Weird what?"

"A couple of minutes ago, a woman knocked on the door, looking for Chris. She's got a little boy with her, and his name happens to be Christopher. He looks to be about six. I'm watching her now."

"Watching her where? What did she say?"

Lily quickly explained the brief encounter and then added, "She's still sitting in her car. Chris just walked into your house… wait…she's driving away…she just turned her car around and is parking on your side of the street…she's getting out of the car. Looks like she's taking the boy out of the back seat."

Instead of continuing to the staircase, Danielle turned and walked into her bedroom. She looked out her window to the street and spied the woman standing by the open door to the back seat of her car, her back to Danielle.

"I can't see her face."

"Let me know what she wants. I'm curious."

"Lily, I came all the way from Europe to see you, and you get on the phone?" Danielle heard a voice say.

"Who was that?" Danielle asked.

"Oh, I forgot to tell you, Dani, Laura's here."

"Your sister?"

"Yeah. I'd better get off the phone. Let me know who the woman is."

No longer talking on the phone, Danielle left her bedroom and started for the staircase again. By the time she was halfway down the stairs, she spied Chris standing in the foyer, talking to Walt. She called out to them. They both looked up and smiled, and then the doorbell rang.

Chris said something to Walt, and the next moment, Chris went to answer the door while Walt walked towards the stairs. Danielle was about to call out to Chris again, she wanted to give him a heads-up about who was at the door, but he had already turned his back to her.

TWO

C hris threw open the door at Marlow House, expecting to see Brian standing on the front porch with dinner, but instead he found himself looking at a young, twenty-something woman, holding the hand of a young boy, with her other hand holding a large manila envelope. The woman said nothing but stared at Chris.

Chris smiled. "Hello?"

"Hello, Chris." The woman's tone was flat, expressionless, her eyes never leaving his face.

Chris frowned. "Do I know you?" Before she could answer, he blurted, "Traci?"

"So you do remember."

"What are you doing here?"

Traci glanced down at the boy at her side before looking back at Chris. "I've brought you your son."

Chris frowned. "Excuse me?"

Motion behind Chris caught her attention—a man and woman stood several feet behind him in the entry hall. The couple appeared to be listening to her and Chris's conversation. She looked at Chris. "Maybe we can go somewhere to talk. Privately."

Chris glanced over his shoulder. Walt and Danielle stood about six feet behind him.

Danielle nodded to the nearby door. "You can use the parlor."

Chris led the woman and child to the parlor while Walt and Danielle retreated to the living room, each wondering what was going on.

Once inside the parlor, Traci told the boy to go sit quietly on a chair on the other side of the room. After shutting the parlor door, Chris turned to Traci and asked, "What is this about?"

"Your son. Although you probably didn't know if he was a boy or girl since you took off the minute you discovered you were going to be a father."

Frowning, Chris looked from Traci to the boy sitting on the other side of the room and back to Traci. "I don't know what this is about, but you and I, never. And with DNA, not sure what kind of scam you're trying to pull."

"Oh stop. Please. Do you even care that Bridget is dead?"

"Bridget? Bridget is dead?"

Traci nodded. "Yes. And I didn't sign up for this. When I agreed to be Christopher's guardian if something happened to Bridget—"

"Who is Christopher?" he interrupted.

"Your son, of course. Just stop. Time to take responsibility for once in your life. When I agreed to be Christopher's guardian, I always assumed there would be money to support him. I can't do it. I can barely support myself." She abruptly pushed the large envelope into his hands before rushing from the room.

Chris stood silently and looked down at the large fat envelope in his hand. A moment later, Walt and Danielle walked into the room. Danielle glanced over to the young boy still sitting quietly in the chair, watching them.

"What's going on? She just left," Danielle whispered.

Shaking himself out of his momentary stupor, Chris turned from Walt and Danielle and raced from the room out into the entry hall and to the front door. He swung open the door in time to see Traci driving down the street in her car, the child still sitting quietly in the parlor. It wasn't until her car was out of sight that he noticed the suitcase and child's car seat sitting on the sidewalk in front of Marlow House.

CHRIS AND WALT stood in the dining room, the papers from the envelope Traci had given Chris now strewn all over the dining room table, as Chris tried to understand what had just happened.

Minutes earlier, Danielle had quietly introduced herself to Christopher and soon discovered he liked chocolate cake. He now sat in the kitchen with Danielle, eating a large slice of chocolate cake and drinking a glass of milk.

"SO YOU AND THIS BRIDGET, never? Are you sure?" Walt asked as he gave the papers a second look.

"Lord, no." Chris cringed and shook his head. "I think I would remember something like that. Oh, she was beautiful, and she made it abundantly clear that if I wanted to—but she was a kid. Barely eighteen."

"As I recall, Seraphina wasn't much older than eighteen," Walt reminded him.

"Yeah, well, Seraphina was worlds more mature than Bridget, and me and Seraphina, well, we didn't either."

Walt let out a sigh. "So there is no chance you could have fathered Bridget's child? Perhaps one time you had too much to drink?"

"And she seduced me?" Chris snorted.

Walt shrugged. "Well, it can happen."

Chris shook his head. "No. I haven't been that drunk since high school. Never liked the feeling of being out of control. And you know drugs aren't my thing. No."

One document on the table was Christopher's birth certificate. Walt picked it up and examined it again. He looked at Chris. "She didn't list you on the birth certificate as the father, and other than naming her son after you, she gave him her last name. If she planned to claim you as the father, why not list you on the birth certificate?"

"From what I understand, an unmarried woman can only add the father's name to the birth certificate if the father agrees. If he doesn't agree, then it requires a DNA test. At least, that's what one of my friends told me when she was dealing with the reluctant father of her child."

Walt tossed the birth certificate back on the table and then picked up another document and silently reread it. The document was an affidavit signed by Bridget Singer, swearing that Chris Johnson, the man who lived at the Dana Point Marina from mid-July to early December 2014, in the sailboat once owned by Tad Gaines, was the father of her son, Christopher Singer, born June 15, 2015.

After setting the document back on the table, Walt picked up a stack of legal-sized pages all stapled together. They appeared to be a copy of Bridget Singer's will. In the will, Bridget assigned Traci Lind as her son's legal guardian.

Walt set the will back on the table and picked up another document, which didn't seem as official as the first affidavit signed by Bridget, swearing to the identity of her child's father, nor her last will and testament, which he had just looked at. This document was a typed statement that read, *I, Traci Lind, the guardian of Christopher Singer, being of sound mind, transfer the guardianship of Christopher Singer to his father, Chris Johnson. And by doing so, I relinquish all responsibility to the child.* Traci signed it, yet it didn't include any contact information for Traci, a date, or any witness signatures. It looked like something she'd written on her computer and printed off at home before signing.

WHEN FIRST SETTING off for Oregon, Traci did not know how any of this would turn out, nor was she certain she would find Chris in Frederickport. She had simply been following the breadcrumbs. The letter she had typed up transferring Christopher's guardianship to Chris had been more of an affirmation exercise, putting out into the universe what she hoped to accomplish. She only added it to the envelope with Christopher's other documents at the last moment, never intending to give it to anyone.

But when she stood in that room at Marlow House with Chris and realized he had not changed—he was still that irresponsible, too handsome for his own good, who thought he could skate by in life using charms and good looks while letting someone else foot the bill —she knew there was no way he was going to step up and do the right thing. At least, not willingly.

So she made an impulsive decision and shoved the envelope into Chris's hands and then ran. By the time she reached her car, she was grateful she had put Christopher's suitcase in the back seat after leaving the motel that morning. It took her just a moment to grab it from the car and leave it on the sidewalk along with his car seat. She had stuffed the car keys in her pocket after parking at Marlow House before shoving her purse under the passenger seat. So she was spared searching for the car keys in the bottom of her messy purse before making her escape.

As she approached the city limits of Frederickport, she started regretting her rash decision. Needing to think this thing through before driving any farther, she made an impromptu right on the next road. She drove a half mile or more before steering her car to the side of the desolate road and parking. For as far as she could see, there were no buildings along this stretch of road. And so far, no other vehicles.

Glancing out the windshield, she wondered when it was going to get dark. Considering it was August, she figured she had at least an hour before sunset. But she needed some fresh air so she could think.

Getting out of her car, Traci walked over to the other side of the vehicle, away from traffic. Not that there was any. But if a car happened by, she didn't feel like getting mowed down. *Is Chris calling the police on me right now?* she asked herself while pacing back and forth beside her car. She paused a moment from her pacing and looked in the direction where she had just come. *Will the authorities see this as child abandonment? Could I get sent to jail?* Traci resumed the pacing, the fingers of her right hand now combing through her hair in agitation. She continued to pace.

She didn't notice the approaching car right away, not until it pulled up behind her vehicle and stopped. *They probably think I broke down and need help*, she thought as she turned to the gray sedan just in time to see a man wearing dark glasses getting out of the driver's side of the car while a second man, also wearing dark glasses, got out of the passenger's side. Both men wore suits.

"I'M OKAY. I don't need help," she called out just before the man who had gotten out of the passenger side of the sedan pulled a revolver from beneath his jacket and aimed it at her. She didn't have time to register what was happening, for in the next moment a lone bullet flew through her forehead, propelling her body backwards. Traci landed alongside her vehicle, her body now hidden, should any cars drive by.

The assassin returned the revolver to the holster under his jacket and sprinted to the woman, whose dead eyes looked up to the sky. By the bloody bullet wound in the center of her forehead, he was certain she was dead. But he would check her pulse in a moment to make sure, but first he needed the boy. He looked in the side passenger window, prepared to open the door, but froze when he saw there was no one in the back seat.

Frantic, he moved to the front passenger door and threw it open. The front seat was also empty. He glanced back to his companion, who stood by their vehicle, prepared to tell any car that might come by that they had everything under control, should someone stop and ask if they needed help. But so far, no cars had driven by.

He knelt down by the woman and checked her pulse. As suspected, she was dead. While kneeling on the ground, he looked back into the car, its passenger car door still open. He spied a purse tucked partially under the passenger seat. He grabbed her purse, rummaged through it, took her wallet, and then shoved the purse back where he had found it. After slamming the car door shut, he reached under the carriage and found the tracking device they had placed on the car at the first motel she had stayed at after leaving San Clemente.

DAZED, Traci opened her eyes and found herself lying on the ground next to her car. Just as she sat up, she saw a pair of gloved hands wrapped around her ankles. Stunned, she watched the man attached to the hands wearing the gloves pick her up. In the next moment, she watched her body lifting from the ground.

None of it made sense. Because her body was still there, on the side of the road next to her car, as it had been moments before the gloved hands grabbed hold of her ankles. For a moment, she seemed to have two sets of legs—and then she had just one again.

Minutes later, she heard what sounded like an engine revving, followed by tires screeching as a car sped away.

THREE

C hris sat at the dining room table and pulled out his cellphone. The papers that had been in the envelope brought by Traci remained strewn across the table. He looked at his phone and began searching online.

"Who are you calling?" Walt asked, still standing by the table.

"Not calling anyone. I'm seeing what I can find out about Bridget. Is she really dead?"

"Do you want me to put the papers back in the envelope?" Walt asked.

Chris nodded while continuing to search on his cellphone. "Yeah. Might as well. I'm done looking at them for now."

Walt gathered up the papers, folding each one neatly before returning it to the envelope, when Chris said, "I found Bridget's obituary. Looks like she died three months ago."

After Walt finished putting all the papers back in the envelope, Chris said, "This explains one thing."

Envelope in hand, Walt looked at Chris. "What?"

Chris set his cellphone on the table and looked up to Walt. "If Bridget was really dead, as Traci claimed, I didn't understand why she had the boy, and not the grandparents. One thing I remember about Bridget, her parents doted on her. She was an only child and spoiled. The last time I saw her, she was still living with her parents and had no plans to get her own place. I suspect her father would have paid for her apartment if she wanted to move out, but she always enjoyed the perks of living at her parents' estate, which included several live-in maids and a chef."

"Sounds like the parents were comfortable."

Chris chuckled. "Not like my parents, but yeah. And if their princess showed up pregnant, I don't see them kicking out their unwed daughter. I can see her mother hiring a designer to remodel one room into a nursery."

"So why did this Traci have the child and not the grandparents?"

"According to the obituary, the parents predeceased her. And my guess it was before Bridget wrote that will. I can't imagine in what world Bridget would assign Traci as guardian to her son as long as her parents were still alive. Which means that kid sitting in the kitchen has lost his mom and maternal grandparents. And just who is his dad?" Chris leaned back in the dining room chair and grabbed hold of his phone again, absently fidgeting with it.

"So tell me about this woman who dropped him off," Walt asked.

"Traci. I assume her last name is Lind, by the papers she left. But frankly, I don't recall ever knowing her last name. She would come down to the *Weekend Warrior* with Bridget. They were best friends."

Walt frowned. "*Weekend Warrior?*"

"Bridget's parents' sailboat. It was docked at the same marina I was at back then. Anyway, I didn't exactly hang out with Bridget or her friends. They would come by my sailboat when I was working on it and talk to me, But I never invited them to come aboard. I'd see them at the barbecues we would have down at the marina on weekends or holidays. Bridget made it obvious she was interested in me and that our age difference didn't bother her."

"And her friend?"

Chris chuckled. "I always got the feeling Bridget was the princess holding court, and Traci was a lady-in-waiting. Traci never said much. Frankly, she said more to me today than in the entire time I've known her."

"And she even gave you a child," Walt snarked.

"I guess with Bridget gone, she's no longer in the mood to do her bidding. And she must have bought Bridget's story that the boy is mine. But I have to assume she's coming back. I suspect this is some stupid idea of hers to force me to spend time with the boy so I'll accept my responsibility as his father."

"Why do you assume she's coming back?" Walt asked.

"For one thing, according to that will, Christopher inherited his mother's estate. That would include what she inherited from her parents, which is substantial. Traci isn't ditsy enough to think she can drop the kid off and go back and keep living in the estate Bridget inherited from her parents and spend his money. She said something to me about assuming there would be money to support him. I suspect she thought she could spend his money as she wanted. And live on their dime. Yet she probably discovered not being able to spend the money as she wants isn't worth the responsibility of caring for a small human."

"If this Traci knew where to find you, then obviously Bridget did, too."

"Not sure how Bridget would have known where I was. But even if she did, she never would have contacted me about her son because we both knew he isn't mine." Chris stood up and shoved his cellphone in his back pocket. "I need to have a talk with that boy sitting in the kitchen, who I imagine wonders if I'm his father, considering what Traci said in front of him when they first showed up at your door."

DANIELLE SAT at the kitchen table, watching Christopher finish the slice of chocolate cake she had given him. Before offering him the cake, she had asked him if he'd had dinner yet, to which he told her he had just eaten a grilled cheese sandwich and fries.

After he finished his last bite of cake, he looked up at Danielle and asked, "When is Traci coming back?"

"Umm, I'm not sure." Danielle glanced briefly at the door leading to the dining room before looking back to the confused child.

The next moment, both the back door and the door to the hallway leading to the dining room opened. Chris and Walt walked into the kitchen at the same time that Heather and Brian entered the back door. Heather and Brian carried the to-go food Brian had purchased.

Heather stopped abruptly when she saw the small boy sitting at the kitchen table. She smiled at him and asked, "Well, hi. Who are you?"

No one answered Heather's question. Instead, Chris walked to Christopher and asked him to come with him back to the parlor so they could have a little talk, and then he asked Danielle to come too. He assumed Danielle had already made friends of sorts with the child, and the boy might be more comfortable if she joined them.

Without saying another word, Danielle and Chris left the kitchen with the boy, leaving Heather and Brian still standing and confused.

IN THE PARLOR, Chris sat with Christopher on the sofa, while Danielle took a chair facing them. Once Danielle sat down, the boy looked up at Chris and asked, "Are you my dad?"

Chris gave the boy a sad smile. "No. I'm not."

Christopher let out a deep sigh and slumped back on the sofa. "Traci said we were going to find my dad." The boy stared across the room, looking blankly ahead.

Chris gave the boy's denim-clad knee a gentle pat and said, "But we have the same name. I think maybe your mom might have named you after me."

Christopher looked at Chris. "You knew my mom?"

Chris nodded. "Yes, before you were born."

"She died," Christopher announced.

"I'm so sorry. Has Traci been living with you since your mom died?"

Christopher shrugged. "Mom and I moved in with Traci after Grandma died."

"What do you mean you moved in with Traci?"

"Mom and I slept on the couch in Traci's living room. It made into a bed. But after Mom died, Traci said I could sleep on the couch. She said it was too much work to make it into a bed for just me."

Chris frowned. "Why did you and your mom move out of your grandparents' house?"

The boy looked at Chris. "Grandma and Grandpa died. Mom said we couldn't live there anymore. But after Mom died, I don't think Traci liked having me live with her. I think that's why she left me here. She isn't coming back for me, is she?"

"Christopher, why do you say she didn't like you living with her?" Danielle asked. "What makes you say that?"

Obviously, because she dumped the poor kid with strangers, Chris thought.

Christopher shrugged. "I think I made her mad. I kept asking her why Mom wasn't coming back. One day Traci took me to this place she called a sen tary. There was a picture of my mom on a big rock thing on the ground. Traci said that was where mom was now. Under that rock."

"Christopher," Danielle said softly, "look at me for a minute."

The boy looked at Danielle.

"Your mom—the person she was—is not under that rock."

Christopher frowned at Danielle. "She isn't?"

Danielle shook her head. "No. When we die, our spirit—the thing that makes us who we are—it leaves our body. Her body is buried under there, but not her spirit—not the thing that made your mom who she is."

"You mean how she's in Heaven?" Christopher asked.

Chris and Danielle exchanged brief glances and then Chris said, "Yes. So Traci also explained about Heaven?"

Christopher shook his head. "No. Mrs. Brown did."

Chris studied the boy. "Who's Mrs. Brown?"

"She's Traci's next-door neighbor. She sometimes watches me when Traci works. Mrs. Brown told me my mom went to Heaven, and I'll see her again when I die."

"CHRIS HAS A KID?" Heather asked as she unpacked the food, arranging it on the kitchen table.

"No. I just explained," Walt said while reaching into the upper cabinet for the dinner plates. Meanwhile, Brian sat at the kitchen table, looking through the documents Chris and Walt had been reading minutes earlier.

"Well, the kid looks like he could be Chris's," Heather said. "Just saying. Beautiful blue eyes, adorable face."

Brian looked up from the papers in his hands to Heather. "You're talking about your boss's beautiful blue eyes and adorable face right in front of your boyfriend?"

Standing at the kitchen table, about to remove the condiment packets from a bag, she looked at Brian. "Oh, come on, we all know how pretty Chris is."

"He is adorable," Walt said with a snort as he set the dinner plates on the kitchen counter.

Brian chuckled. "Well, these days with DNA, it makes it difficult to pass someone's kid off on the wrong guy regardless of how much they look alike." Brian glanced over to Walt and asked, "So she just ran out, left the poor kid here?"

Walt turned to face the kitchen table, leaned back against the counter, and folded his arms across his chest as he looked at Brian and Heather. "According to Chris, she's convinced he's the father, and she'll be back because this is a stunt to force him to get to spend time with his son so he'll accept his responsibilities. What she doesn't realize, he isn't the father. I have no idea how she's going to handle that when she comes back."

"Do they know he's really Chris Glandon?" Heather asked.

Walt shook his head. "Chris said no one at the marina did. Not even the owner of the boat Chris lived on."

FOUR

Across the street at the Bartleys', they had a full house. Lily's parents, Tammy and Gene Miller, had arrived late that afternoon from California to meet their new granddaughter, Emily Ann. Less than two hours after the parents' arrival, Lily's sister, Laura, showed up unexpectedly at the front door. She had been in Europe, and Ian's sister, Kelly, offered to pick Laura up at the Portland airport and had brought Laura to the Bartleys' house.

But now, Ian and Gene sat at the breakfast bar, with the men chatting while Connor sat nearby in his highchair, eating his dinner. Realizing Laura's unexpected arrival meant they would probably have dinner later than they initially planned, Ian had decided to feed their young son.

Not long after Laura's arrival, Lily gave her sister a quick tour of their home, as Laura hadn't seen it since the remodel. During the tour, baby Emily Ann woke up, so now the sisters, along with Kelly and Tammy, gathered in the living room while Laura held her new niece.

"She is so pretty," Laura cooed for the third time, her eyes focused on the infant.

"I still can't believe you're actually here," Lily said. "You never mentioned you were coming back this soon."

Laura glanced up at her sister. "I was over there for almost four months."

Lily shrugged. "When you left, I thought you planned to spend at least a year in Europe. But I'm glad you're back. Yet I still can't get over the fact you're here."

"I needed to meet my new niece." Laura smiled down at the newborn.

"To be honest, from what you told me about the guy you were seeing, I wondered if you might stay longer." Lily smiled mischievously at her sister. "Or should we be expecting someone else to show up?"

Laura shook her head. "No, that didn't work out."

"Your father and I had no idea Laura was coming until last night. We would have figured out some way to pick her up at the airport, but Kelly was so nice to do it," Tammy said.

"That would have been too much driving for you," Kelly insisted. "Not after driving up here from California."

"Mom and Dad are staying in our new guest room," Lily told Laura. "Do you want to sleep in the living room, or I could put a blowup bed in Connor's room?"

"That won't be necessary," Kelly answered for Laura. "We already discussed it on the way back from the airport; Laura is staying with Joe and me in our guest room."

Lily looked at Laura. "Really? You don't want to stay here?"

"It'll be easier this way," Laura said. "And I don't want to bother Walt and Danielle again and ask to stay over there. I imagine they have their hands full these days."

"Don't forget to give your sister your new phone number," Kelly reminded her.

"What new phone number?" Lily asked.

Laura looked up from Emily Ann. "I lost my cellphone at the airport in London, so I got a new one in New York."

Lily frowned. "Umm...I understand getting a new phone, but why not keep the same phone number?"

Laura shrugged. "I just figured if I was getting a new phone, I might as well get a new number."

"I was telling Laura, on the way back from the airport, that Chris doesn't seem to be seeing anyone," Kelly said.

"Not that we know of. According to Heather, Chris does his share of dating, just not locally." Lily glanced over to the living room window that looked towards Marlow House and wondered about the woman who had showed up at her front door an hour earlier looking for Chris and had then gone across the street to Marlow House. After showing Laura around the new upstairs earlier, Lily had glanced out the front window and noticed the woman's car was now gone.

"But no one serious, since he hasn't introduced anyone to his friends here," Kelly countered.

"How long are you planning on staying?" Lily asked Laura.

"I'm not sure. I don't really want to go back to California." Laura looked at her mom. "I hope you understand, Mom, but I just feel like that's going backwards. And if I decide to stay in this area, I obviously will need to find my own place. I don't think Joe would appreciate an extended houseguest."

"You might stay in Frederickport?" Lily sounded surprised.

Laura shrugged. "I don't have a definite plan yet. But one thing I need to do while I'm up here is buy a car, and I'd rather do it here in Oregon, where I don't have to pay sales tax." Laura had sold her previous car before going to Europe.

"What happened to that job you got?" Lily asked. "You said you really liked it."

"I did. But it was temporary. It's not like I planned to stay there forever."

"I loved the pictures you posted," Kelly said. "It was like traveling with you."

Tammy chuckled.

They all turned to Tammy. "What's funny?" Laura asked.

"Oh, when Kelly mentioned the pictures you posted, it reminded me of something that I thought about not long after you arrived in Europe and started posting on your blog."

"What was that?" Lily asked.

"And why was it funny?" Laura added.

"It's not funny, I suppose. But I guess when you get my age, you move along in life, things keep changing, and one day it hits you that something that was common when you were a kid is something your own children will never know was a thing. It's not that it is an especially important thing, but it does remind a person they are getting old." Tammy chuckled again.

"What thing were you reminded of?" Lily asked.

Tammy leaned back on the sofa. "Not sure if it was common throughout the US or just where we lived, but where I grew up, when someone traveled abroad, took a trip to Italy or Spain or whatever, it wasn't uncommon for them to have a slideshow, maybe at the Woman's Club or some other local civics group. And the public was invited."

"So they would watch strangers' vacation pictures?" Laura frowned.

Tammy laughed. "Sort of. But not exactly. Remember, we didn't have cable television or the internet in those days, and, like now, not everyone can afford to travel. It was a way to learn about the world. I think they might have been called travelogues. But it was something my parents would occasionally go to. Instead of going out to dinner or the movies, they'd watch a slideshow of some stranger's trip abroad. I suppose it also included some sort of narration. While I never went myself, Mom and Dad attended a few when I was younger."

"Laura, most of the people looking at your vacation pictures were strangers, too. Your blog is a modern version of Mom's travelogues," Lily said.

"Well, they weren't exactly my travelogues," Tammy said.

TRACI STOOD ALONE by her car, confused and disoriented. She remembered pulling off from the highway onto the desolate road after second-guessing her rash decision to leave Christopher with

25

his father. It didn't seem wise to keep driving down the highway, not since realizing leaving the child might be seen as abandonment. So she had impulsively turned off on the road, making it easier to turn around should she decide to return to Marlow House.

She remembered the car that had pulled up behind her. There were two men, and one pulled something from his pocket, but after that everything seemed to go blank, and then a blur, where she had this odd sensation that someone was picking her up off the ground. But then no one was there, and then she was alone, sitting on the ground next to her car.

None of it made sense.

Traci looked into the window of the front passenger door and saw her keys still hanging in the ignition.

"Do I go back to Frederickport and talk to Chris?" Traci asked aloud. "Or should I get back in my car and keep driving?"

Traci closed her eyes and played back all that had happened that day, from leaving the motel, driving for hours, talking to the purple-haired lady at the diner, and then the first house she had stopped at, where the redheaded woman had answered the door. She opened her eyes and, to her shock, found herself no longer by her car on the desolate road, but standing on the doorstep of the first house she had visited.

CONNOR HAD JUST FINISHED EATING his dinner, while his father and grandfather sat at the nearby breakfast bar, still visiting, each with a now empty cocktail glass sitting before them. Sadie, the golden retriever, sat on the floor beneath the highchair, ready to clean up any food Connor might drop from the highchair tray, when a woman stepped through the wall into the kitchen and looked around the room.

Sadie didn't notice the woman immediately; it wasn't until Connor started slapping the palm of his hand on the tray while pointing to the lady with his other hand. The dog immediately jumped up, saw the unfamiliar woman standing in the room, and started barking.

Connor's abrupt assault on the highchair tray, immediately followed by the barking, interrupted the men's conversation, and they both turned to the commotion.

TRACI WONDERED how she had gotten into these people's kitchen. Someone must have left a door open, and she'd mistakenly walked in when trying to find her way back to her car. Two men had been sitting at the breakfast bar when she first walked in, yet they hadn't seemed to notice her yet. Instead, they focused their attention on the child pounding on the highchair tray, pointing at her and the barking dog.

Once they noticed her, she was certain she would die of embarrassment. *Could this day get any more messed up?* she asked herself. Since waking up that morning, she seemed to make one poor decision after another. First abandoning Christopher without having more of a conversation with Chris, forgetting where she left her car, and now barging into the home of strangers.

The younger looking of the two men at the breakfast bar stood up and shouted, "Sadie, quiet," while placing his hand over his son's, preventing any more pounding,

No longer barking, the dog sat beside the highchair, staring at her as the man removed the squirming boy from the highchair. Both boy and dog continued to stare at her, while both men seemed oblivious to her presence. Traci stared at the dog, and she could almost swear it asked, "Who are you?"

THE TWINS HAD FALLEN ASLEEP, and Marie decided to pop downstairs and tell Danielle everything was fine. But then she thought about Connor's family across the street. Lily's parents had arrived today for a visit, and Marie intended to avoid visiting

Connor and Emily Ann during their stay. She felt it best if Tammy could have her grandson's entire attention, and he would not be distracted by the woman he knew as Grandma Marie. To Connor, she was an extra grandmother, and to his actual grandmothers, she was nothing more than an imaginary friend.

While she didn't intend to stop by the Bartleys' as frequently as normal, she decided it wouldn't hurt to pop in for a moment and see how the visit was going before returning to Marlow House. One nice thing about being a ghost, traveling from one house to another took just a moment.

A FEW MINUTES before the barking started in the kitchen, Marie had popped into the Bartleys' living room, where she found four women sitting in the living room with Emily Ann. While she recognized all the women, she was surprised to see one of them. "Laura's here?" Marie asked deaf ears. "Danielle didn't mention Laura was coming back from Europe."

Marie heard barking and pounding coming from the kitchen. The next moment, Marie stood in the kitchen and saw a strange woman standing in the middle of the room while Ian attempted to quiet his son and dog.

But it wasn't Ian who got the dog to stop barking and sit quietly; it was Marie, who silently conveyed the command to Sadie, to which she complied. Marie's attention focused on the young woman, whom Ian and Gene ignored. Marie was fairly certain she knew why. It had something to do with that bloody gunshot wound in the woman's forehead.

"Who are you?" Marie called out to the woman.

Startled, the woman looked over at Marie. By her reaction, it was clear to Marie the mystery woman—or ghost—hadn't seen Marie enter the kitchen.

"Who shot you?" Marie asked.

The next moment, the woman vanished.

FIVE

After Christopher told Chris and Danielle that Traci's neighbor, Mrs. Brown, had explained his mother was in Heaven, and he would see her again one day after he died, Christopher asked, "Is Traci picking me up? I thought she left me here because you were my dad. If you're not my dad...she said she is taking me to my dad."

Chris turned on the sofa to look directly into the young boy's eyes. "Christopher, your mom is a friend of mine. I knew your grandparents. Traci needed to do something, so she left you here with me, where you would be safe." It wasn't exactly a lie.

"You mean while she looks for my dad?"

"Maybe. I'm not really sure. You will be safe with me until Traci gets back, and we figure this all out."

Chris gave the boy's knee a pat, stood up, and looked at the suitcase he had brought into the house earlier after seeing Traci speeding away from Marlow House. "Let's find out what Traci packed for you." Chris walked over to the suitcase, picked it up, and set it on the desk, preparing to open it.

Christopher wasn't interested in what was in the suitcase.

Instead, he looked over at the television on the other side of the room. "Can I watch TV?"

"Sure." Danielle stood up and walked to the television. As she turned it on, the boy changed positions on the sofa to better view the set. After he did, he spied the basket of toys in the corner.

Glancing back to the boy, Danielle caught him eyeing the toys. She smiled and walked over to the corner and grabbed the basket, pulling it to the sofa. It was filled with toys both Connor—who was a few years younger than Christopher, and Evan, who was significantly older, enjoyed, such as toy cars, trucks, building blocks and other random toys.

After inviting Christopher to check out the basket's contents, Danielle returned to the television and found a show he liked. She joined Chris at the desk, who currently looked through the now open suitcase.

Danielle watched as Chris sorted through the clothes, which included several T-shirts, pants, socks, and underwear that appeared to be in Christopher's size.

"I guess he doesn't brush his teeth or hair," Chris noted as he tossed the pair of socks in his hand back into the suitcase.

"Why do you say that?"

Chris shrugged. "She only left clothes, and only a couple of days' worth. His toothbrush is probably with hers, assuming he has one. And since this suitcase isn't full, I wonder if there are some dirty clothes of his in some pillowcase in the back of her car that he wore on the trip up here. There is nothing personal in the suitcase, no favorite stuffed animal or blanket. Connor likes that Winnie the Pooh of his. When I was a kid, I always had to take my favorite blanket with me when we traveled."

Danielle smiled, imagining a Linus version of a much younger Chris.

Thoughts of the contents of Christopher's lone suitcase was interrupted when Walt stepped into the room. Walt glanced over to the boy now watching TV and exploring the contents of the toy basket, before looking back at Chris and Danielle, who stood by the nearby desk. The two looked over at him.

"Everything okay?" Walt asked in a low voice.

"I suppose." Danielle glanced briefly at the boy and back to her husband.

"Everyone is in the living room. I decided to have them bring the food in there. What do you want to do?" Walt asked.

Chris was about to close the suitcase when Max, Danielle's black cat, jumped up on the suitcase, making himself comfortable in the pile of clothes. He had followed Walt into the room. The cat looked over at the unfamiliar human sitting on the sofa and back to Walt.

Ignoring Max, Chris said, "I wouldn't mind something to eat. Our visitor will be okay in here for a while." He glanced briefly at the boy.

Walt focused his attention on Max, who had been staring at him, and said, "It's complicated, Max. Consider him a new house-guest. Why don't you make friends with him, and if he gets restless or leaves the room, come tell me. We'll be in the living room."

The next moment, the cat jumped down from the suitcase to the floor and sauntered toward the sofa and the little boy.

Walt looked at Chris. "Hunny was trying to find you." Chris had left his pit bull, Hunny, at Marlow House earlier that day, and the dog had been napping in the side yard when Chris had returned. After Heather and Brian showed up with the food, the dog had tried following the pair into the house, but they unintentionally closed the door on her, and the doggy door had somehow gotten latched, locking Hunny outside. It took Hunny scratching on the doggy door before Heather realized what had happened.

"I told her you were busy, and to stay in the living room."

Chris nodded and looked back to the boy, who had turned his attention to the purring cat now curled up next to him on the sofa.

After telling Christopher where he was going, Chris stepped into the entry hall with Walt and Danielle and, before going into the living room, stopped a moment to fill Danielle in on what he and Walt had learned from the documents left behind by Traci. Danielle had been in the kitchen with Christopher when Walt and Chris had first looked through the papers, and after she joined Chris in the parlor, he hadn't had a chance to explain all that had been in the documents.

"AT FIRST, I figured Traci would probably come back to get him. That this was just her way of forcing me to get to know my son so I would start taking responsibility. In some ways, I understand. If he were my son, I couldn't just walk away from him. But he's not." Chris sat in Marlow House's living room, eating Thai food with Walt, Danielle, Heather, and Brian, while Christopher remained in the parlor, watching television. They had left the doors open in both the living room and the parlor so they could hear Christopher should he call for them. Plus, they needed to leave the doors open if they wanted Max to come get them should Christopher decide to go exploring.

Danielle had been tempted to run upstairs and check on the twins before eating dinner, but she knew Marie was in the nursery, and it would be at least an hour before the babies would need to be nursed again.

"You no longer think she's coming back?" Heather asked.

Chris shrugged. "According to the boy, he and Bridget moved in with Traci after Bridget's parents died. He told me he had to sleep on the couch in the living room. Why? Bridget should have inherited a fortune, and according to her will, her estate went to her son. Admittedly, the will didn't list her assets; it was broadly phrased. I assumed there was some sort of trust fund set up to oversee the inheritance. Did something happen to the money?"

"Do you think Chris needs to call someone?" Heather asked Brian.

Brian frowned at Heather. "Call someone, who?"

"I don't know. The chief." Heather shrugged. "A woman just abandoned that poor little boy with strangers."

"I've been in foster care," Chris said. "The only thing the chief —or Brian—could do is call child protective services, and I don't want to do that right now. For the moment, I'm babysitting Christopher. I even have a letter—of sorts—showing his guardian has put him in my care. I don't want to put a child in foster care."

Heather frowned at Chris. "You're going to keep him?"

Chris rolled his eyes. "I can't keep him. He's not a puppy. But I need to sort this thing out. Unfortunately, tomorrow is Sunday, but on Monday, I can contact my attorney and see what they can find out about Bridget and her parents. I can start from there."

"I agree with Chris," Brian said. "We could definitely call child protective services—and if he came to me officially with this—then I might feel compelled to do that myself."

Danielle looked at Brian. "Why do you say that?"

Brian gave a shrug. "Think about it. Chris claims he's not related to the boy. A woman he barely knows just dumps the kid on him. If she's really the child's guardian, should she be? I suspect child protective services would seek to remove him from her care."

"She already did that herself," Heather grumbled before taking a bite of her food.

———

AFTER THE MYSTERY GHOST VANISHED, Marie remained at the Bartleys' home for a few moments, first to ask Sadie about the apparition, and then to call out to her. Yet the ghost was no longer there. When Marie returned to Marlow House, she headed first to the nursery to check on the twins. They still slept.

Marie wasn't sure what room Danielle and her friends planned to eat in. Since only Heather, Brian, and Chris were coming over, it might be any room downstairs, so she thought to check the parlor first.

What Marie didn't expect to find in the first room she looked at was a little boy sitting on the sofa, watching television, surrounded by toys, while Max sat on his lap, purring.

"Who are you?" Marie asked the moment she appeared before the boy and Max.

Marie was fairly certain whoever the boy was, he wasn't a medium, nor young enough to still see spirits, considering he never flinched at her sudden appearance, and he continued to watch the television, which she blocked.

"Well, I guess that answers one question." She turned her attention to Max, who quickly told her what he knew.

"WHO IS that child in the parlor?" Marie asked when she appeared the next moment in the living room. Before anyone could answer, she looked at Danielle and added, "I was just in the nursery; Jack and Addison are sleeping."

"His name is Christopher," Chris said before explaining to Marie what had happened.

"Oh my." Marie glanced toward the open doorway leading to the entry hall and parlor. "This has been an eventful day. I just popped in to check on Lily." Again, Marie looked at Danielle and added, "I was only gone for a moment and immediately checked on the twins when I returned."

"Did something happen at Lily's?" Walt asked.

"Aside from her sister, Laura, being there, I didn't realize she was coming with her parents; I thought she was still in Europe."

"Laura's here?" Heather asked.

"Yes. And then there was that ghost in Lily's kitchen," Marie said.

"What ghost?" Danielle asked.

"No clue who she is. Right after I got there, I heard Sadie barking and something pounding from the other room, so I popped into the kitchen and found a strange woman standing in the kitchen with Ian and Gene. Connor was sitting in his highchair, and Sadie was barking up a storm. The ghost saw me and vanished. According to Sadie, the woman popped in, then popped out again. Of course, I knew she was probably a ghost before I saw her disappear."

After Heather told Brian what Marie said, he asked, "Why did Marie assume she was a ghost when she first saw her?"

"It had something to do with that bullet wound in the center of her forehead."

"Oh, my god! Who was she?" Danielle gasped, as Heather told Brian what Marie said.

Marie described the woman, including what clothes she wore. Once she finished, the mediums exchanged worried glances.

"That sounds like Traci," Chris said.

"If it is, I don't think she's coming back for the child," Brian said.

SIX

"Do you think this Traci is really dead?" Heather asked in a whisper, not wanting the child across the entry hall to hear, although he probably wouldn't have even if she had shouted the words.

Chris shrugged. "It sounds like what she was wearing."

"I wish we had a picture of her so we could show Marie and make sure," Danielle said.

"A picture?" Chris considered for a moment. "I might." He picked up his cellphone and started scrolling through his photos. After a moment, he held out his phone to Marie. "Look at this."

Marie took the phone from Chris. From Brian's perspective, Chris's phone floated in the air a few feet from Chris's face.

"I took that picture over four years ago, before I moved here," Chris explained. "It was Bridget's birthday, and her parents had a party at their boat. Bridget asked me to take a picture of her and Traci with my phone. Traci's the one on the right. It's been a few years, but I don't think Traci's changed that much."

"It's her." Marie sent the cellphone floating back to Chris. Heather told Brian what Marie said.

"Do I understand correctly, the ghost had a bullet wound in the center of her forehead?" Brian asked.

"That's what it looked like to me," Marie muttered.

"Yes," Heather said.

"If that's the case, it sounds like this Traci didn't come here just so Chris could meet his son. It sounds like her intent was to leave the boy with someone who would take care of him, before killing herself," Brian said.

"You think she committed suicide?" Heather asked.

"Brian is probably right," Chris said. "I can't believe Traci left here and someone murdered her. Who? Why? Suicide sounds more plausible."

"I think we'd better call the chief after all," Brian said.

WHILE BRIAN CALLED THE CHIEF, Danielle, cellphone in hand, headed upstairs to check on the twins. When she entered the nursery, she found both babies still sleeping in their cribs, but by Jack's restless sleep, she suspected he might wake up soon and would be hungry. While waiting for her babies to wake up, Danielle took a seat on the rocker and called Lily.

"Hey, Dani," Lily said when answering Danielle's call.

"Hey. Is everyone right there?" Danielle asked in a low voice.

"Do you mean am I sitting in a room with my parents, Laura, and Kelly? No. Kelly and Laura left a few minutes ago so Laura can drop her things at Kelly's place before she comes back over here. And Mom and Dad are upstairs in their room, unpacking."

"Laura's staying with Kelly?" Danielle asked.

"Yeah. I'm actually kind of bummed she isn't staying with us. I sorta liked the idea of late night talks with my big sis while she's here. But I guess I understand. So what was the deal with that woman looking for Chris? Yes, I am nosey." Lily chuckled at her own admission.

"Actually, that's why I'm calling." Danielle then told Lily all that had happened since Traci showed up at her door.

"Holy crap, Dani. And her ghost was in our kitchen? I asked Ian why Sadie had been barking. He had no clue. But he did wonder if it might be Marie by the way Connor was pointing, but Sadie doesn't bark at Marie or Eva." Lily went silent for a moment before letting out a gasp.

"What?"

"If it's the ghost of the woman who went to your house, that means I was one of the last people to see her alive. She knocked on our door, looking for him. What are you going to do?"

"Like I said, Brian is calling the chief. Not sure what they'll do. While you can tell Ian what I told you, please don't say anything about the woman to anyone else, not until we know more."

POLICE CHIEF MACDONALD had just arrived at Marlow House when Danielle came downstairs after feeding the twins. Marie, who had showed up in the nursery around the time the twins woke up, had stayed with the babies after Danielle finished nursing.

Danielle found the chief in the living room, being apprised of the current situation.

"I'd like to talk to the boy first," the chief said.

"What are you going to do?" Heather asked.

The chief looked at Heather. "I understand everyone assumes this woman killed herself, considering the circumstances. But we don't know if she came up here from California with just the boy, or if she came with someone else. Or even if she came from California. Chris said he didn't ask the child about his trip to Frederickport."

"Are you saying she might have been murdered? And the killer is still in town?" Heather asked.

The chief shrugged. "I am only saying we don't have enough information to determine anything."

"We know she's dead," Heather said. "Shot in the head."

"Taking into consideration when Marie claimed to have seen her ghost, and when the woman was last seen alive, it is entirely possible she kept driving after leaving Marlow House and was miles away from Frederickport when she was killed—or when she killed herself. But like I said, I want to talk to the boy. I also want to start this investigation by stretching the truth a little." The chief looked at Chris.

"What are you thinking?" Chris asked.

"The only people who overheard the conversation between you and Traci were Walt and Danielle. We will stick as close to the truth as possible with a few changes. When Traci runs out of the parlor, instead of leaving Marlow House without saying anything, we'll say she told Walt and Danielle to tell Chris she will be back in an hour. That she just wants Chris to get to meet his son. When she doesn't show up in an hour, it's reasonable for us to put out a bolo."

"That makes sense," Chris said. "Christopher was there when she told me I'm his father. And he also saw her run out of the room. But he wouldn't have heard what Traci said to Walt and Danielle before she drove off."

"I need that photo of Traci, along with a description of the car, so I can get someone out looking for it." He looked at Brian. "I want you to go down to the station. Get on the computer and find a vehicle registered to Traci Lind in California, one that matches the car she drove to Marlow House, along with a license plate number. I assume when we find the car—if we find the car—we will find her body. While you're doing that, I'm going to talk to the boy."

FIFTEEN MINUTES LATER, the chief entered the parlor with Chris and Danielle. Danielle turned down the volume on the television while Chris introduced the chief to Christopher. The chief took a seat next to the boy, while Danielle and Chris sat in the chairs across from the sofa. Danielle didn't remove Max from the boy's lap, noting the way he absently petted the purring cat. She suspected Christopher might benefit from an emotional-support cat.

"Chris tells me you've been living with Traci since your mother died," the chief asked.

The boy stared into the chief's eyes while his right hand continued to stroke the black fur along Max's back. He nodded and whispered, "Yes."

"What town did you live in?"

Christopher shrugged. "I don't know."

"Christopher, do you remember living at your grandparents' house?" Chris asked from the chair across from the sofa.

The boy looked over at Chris. He stared for a moment before finally saying, "Traci called it a castle. Sometimes, when we would go out for ice cream, Traci would drive by it and say there's the castle you used to live in."

"Bridget's parents lived in San Clemente," Chris said.

The chief glanced at Chris. "Sounds like he was still living in that area." He turned back to the boy. "The place you were living with Traci, you never moved?"

Christopher frowned at the chief. He clearly did not understand the question.

"After you and your mom moved from your grandparents' house and moved in with Traci, did you stay there until you came here?" the chief rephrased.

Christopher nodded. "Yes. Traci told me we were going on a trip so I could meet my dad. But Chris says he's not my dad. We only have the same name."

"Did anyone else join you on this trip?"

Again, the boy frowned. "What do you mean?"

"Was it only you and Traci in the car driving up here from where you lived with Traci? Or perhaps someone in another car? Someone who stayed at the motel with you. Or had dinner at the restaurants with you on your trip."

Christopher shook his head. "No. It was only Traci and me. We didn't eat at any restaurants. Not until today. Traci made us peanut butter sandwiches. She said it was more like a picnic. When is she coming back?"

JOE MORELLI HAD JUST PICKED up a cup of coffee and returned to the squad car when he received a notice to be on the lookout for a vehicle in the area. It gave the description of the car, license number, and a picture of the driver.

Now sitting in the driver's seat, sipping on his coffee, Joe looked at the photograph. Unbeknownst to Joe, it was a cropped photo from Chris's phone that had once included two women instead of only one.

Joe glanced at the clock on the dashboard and saw it was about forty-five minutes before his shift ended. He wasn't eager to get home. It wasn't that he disliked Lily's sister, Laura, he just wished Kelly hadn't offered for her to stay with them. Lily and Ian had plenty of room now, even with her parents staying. And Laura could always stay across the street at Marlow House, after all, they had extra bedrooms, and Laura had stayed there the last time she had been in town.

Joe turned on the ignition and pulled out onto the street. It would be dark in about thirty minutes. Maybe he could track down this missing car. Twenty minutes later, just as Joe was getting ready to head back to the station, he took a turn down a side street. He didn't really expect to find anyone, as this stretch of road was fairly desolate, and there were no homes, just pastureland on either side of the road.

Moments after making the turn, he spied a vehicle up ahead; it matched the description of the car in the bolo. Pulling up behind the car, he checked out the license number.

Before turning off his ignition, he got on the radio and called into the station, letting them know he had found the car. A moment later, he parked, turned off the ignition, and got out of his vehicle.

His first assumption while approaching the car, it had broken down, and someone had picked her up. But when he got to the driver's side of the car, he saw the keys still hanging in the ignition. He glanced around and then tried the car door. It was unlocked.

With a frown, he circled around to the other side of the vehicle. Daylight was fading, yet he could still see clearly and hoped backup would arrive soon. At the passenger side of the car, he found that door unlocked, too. After opening the car door, he peeked down and saw a strap on the floor coming from under the passenger seat. He knelt down, reached out, and found the strap was attached to a woman's purse shoved under the seat. He grabbed the purse, opened it, and looked through it. If the woman had a wallet, it wasn't in her purse. He tossed the purse on the passenger seat, stood up, and shut the car door.

Just as he turned around, he saw something in the dirt next to the car. Because of the dwindling sunlight, he wasn't sure what it was, so he knelt down and picked it up.

It was moist, soft, and sticky.

SEVEN

Not long after Joe called into the station about locating the vehicle, responders started appearing on the scene and now parked along Traci's vehicle, their lights flashing as the sun faded into the west. After hearing what Joe found on the ground next to the parked car, the chief arrived with Brian at the same time as the vehicles from the coroner's office showed up.

Somewhat traumatized by what he had carelessly picked up, Joe now sat on the back end of a paramedic rig, its back doors open. He absently wiped and rewiped his right hand with a damp rag while watching the commotion around the perimeter of Traci's car. With responder vehicles blocking one lane, traffic control officers monitored the one free lane, should any car need to pass by. Yet there were few cars passing by on this stretch of the road.

A few minutes later, he heard someone call out, "We found her!"

Twenty minutes later, Joe sat in the passenger seat of his squad car while Brian and the chief stood outside by the front of the vehicle. Brian glanced briefly through the squad car's windshield, looking at Joe, who sat stoically in the passenger seat, staring blankly ahead. Brian looked back to the chief and said, "After I drive him home, I'll get Heather to pick me up at the station."

The chief nodded, his attention now focused on the activity on the other side of Traci's car, where responders carried a body out on a stretcher from beyond the bushes along the side of the road. "If Joe didn't pick up—what he picked up—we might not have found her right away."

"Why do you say that?" Brian asked.

"At first glance, it looks like she stopped and someone picked her up."

"With her keys still in her car, along with her purse, it would make me assume abduction."

The chief nodded. "If Joe hadn't reached down and picked up part of that poor girl's brain, we might be looking for a kidnap victim, not a body."

"And I guess this isn't a suicide." Brian let out a sigh.

"Someone obviously shot her when she was standing by her car. And there was no way she crawled over those bushes to where they found her. Not to mention, we haven't found the weapon."

Brian shrugged. "We still may find the weapon. But she didn't shoot it."

BEFORE THE CHIEF left Marlow House, after receiving the news Joe found Traci's car, there had been a discussion regarding where Christopher should sleep that night. Chris was emphatic. He did not want to call child protective services.

"There is no reason for them to get involved right now," Chris had insisted. He also pointed out that Christopher's legal guardian had left him in charge, and the fact they had misconstrued what actually occurred at Marlow House meant there was no reason for CPS to find out Traci had abandoned the boy—not unless they told them.

Danielle had offered to let Christopher stay at Marlow House for the night. They had plenty of bedrooms, plus the boy had gotten attached to Max, who had remained by his side since their first introduction. And when Hunny was introduced to

Christopher, the boy reacted similarly to the dog as he had the cat.

After much back-and-forth, it was decided Christopher would stay at Marlow House, but in the downstairs bedroom, and Chris would sleep in the living room on the sofa, in case Christopher woke up in the middle of the night and needed something or was afraid.

After the chief left, Chris took the boy upstairs for a bath. Danielle, who kept extra toothbrushes on hand for guests who might forget theirs, gave Chris a new toothbrush so the boy could brush his teeth before going to bed. After Chris finally put Christopher to bed in the downstairs bedroom, the boy did not sleep alone. Both Hunny and Max were on the mattress with him.

"HE DEFINITELY LIKES ANIMALS," Danielle said after her houseguest was securely tucked in for the night. She sat in the living room with Walt, Chris, Heather, and Marie while she nursed the twins. She and Walt shared the love seat, making it easier for Walt to help her with the babies.

"Max told me the boy is very kind. Gentle. Apparently, he likes to kiss Max on the top of his head." Walt chuckled.

Heather's cellphone rang, and she answered it. They all listened. By her side of the conversation, she was obviously talking to Brian. When the call ended, she looked over at her friends and said, "They found her body. It wasn't far from where they found her car. And according to Brian, it wasn't suicide. Someone murdered her and then moved her body out into the bushes off the side of the road. Joe is the one who found the car, and I guess when he did, he…" Heather went on to tell them what Joe had inadvertently picked up and then added, "At least when I find bodies, I don't touch them."

"Joe didn't actually find the body," Walt reminded her. "Just a part of it."

"I'd better go look for that poor girl's spirit. Find out who murdered her." Marie disappeared.

"This makes little sense. Was this a robbery?" Chris asked.

"Possibly. Brian said there wasn't a wallet in her purse or anywhere in the car," Heather said. "No driver's license, money, or credit cards."

"It could have been a robbery," Danielle said.

"So what are you going to do now?" Heather asked Chris.

Chris leaned back in the chair and let out a sigh. "I need to go home, get a change of clothes, my shaving kit. Grab my pillow and then come back here."

Heather rolled her eyes. "You know what I mean."

Chris let out another sigh. "I figure I'm sort of this kid's de facto guardian. I imagine if some by-the-rule-book supervisor over at CPS found out Christopher's guardian had been murdered, they might insist on dragging him into their care. Which would ultimately mean finding an emergency foster home for the night. And then he bounces around for a while from home to home—or indefinitely, like some of my friends. Or like my brother. But I don't see the chief calling them right now. As it is, Christopher has lost his grandparents, mom, now his guardian, in a relatively short time. I understand he just met me, but I don't want him shipped off to a series of foster care homes while he waits for this to get sorted out."

"So he is like a puppy?" Heather asked.

Chris frowned at Heather.

Heather arched her brow at Chris before saying, "You're keeping him."

Chris reluctantly smiled. "I suppose I am—temporarily. Until we find his people. He obviously has a father out there."

"A father whose identity his mother didn't even disclose to her best friend," Danielle reminded him.

"Yeah, that bothers me. Why did she lie?" Chris shook his head at the possibilities and then added, "But we also have Bridget's side of the family to look at. While I know Bridget was an only child, she might have some cousins or other family members out there who would want to take Christopher into their home. I also want to find out what happened to the Singer estate. I have to assume something happened to it if Bridget moved out after her parents died and moved in with her friend. It sounds like they were living in a condo or apartment. But considering what I knew about Traci and her circumstances, I find it difficult to believe she owned her own condo. I assume she was renting."

"I'm also curious how the parents died," Danielle said. "The last time you saw them was over four years ago, so it's possible the parents died several years apart."

"Or did they die like our parents did," Chris asked. "Together?"

Danielle understood what Chris meant. Her parents had died together in an airplane crash, while Chris's had died in a boating accident.

LATER THAT EVENING, across town, Kelly Morelli joined her houseguest, Laura Miller, in her living room, while her husband, Joe, took a shower at the other end of the house.

"And he touched it?" Laura asked as she sipped the glass of wine Kelly had given her.

"It really freaked him out. It took him a minute to realize what it was." Kelly shivered at the thought.

"So who was she?"

"I guess she was a friend of Chris's."

Laura's eyes widened. "Chris Glandon?"

Kelly nodded. "But you'd better say Johnson. If your sister hears you say his real name, she'll be all over you."

"Wow. How does Joe know she was a friend of Chris's?"

"I guess she showed up at Marlow House to see Chris. Sounds like it wasn't long after I brought you back from the airport. Joe said she had a kid with her, asked Chris to watch him for an hour, and then when she didn't return, Chris called the chief."

"Wow." Laura took another sip of the wine.

"Joe said it looked like a professional hit." Kelly shivered again.

"A professional hit? That's scary. I wonder if she was involved in drugs or something. I had a friend from high school. When I was in college, I heard they found his body on a beach. He had been shot; they said it looked like a professional hit. Later it came out he had gotten involved with some drug dealers. The thing that always blew my mind, back in high school he never did drugs. I never saw that one coming."

Kelly shrugged. "Joe said nothing about drugs. Just that it looked like a professional hit."

"That poor kid. Someone killed his mom."

Kelly shook her head. "According to Joe, the boy isn't her son, but she was his guardian. His real mom died a few months ago."

"How did his mother die?" Laura asked.

"Joe didn't say. Not sure if he even knows."

"You think his mother was murdered, too?" Laura asked in a whisper.

Kelly frowned. "Why would you wonder that?"

"Think about it. Two close friends died three months apart?"

"That's a chilling thought." Kelly shivered at the idea.

"Where's his father?"

"I have to think he doesn't have one if the murdered woman was his guardian."

"So what happens to him now?"

Kelly shrugged. "I guess he's staying with Chris for now until they can contact someone from the boy's family."

Laura picked up her cellphone off the end table.

"Who are you calling?" Kelly asked.

"My sister. You said the woman stopped over at Marlow House to see Chris. I'm sure Danielle has already filled my sister in on all the details."

"Isn't it kind of late to be calling Lily?" Kelly asked.

Laura paused a moment and then reconsidered the call. Finally, she shrugged and reluctantly sent a text instead of calling. A moment later, Lily replied.

"What did she say?" Kelly asked.

Laura let out a sigh. "Said she really doesn't know anything. We could talk in the morning, and that she was in bed." Laura tossed her cellphone back onto the end table.

EIGHT

Traci stood on the beach, looking out at the ocean, listening to the sound of the waves breaking along the shore as the full moon overhead lit up the night sky. She wasn't sure how long she'd been standing there, watching the waves and contemplating recent events.

It had been reckless and out of character to leave Christopher with a virtual stranger. Did she even say goodbye to the child? What would Bridget have thought? Bridget, who had adamantly refused to track down Chris and make him take some responsibility for his son.

Although she suspected if not for Mr. Singer, Bridget would have looked for Chris. Traci had seen how crazy Bridget had been for him. He was all she'd ever talked about. While she'd dated other men, those closer to her age, she'd wanted Chris.

But when Bridget had learned of her pregnancy and Mr. Singer found out Chris was the father, he was outraged. Of course, Mr. Singer could do nothing legally to Chris aside from pressuring his daughter to seek child support. But Bridget was a legal adult. While he might have been able to bribe Chris into marrying his daughter, Mr. Singer didn't want that.

Traci had once overheard an argument between Mr. Singer and

his daughter. She had been visiting Bridget and left to go home. But when she reached her car, she realized she left her cellphone in Bridget's bedroom. After returning to the house, she let herself in and started for her friend's bedroom.

"You are not to see Chris Johnson again," Mr. Singer shouted from the den. "It's not because he's too old for you. Hell, if he acted his age and did something with his life, I'd be happy to pay for your wedding. But he's a parasite and a freeloader. A perpetual charming Peter Pan. What are you going to do, live on Tad's sailboat with him while taking care of a baby? Does he even own a car? And if you think I'll foot the bill so you can be with him and play house while he coasts through life, you are sorely mistaken. Unless you want to be cut off financially, you will never see him again. You can continue to live here, or you can find a suitable husband and father for your child, one that I approve of."

After that, Traci understood why Bridget had never tried to find Chris. But after all the drama happened following Mrs. Singer's death, Traci had assumed Bridget would want to look for Chris. But she had been wrong.

"It's been over four years; he'll hate me," Bridget had insisted.

Traci had eventually stopped trying to convince Bridget to find Chris. But at Bridget's funeral, Traci had run into one of Chris's old acquaintances. It was Ken Palmer. At first, Traci didn't recognize him, but he recognized her. After they exchanged small talk at the memorial for a few minutes, she realized who he was. He was the old dude who owned a boat down at the marina, but she and Bridget had stopped going to the marina after Bridget got pregnant.

On impulse, Traci had asked, "Do you have any idea whatever happened to Chris Johnson? He used to live on a boat that belonged to one of his friends. He left before Christmas, about four years ago."

"Sure, Chris. I haven't thought about him in a long time. He lived on Tad Gaines's boat. Tad sold it because of his divorce. Last time I saw Chris, he was on his way to Oregon to spend Christmas there. In fact, I drove him to the airport."

"Really? Chris has family in Oregon?"

"No, he wasn't going to see family. He was planning to stay in some little bed-and-breakfast there, Marlow House. It's in Frederickport. I only remember because after I came home, I looked it up online. An old Victorian, right across the street from the ocean. Owned and operated by a single lady. Nice-looking woman. I told my wife, just watch, now that Chris doesn't have Tad's boat, landing at a B and B with a short walk to the beach would be perfect for him. He was a handy guy, helped all of us down at the marina. Bet he finagled himself into a handyman job up there."

As soon as Ken had walked away, Traci added the name of the town and B and B to Notes on her iPhone. She forgot about it until several weeks ago, when she could no longer deal with her new reality.

Traci closed her eyes and replayed all that she remembered of the day. A jumble of confusion, starting with her irrational abandonment of Christopher, losing her car, and then wandering into a stranger's house. Incapable of a clear stream of thought, Traci thought it reminded her of the time she and Bridget had gone to that party at Scarlet Larson's house, and someone put something into her drink.

Traci's eyes flew open. Was that what had happened to her? But where, when, how? For the last few days, they had been eating nothing but the peanut butter sandwiches she had made, and drinking water from the bottled water she had purchased back in California. But they had eaten at that restaurant on the pier. Had someone put something in her food there that made her mind feel so jumbled? Something that made her make foolish decisions and forget things?

LILY SAT ALONE in her kitchen at the breakfast bar, drinking coffee early Sunday morning. She wore her pajamas and a robe, while Sadie napped nearby. She had finished nursing Emily Ann ten minutes earlier, and Ian had offered to take the baby with him into their bedroom so she could have some quiet time before her family descended on her. They'd had a rough night with the baby, and she had gotten little sleep. But Connor was still sleeping in his bedroom, and her parents were upstairs in the guest room, she assumed, still sleeping.

Just as Lily prepared to take another drink of coffee, Sadie jumped up and looked toward the front door, wagging her tail without barking. The dog rushed toward the front entry. She returned a moment later, still not barking, Laura by her side.

"You're awake," Laura chirped. She held up a key. "Kelly gave me this so I wouldn't have to knock and wake you up."

"Please, not so loud," Lily groaned. "Connor is still sleeping, and it's possible Ian got Emily Ann back to sleep. She didn't sleep much last night."

"I'm sorry." Laura dropped the keys on the breakfast bar and then walked to the coffeepot to pour herself a cup.

"You're here early," Lily said.

"Kelly dropped me off. She and Joe were going to Pier Café for breakfast before he goes into work. They invited me to join them, but I thought they probably wanted some alone time."

"I heard Joe found that woman's body."

Now, with a full cup of coffee in hand, Laura turned to her sister and walked to the breakfast bar. She took a seat next to Lily. "I imagine Danielle told you?"

"Yeah." Lily took another sip of coffee.

"So who was this woman? How good a friend of Chris's was she?"

"Just someone he knew when he lived on that boat. I guess she was in the area, heard he was up here, and dropped in to say hi. Don't know why, but she thought he might be at Marlow House. Probably because that's where he stayed when he first moved up here. That's who was at our door right after you arrived."

Laura arched her brows. "That was her?"

Lily shrugged. "Apparently. She said she was looking for his house."

"Someone said there was a little boy with her."

"Yeah, the son of one of their mutual friends. Chris didn't know the girl had died—or that she'd had a son. Anyway, she asked Chris if the boy could stay with him for an hour because she needed to do something. He said yes, and when she didn't come back, he felt he needed to involve the police," Lily lied.

"Does Chris have any idea who killed her?"

Lily shook her head. "No. Chris said they were just acquaintances."

"That is wild. I swear, Lily, every time I come here, something crazy happens."

Lily turned to her sister and set her now empty mug on the breakfast bar counter. "I want you to tell me about your trip."

Laura shrugged. "You read my blog, didn't you?"

"Yeah, but I imagine there are some things you didn't put on the blog. Like, how about that guy you were dating?"

"I told you, that didn't work out. It was nothing." Laura shrugged again and sipped her coffee.

"It didn't seem like nothing the last time we talked on the phone. Oh, and about that, why would you get a new number?"

"Why not?"

"For one thing, all your friends have that number."

"The friends I want to keep in touch with, I'll give them my number."

Lily frowned. "Okay."

Laura turned to her sister. "Another thing, if anyone calls for me, don't tell them I'm in town. Tell them I'm traveling, but that you'll be happy to pass on their name and number if they want me to call them."

"Is there someone you're trying to avoid?"

"No. I just like my privacy. And come on, aren't there some people you knew before you moved up here that you simply have nothing in common with anymore, so there's no reason to keep in touch? You got a new phone number when you moved up here."

"Yeah, because everyone assumed I was dead, and Mom cancelled my phone."

WHILE LILY and Laura talked in Lily's kitchen on Sunday morning, Kelly and Joe sat together in a booth at Pier Café, preparing to put in their order with Carla.

"Is it true they found some woman on the outskirts of town, shot along the side of the road?" Carla asked them.

"Joe found her," Kelly blurted.

Setting the coffeepot she held on the table, Carla turned to Joe, hand on hip, and asked, "Who was she?"

"We can't release that information until we contact the family. But she wasn't from Frederickport; I doubt you knew her."

"Is it true she was a friend of Chris's and that she had a little boy with her?" Carla asked.

Joe frowned at Carla. "Who told you that?"

Carla shrugged in response. Joe silently guessed some responders had stopped into the diner last night after they got off work and talked to Carla. It was possible one of them might have overheard the chief talking to Joe and Brian about the child staying with Chris. *You can't keep anything secret in Frederickport,* Joe told himself.

"Because if it is…" Carla paused a moment and leaned closer to Joe, "then I saw her last night right before someone murdered her."

"You did?" Joe asked.

Carla nodded and picked up the coffeepot. She flipped over two clean coffee cups on the table and started filling them as she said, "Yeah. She came in here asking about Marlow House and Chris Johnson. Said he was an old friend. I told her his house was on Beach Drive and that he worked for the Glandon Foundation. She seemed surprised. So not sure how good of friends they were. I got the impression she hadn't seen Chris since he moved up here. But I noticed one thing."

"What was that?" Joe asked.

"That little boy with her. He looked just like a Chris mini me."

Kelly frowned. "What are you saying?"

Carla shrugged. "Just that I wouldn't be surprised if the little boy is Chris's. Not only does he look like Chris's spitting image, she calls the boy Christopher."

NINE

After picking up Brian from the police station on Saturday evening, Heather brought him back to her house for the night. They both slept in on Sunday morning. Heather woke first. She quietly slipped out of bed and headed to the bathroom. While in the bathroom, she brushed her hair, pulling it into a high ponytail before brushing her teeth. She quietly reentered the bedroom, where she put on her running clothes and gathered up the clothing Brian had worn on Saturday. Heather left Brian sleeping in her bed as she stepped out of the bedroom into the hallway, still holding Brian's clothes. The moment she closed the bedroom door behind her, she heard a meow. Heather looked down and saw her calico cat staring up at her, its tail swishing.

"Good morning, Bella," Heather whispered. Bella followed Heather downstairs, where Heather put Brian's clothes in the washing machine, fed the cat, and left the house to take her run.

Standing outside on the sidewalk in front of her house, Heather looked both ways before sprinting across the street. Once on the other side of Beach Drive, she used the path between two of the houses to reach the sand.

Now standing not far from where the breakers rolled up onto

the shore, Heather took a few minutes to warm up before she started her run. She had passed Chris's house when she noticed a woman standing about a hundred feet away, looking out at the ocean; her left side faced Heather.

Heather was about twelve feet from the woman, preparing to go around her, when the woman turned and faced Heather, her expression blank.

Heather stopped abruptly and stared at the woman. While she had never seen her in person, her identity was no mystery, considering the bloody hole in the center of her forehead.

The two women stared at each other. Finally, Heather said, "Traci?"

The woman frowned at Heather. "Who told you my name?"

"Chris has been looking for you."

Traci cocked her head, looking curiously at Heather. "Who told you that?"

"I'm a friend of Chris's. My boyfriend and I had dinner with him last night at Marlow House after you left."

"Did he tell you about Christopher?"

Heather nodded.

"I shouldn't have left him there without saying goodbye. Or explaining. How is he?"

"He's okay, considering everything. Confused. He spent the night at Marlow House."

Traci frowned. "Chris didn't take him home with him? Someone said Chris has his own house on Beach Drive."

"He does. But Chris spent the night at Marlow House, too."

Traci glanced around, as if looking to see if anyone else was nearby. The beach was virtually empty. She looked back at Heather. "You said Chris was looking for me? Did he call the police on me?"

"Why would he call the police?" Heather was fairly certain Traci didn't realize she was dead. Heather wanted to blurt the question *Who shot you?* But that would probably scare her off.

Traci shrugged. "I figured he might tell the police I abandoned Christopher. But Chris is the father, and he should take responsibility for his son. I can't do it anymore."

"I understand Christopher's grandparents were wealthy. What happened to all their money?"

Traci stared at Heather. Instead of answering the question, she disappeared.

TRACI STOOD in the middle of Marlow House's entry hall. She glanced around, somewhat confused and unsure how she had gotten here. Moments earlier, she had been standing on the beach, talking to a woman who claimed to be Chris's friend. When the woman asked about Bridget's parents, it got Traci wondering about Chris and how much he actually knew about the Singers' fate. When talking to him at Marlow House, Chris had acted surprised to learn of Bridget's death. She wondered what Chris might be hiding and decided she needed to return to Marlow House and see Christopher.

Traci spied an open doorway on the other side of the hallway. Without a second thought, she found herself standing in its doorway, looking into what was obviously the living room. She immediately spied someone who appeared to be sleeping on a sofa. She moved closer. It was Chris.

Instead of waking him, Traci backed up and moved out of the room. She needed to find Christopher. Perhaps it would be best if she took Christopher. But first, she needed to find him. If he was still asleep, she could wake him up and sneak him out of the house before Chris woke up. *This was a bad idea. I should never have come to Oregon*, she thought.

Back in the entry hall, she walked to another room. Traci peeked into the open doorway; she saw it was a bedroom. Stepping inside the room, she found Christopher sleeping soundly on the bed. Traci moved closer to the bed and found the boy was not alone. A dog slept on the foot of the boy's bed. It was not just any dog—it was a pit bull. Traci's eyes widened at the sight.

She glanced around the room and spied Christopher's suitcase sitting in the corner and then looked back to the bed. Reaching her hand out toward Christopher, intending to nudge his arm to wake him and not the dog, her plan was dashed when in the next moment the dog lifted its head and looked at Traci.

Traci jumped back from the bed, her eyes never leaving the dog, who had just sat up and now stared at her.

Surely that dog didn't just ask who I am, Traci asked herself before disappearing.

TRACI STOOD in the middle of the diner where she and Christopher had eaten dinner. Like with Marlow House moments earlier, where she couldn't recall traveling from the beach to Marlow House, she had no memory of leaving Marlow House to come here —she was simply here. But this is where it had all begun—the irrational loss of memory and her rash behavior. She needed to find out what someone had put into her food.

She spied the server with the purple hair who had waited on her. She was currently delivering food to a table. The next moment, Traci found herself sitting at the table with the couple. They didn't seem to notice her.

"Here we are," the server said as she set down the plates. "Do you need anything else?"

After picking up their silverware, the couple looked over their food.

"Looks good," the woman said.

The server started to turn away, but stopped and turned back, her hand on one hip as she looked at the man. "Joe, what's going to happen to Christopher?"

The man looked up at the server. "Christopher?"

The server nodded. "Not Chris, but the kid. The little boy who looks just like him. When I was putting your order in, I remember he called her Traci. So I assume she's not his mother. I imagine when you said they're looking for her next of kin, you're probably looking for his mother, too."

The man called Joe set his silverware on the table and looked up at the server. "From what I understand, Chris and the woman who was killed—"

"Traci. Her name was Traci. I just remembered," Carla reminded him.

"Yes, that was her name. From what I understand, she and Chris were mutual friends of the boy's mother. But the boy's mother is also dead."

"Someone shot her, too?" Carla gasped.

Joe groaned. "No. I don't know how the boy's mother died. I just know the murdered woman was the boy's guardian."

"What are you talking about? I'm Christopher's guardian!" Traci blurted. But they continued to ignore her.

"And his father? It's Chris? Isn't it? I was right. They look just alike," Carla said.

"Carla, please, don't be telling people Chris is that child's father. From what the chief told me, the woman was a friend of Chris's from when he lived in California. While in town, she decided to stop and say hi while she was passing through."

"She didn't realize he lived here," Carla said. "She just said he once stayed at Marlow House."

Joe shrugged. "I understand she stopped by to say hi while she was in the area, and Chris agreed to watch the boy for an hour, and she never came back."

"That's not true," Traci insisted. They continued to ignore her.

"If she pulled off the highway, like they said she did, she probably knew her killers," Carla said.

"What killers?" Traci demanded.

WHEN HEATHER RETURNED HOME, she found Brian sitting in her kitchen, drinking coffee while wearing one of her robes. It was one of her more feminine robes, one with lace. She was fairly certain he hadn't specifically chosen that one. As she recalled, it had been hanging on the back of her closet door. She paused a moment in the doorway and gave him a once-over.

Brian looked up from his coffee and gave her a brief salute with his mug. "You stole my clothes."

She walked to him and gave him a quick kiss before saying, "I threw them in the wash before I left. I didn't think you'd want to put on day-old briefs."

"Yeah, I know. I already put them in the dryer. Thanks."

Heather walked over to the counter and poured herself a cup of coffee while saying, "I saw Traci on my run."

Brian set his cup on the kitchen table and looked over to Heather, her back to him. "Her ghost?"

Heather turned around, now facing him, a filled cup of coffee in hand. "I don't imagine the coroner's office dumped her body on the beach last night. So yeah, her ghost. And I don't think she knows she's dead." Heather walked to the table with her coffee and sat down.

"Did you recognize her from the picture Chris showed us?"

Heather shook her head and pointed to her forehead. Brian understood her meaning: The ghost had a gunshot through her forehead.

"If she doesn't understand she's dead, I guess you didn't ask who killed her."

Heather shook her head. "No." She then told Brian about her exchange with the spirit.

"Do you think she's moved on?"

"I doubt it. From what I've learned, confused spirits don't move on. They have to accept their death before they take that step. Unless they were a really horrible person, then the universe might suck them up and do whatever they do to defective souls." Heather shrugged and took a sip of coffee.

Brian glanced at the clock and looked back at Heather. "I called down to the station while you were out. They still haven't been able to locate any family for Traci. Much less for the boy."

"I'm dead, aren't I?" a new voice demanded of Heather.

Heather's eyes widened as she shifted her gaze from Brian to the apparition standing next to him. She slowly lowered her coffee cup to the table and said, "Please don't leave."

60

"I wasn't planning on it," Brian said.

"I'm not talking to you, Brian. I'm talking to her." Heather pointed to the space next to Brian.

He turned, looked at the space, and then looked back at Heather. "Marie? Eva?"

"No. Traci."

TEN

"I'm dead, aren't I?" Traci repeated. "And you can see me. Why is that? No one else could."

"I'm a medium," Heather told her. Brian sat quietly, watching Heather and occasionally looking to where he imagined the spirit stood—or sat. *Hell, she could be floating in the air next to me*, Brian told himself.

Traci glanced briefly at Brian. "He can't see me, can he?"

Heather shook her head. "No."

Traci took a second look at Brian. "That's a nice robe. I guess I interrupted something."

"It's okay. He's waiting for his clothes to dry." Heather grinned.

"So I am dead."

"How did you figure it out?" Heather asked.

"Strange things kept happening that I didn't understand. Like one minute I'm standing on the beach, and the next, I'm in Marlow House. Nothing makes sense. I ask myself why, and suddenly I'm in the diner where Christopher and I had dinner. But no one can see me. But they're talking about me, and they say someone murdered me. I'm dead."

"You went to Marlow House after you left me on the beach?"

"Yes. Briefly. But no one was awake downstairs." Traci studied Heather for a moment before asking, "When you spoke to me on the beach, you knew I was dead, didn't you?"

"Yes. But I didn't want to say anything because you obviously didn't understand, and I didn't want you to disappear. I needed to ask you some questions. But you disappeared anyway."

"What did you want to ask me?"

"For starters, who killed you?"

"At the diner they said someone shot me. But that can't be true."

"Yeah, well, about that. There is a big hole in your forehead that says something different."

"I have a hole in my head?" Traci reached up to touch her forehead, but her hand simply moved through it.

"From a bullet," Heather explained.

"I can't believe that. Where's your bathroom? I need to find a mirror."

"I'm afraid that won't help. Spirits don't have a reflection."

Traci shook her head. "I don't believe that." The next minute, she vanished.

"Damn, she disappeared again," Heather grumbled.

"Where did she go?" Brian glanced around the kitchen.

"She has either moved on—now that she knows she's dead—or she's looking for a mirror."

The next moment, Traci reappeared in the kitchen. "You were right. I don't have a reflection."

Heather shrugged. "Told you."

"Told me what?" Brian asked.

Heather smiled at Brian. "I wasn't talking to you. Traci is back."

"Please ask her to tell us who killed her before she leaves again."

"This is Brian," Heather introduced. "And I'm Heather. Brian is a police officer with the Frederickport Police Department. He was there last night when they found your body. And he's trying to find your killer. It would make it easier if you told me what happened." Heather leaned forward and pulled a chair out from the table and motioned to it. Traci sat down.

"I don't know what to tell you."

"Start with what happened after you left Christopher at Marlow House," Heather suggested.

Traci shrugged. "I headed out of town and then realized it was a stupid thing to do, to just leave Christopher with his father and take off. So I pulled off on a side road, to pull my thoughts together." Traci froze for a moment, as if she had remembered something.

"What is it?" Heather asked.

"I remember I parked my car and got out. There was no one on the road. A car pulled up. Two men got out of the car. They were wearing suits and dark sunglasses, so I didn't get a good look at their faces. I assumed they thought I had broken down and were offering to help. Right after I told them I was okay, one man pulled his hand from his coat, and the next thing I remember, I'm lying on the ground next to my car."

"I assume it was a gun he pulled out of his pocket."

"But why? Why kill me?" Traci paused again, her eyes widening. She stared at Heather a moment and asked, "Did they do anything…um, weird with my body?"

"Aside from shooting you and moving your body off into the bushes along the road, no."

"What is she saying?" Brian asked.

Heather repeated for Brian what Traci had said.

"So she didn't recognize her killer?"

Traci shook her head, and Heather said, "No. She didn't."

"Heather, ask Traci—" Brian paused a moment and turned to face the chair where he assumed Traci sat. "Traci, tell Heather what you remember about the car, the men. Anything you remember."

Traci stared at Brian a moment before looking back at Heather. "He still can't see me, right?"

"No." Heather smiled. "But tell me what he asked."

"Not sure what I can tell you that will help. They might have been white. But not Black. Like I said, they were wearing dark glasses, and I only glimpsed them for a moment—and then I was lying on the ground. But I remember sitting up and seeing someone grab my ankles. But the next minute, they weren't there. And I still was."

"What about their car?" Heather asked.

"It was gray, maybe. Yet not sure. I just saw it for a moment. It wasn't a van or a truck. Just a car."

"And you've never seen this car before or the men?"

Traci shook her head. "Not that I remember."

Heather repeated her words for Brian.

"Does she know of anyone who would want her dead?" Brian asked.

"Why would anyone want me dead?" Traci gasped.

"Someone obviously did, considering they shot you through the head," Heather snarked.

Traci frowned.

"Please don't scare her off," Brian begged.

Heather rolled her eyes at Brian and said, "Traci, the police are trying to find your next of kin to notify them of your death. Who should they contact?"

Traci shrugged. "My parents divorced when I was a freshman in high school. Mom lives in Hawaii with husband number three—or is it four? I don't talk to her very often. We were never close. I don't think she wanted kids. My dad remarried my stepmother right after the divorce. Mom left to find herself, and I stayed with Dad and his new wife. She and I never got along very well. I guess I look too much like Mom. Right after I graduated from high school, I moved out. I talk to them maybe twice a year. They moved to Florida a couple of years ago."

"Do you have any siblings?" Heather asked.

"I have an older brother. I lived with him after I moved out of my dad's house. He's probably the one you should call. He's the only one who will care." Traci then gave Heather his name and phone number. Heather got up from the table, grabbed a pad of paper and pen from a kitchen drawer, and then had Traci repeat the name and number. When done writing the name and number, Heather ripped the top sheet of paper from the pad and handed it to Brian while saying, "This is Traci's brother. He's the one you should call."

Sitting back down at the kitchen table, still holding the pad of paper and pen, Heather asked, "Now we need some contact information for Christopher's next of kin."

"That would be Chris. He's his father."

Instead of pointing out Chris was not the father, Heather said, "Aside from his father, doesn't he have some cousins? I know his mother was an only child, but didn't Bridget have some aunts and uncles? Cousins?"

Traci stared at Heather for several moments. When she didn't answer, Heather repeated the question.

"Are you suggesting Chris isn't going to step up to the plate and take care of his son? Christopher's mother and grandparents are gone, and now me. Surely Chris is going to do the right thing."

Heather let out a sigh and set the pad of paper and pen on the kitchen table. "The thing is, Chris swears he is not the boy's father. He and your friend, well, they never hooked up."

Traci shook her head. "That's not true. Why would Bridget lie to me? And he looks like Chris. How can he deny his son like that?"

"Did you ever see your friend and Chris together as a couple? Did they ever hold hands or kiss in front of you? Discuss their hookups when you were with them?"

"No. Of course not. They had to keep their relationship a secret. For one thing, Bridget's father would have had an absolute fit. And when he found out about the pregnancy and who the father was, he threatened to cut Bridget off if she tried contacting Chris. Chris had already left town by then. He took off right after she told him she was pregnant."

"Chris would never abandon a child that he believed was his," Heather insisted. "For one thing, he was in foster care for about six years before he was adopted, and his older brother was stuck in the system. No. There is no way Chris would turn his back on a child he believed was his."

"I never knew he was adopted. Or that he had been in foster care. But I suppose I can understand why he took off after Bridget told him she was pregnant. Chris didn't have a job and was living on some guy's boat for free in exchange for maintaining it. He'd help people around the marina for a free beer. He was barely taking care of himself, and he obviously didn't want the added responsibility of a kid. But the waitress at that diner told me he has a job now, and he even has a house on this street. So he has no excuse."

Heather leaned back in the chair, folding her arms over her chest as she stared at Traci.

"What's going on?" Brian asked.

"If you weren't dead, I wouldn't tell you any of this. Chris didn't leave your friend because he didn't want to take responsibility. With his money, he could easily have paid her off and set Christopher up with a trust fund and never bother with either one again, if he was that sort of person. Which he's not, considering how passionate he is about helping people."

Traci frowned at Heather. "You aren't making any sense."

"Chris's real name is Chris Glandon, not Johnson. Not only is he stupidly good looking, he is stupidly rich. The Glandon Foundation he works for—that I work for—is his foundation. Chris gives away millions of dollars every month. He is a philanthropist."

Traci's eyes widened. "Are you serious?"

"Very. Christopher needs to be with his real family. And that is not Chris."

"That can't be true. Bridget said…"

"You obviously have no idea who Chris really is. Because of our work, we have spent a lot of time together, and women are always throwing themselves at him—even without knowing his net worth. But young girls fresh out of high school, they aren't his thing. I'm sorry to tell you, your friend lied to you. I have a feeling she hooked up with some guy who looked like Chris because Chris wouldn't take her up on her offer."

"Peter," Traci muttered under her breath.

"Who's Peter?" Heather asked.

"Nobody. But if what you say is true, I'd still rather Christopher stay with Chris. Sounds like he won't starve, and he'll be better off with Chris than any relative of Bridget's. If he doesn't want to play father, he can send him to a good boarding school. He can be one of Chris's new charities." Traci smiled and added, "If it wasn't for being dead, coming up to Oregon was probably a good idea." The next moment, she vanished.

ELEVEN

After Kelly and Joe finished breakfast at Pier Café on Sunday morning, Kelly dropped Joe off at the police station before going to her brother's house. When she arrived, she found Ian in the kitchen with Gene and Connor. Connor sat in his highchair, eating breakfast, while the two men sat at the breakfast bar, drinking coffee and visiting with each other.

Kelly greeted Gene and Ian, dropped a kiss on Connor's brow, and then headed on to the living room, where Ian had told her she would find the ladies. In the living room, she found Tammy holding Emily Ann while Laura sat next to her on the sofa, talking to her mother.

"Morning," Kelly greeted. "Where's Lily?"

"Morning." Tammy flashed her a smile.

"She's in her room getting dressed. How was breakfast?" Laura asked.

"Aside from Carla grilling Joe about the woman who was murdered, it was fine." Kelly took a seat on the nearby recliner.

Tammy looked up from her granddaughter. "Who's Carla?"

Kelly leaned back in the chair and crossed one leg over an opposing knee. "A waitress who works at Pier Café. She's something of a busybody. But I have to give her credit. That girl has a knack for finding things out. She should start a podcast about local gossip." Kelly chuckled at the idea.

"What kind of things?" Laura asked.

Before Kelly could answer the question, Lily walked into the room. "Morning, Kelly."

"Morning, Lily. Have you talked to Danielle this morning?" Kelly asked.

"Umm, yeah. Why?" Lily took a seat on the sofa, next to her mother. Tammy now had a daughter on either side of her and her granddaughter on her lap. Lily smiled over at her baby and reached out, gently caressing the sleeping infant.

"When Joe and I had breakfast at Pier Café this morning, Carla was full of all sorts of information."

"Isn't she always?" Lily scoffed.

"Seems Carla waited on the woman who was murdered last night, before the woman stopped at Marlow House." Kelly shared what Carla had told them at breakfast regarding the murdered woman coming into the diner with a small boy a few hours before her murder.

"Do you think it's true?" Laura asked her sister when Kelly finished her telling.

Lily frowned. "Do I think what's true?"

"Is the little boy Chris's son?"

Lily shook her head. "No. According to Dani, he's not. When the woman first showed up at Marlow House, she told Chris she brought him his son."

"You didn't tell me that this morning," Laura said.

"I didn't know this morning when I talked to you," Lily lied. "I talked to Dani a few minutes ago. Chris says he never had an intimate relationship with the boy's mother. She was only eighteen when he moved up here. And knowing Chris, I don't see him dating someone so young."

"Not like Brian," Kelly said with a snort.

Lily frowned at Kelly. "What is that supposed to mean?"

"Brian is old enough to be Heather's father," Kelly reminded her.

"It's not the same thing. Heather was a full-grown woman when they got together. Not exactly a kid. Eighteen is barely out of high school," Lily said.

"There is still a big age difference," Laura argued.

Lily shrugged. "True. But with Heather and Brian, despite the age difference, there isn't that balance-of-power thing."

Kelly frowned. "I don't get what you're saying."

"When an older guy dates a much younger woman, it's often because he wants to control her. Or train her, which sounds really gross. Guys like that often go for the barely legal or almost legal woman. I don't believe Brian is foolish enough to imagine he could ever control Heather." Lily chuckled at the idea.

"You have a point," Kelly conceded. "Why do you think Heather seems to go for the older guy?"

Lily shrugged. "Perhaps she doesn't want to put up with the bullshit from some younger guys. And she's always been clear about not wanting kids. Maybe she figures older guys aren't looking for a woman who wants babies. Or maybe she simply finds older guys hot."

They chatted for a few more minutes about the tragic events of the previous day before the topic shifted to what everyone had planned for the day.

"Kelly's going to take me shopping," Laura said. "I need to get some exciting things, like a new toothbrush, some makeup, and a few other fun purchases."

"Do either of you want to go? I have room in my car," Kelly offered.

"Thank you, dear. But I spent a lot of time in a car yesterday, and I just want to sit here and hold this angel." Tammy finished her sentence by kissing Emily Ann's right cheek.

"I'm going to stay here with Mom," Lily said. "But thanks for the offer."

KELLY AND LAURA had been gone for about thirty minutes, and Lily had just finished nursing the baby when Lily's cellphone rang. Tammy took the baby from her daughter. Lily picked up her cellphone from the coffee table and looked at it. She didn't recognize the number, but she answered it anyway.

"Hello?"

"Hi. Is this Lily, Laura's sister?" asked an unfamiliar male voice in a British accent.

"Yes. Who is this?"

"Hi. I'm a friend of Laura's. I've been trying to call her, and I'm not getting an answer. I'm hoping nothing's wrong. Have you heard from her?"

"Who is this?" Lily repeated the question.

"I'm sorry, my name is Dane."

Lily remembered that was the guy Laura had been seeing in London. "No. Laura's not here."

"Is she alright?"

"Laura's fine. I talked to her about an hour ago. She just has a new number. But I can tell her you called."

"So she is in Frederickport?"

"Umm, no. She's traveling. But I talked to her on the phone this morning," Lily lied.

"Could you give me her new number, please?"

Lily didn't answer immediately. She considered the question a moment and then said, "I'll be happy to tell her you called the next time I talk to her. Does she have your number?"

"I suppose I can understand not being comfortable giving out her number to someone you don't know. So yes, please tell her I called, and I'd really like to talk to her."

———

NOT LONG AFTER the phone call, Lily told her mother she was running over to Marlow House and wouldn't be gone long. Tammy told her Emily Ann would be fine. When Lily arrived at Marlow

House, she entered through the kitchen, where she found a little boy sitting at the kitchen table, coloring.

He wasn't alone. Max lounged on the kitchen table, watching him color, his tail swishing back and forth, while Hunny, who had been curled up on the floor next to the boy's chair, jumped up to greet her. Lily absently reached down to pet Hunny while approaching the boy.

She looked at Max and raised her brows, wondering if Danielle knew he was up on the table. The boy stopped coloring and looked up at her.

"Hello. You must be Christopher. I'm Lily. I live across the street." She glanced around the kitchen. "Where is everyone?"

Christopher pointed to the door leading to the hallway. "In there." He resumed his coloring.

Lily smiled down at the boy, gave Max a cursory pet, and headed for the doorway. Before leaving the room, she turned to look at the boy, who seem uninterested in her presence. She also noticed Hunny had returned to where she had been when Lily first entered the house, and the dog made no attempt to follow Lily out of the room.

Lily found Chris, Heather, Walt, Danielle, and the twins in the living room. Both babies were swaddled and sleeping, with Walt holding his daughter and Danielle holding her son.

"You know, you're going to spoil those babies by always holding them," Lily teased.

"Hi, Lily," several of them chorused while Heather asked, "Where's Emily Ann?"

"Grandma's currently holding her," Lily said with a chuckle before taking a seat.

"Heather was telling us about her visit from Traci," Danielle said.

"Traci? The woman who was murdered?" Lily asked.

"She stopped in this morning. Brian was there. After Brian left my place, he headed over to the chief's house to give him an update," Heather explained.

"Did she tell you who killed her?" Lily asked.

"No."

Before Heather could elaborate, Chris stood and announced, "I need to go home and get on the computer, see what I can find out about Bridget's family. Call a few people who can help."

"Want to leave Christopher here?" Danielle asked.

Heather stood. "Let me take him shopping."

"Shopping?" Chris asked.

"The kid's going to need some more clothes. And some toys. Kids need toys. I'll use your credit card." Heather flashed Chris a grin.

Fifteen minutes later, Lily sat alone with Danielle in the living room, each holding a baby. Walt had gone up to his office after the others had left, and Danielle had just finished telling Lily all that Heather had told them about their encounter with Traci's spirit.

"That's chilling," Lily said. "Someone just drives up to a parked car and kills the driver. Someone they don't even know?"

"It's insane. It sounds horrible, but I hope it was someone targeting her specifically. Although it doesn't sound like it."

"I understand what you're saying."

Danielle nodded and then said, "So how are your parents? Laura? I'm surprised you are over here."

"I wanted to come over to find out what was going on with Chris. Laura's with Kelly doing some shopping. And Mom is playing grandma. I could have called you to see what was going on, but I sorta wanted to talk to you about something, and I didn't want Mom to overhear."

"What's wrong?"

"It's Laura. Remember that guy I told you Laura met in London?"

"Yeah, the way you talked about him, I thought it might be serious. I guess if Laura cut her trip short, it wasn't."

"Laura used to tell me everything about the guys she dated."

Had Danielle been wearing eyeglasses, it would have looked as if she were peering over the lenses the way she looked at Lily. "You mean like she did with Charlie? I mean Frank?"

"Yeah. She didn't tell me anything about him, which is why it drove me nuts."

"As it turned out, you had a good reason to be worried," Danielle reminded her.

"I just think that whole deal with that guy traumatized her more than any of us realize. I think she really liked him. And he tried to kill her."

"What does this have to do with the guy in London?"

"I get the feeling she ran away from that relationship. Did I tell you she lost her cellphone at the airport when coming home?"

"No. Wow, wasn't that the cellphone Chris bought for her right before she left? She'd better be careful, or she's going to go through cellphones as fast as me." Danielle snickered at the thought. She and Laura had both lost their cellphones when Charlie had kidnapped Laura and tried to extort Danielle. It was not the first time Danielle had been forced to replace a cellphone after a harrowing event.

"When Laura bought a new one, she got a new number. And she told me that if anyone calls for her, not to give out her number or tell them where she is. Just to say she's traveling. A little while ago, that guy she had been dating called me, looking for Laura. He hadn't been able to get ahold of her, and he wanted to make sure she was okay."

"Sounds like Laura doesn't want to talk to someone."

"Yep. Sounds like it. And if Laura doesn't want to see this guy anymore, I just hope it's not because she's afraid to get close to anyone again after what happened with Charlie."

"Or perhaps he had some red flags, and she paid attention this time."

TWELVE

Heather didn't imagine a four-year-old would love spending the afternoon clothes shopping with a woman he just met, so she called the chief and asked if she could elicit the help of his sons. She had seen how Connor responded to Evan, and she assumed Christopher might feel more comfortable with another child, even one who was older. The chief was happy to find something constructive to occupy Eddy and Evan's day, especially since he had an open murder investigation currently occupying his time.

Once he heard Christopher's story, Evan was more than willing to help Heather. He understood what it was like to lose a mother, and at least he had a father. While Eddy Junior was also emotionally swayed, he would have gone even if Christopher didn't come with a sad story. Fact was, he had something of a crush on Heather Donovan. Not only did she look fine, but she also talked to ghosts.

After picking up Evan and Eddy from their house, Heather's first stop was the drugstore. She planned to let the boys take Christopher to the toy section and pick out a few games and toys while she shopped for some child-appropriate toiletry items. Danielle had given Christopher one of the extra toothbrushes she kept on hand for guests; Heather figured he would be more comfortable with a smaller-sized child's toothbrush, along with some kids' toothpaste. He also needed shampoo made for young children, the kind that didn't sting if it got into their eyes, and it wouldn't be a bad idea to pick up a first aid kit. Little kids were always scraping knees or getting cuts.

Heather was thinking of all the things she needed to buy as she walked with the boys up to the store's entrance, telling herself she should make a list. Right before they entered the store, she stopped and looked at Christopher.

"Do you have a favorite cartoon character?" Heather asked him.

Christopher looked up at Heather and named several.

"Why did you ask that?" Eddy asked.

Heather turned to Eddy and smiled. "If they have cartoon-character toothbrushes, I might as well get him his favorite."

"IS that Heather with the chief's boys?" Kelly asked aloud. She stood with Laura, who was checking out makeup on one display, in clear view of the store entrance.

Laura stopped what she was doing and looked in the direction of Kelly's gaze. "Who is the younger one?" Laura asked.

Kelly shrugged. "Not sure."

While Heather and the boys headed in their direction, they clearly had not yet spied the two women. Laura and Kelly watched as Heather stopped, said something to the three boys, and then the boys headed off in another direction in the store. After a few minutes, Heather started toward the section selling toothbrushes. Kelly called out her name. Heather stopped walking and looked at them.

Kelly and Laura approached Heather.

"Hi, Kelly." Heather turned to Laura and said, "Hey, Laura. Danielle said you were back. Had to meet that new niece of yours, didn't you?"

Laura smiled. "She's adorable."

"I thought you were going to be in Europe for at least a year," Heather asked.

Laura shrugged. "I got homesick. And like you said, I really wanted to meet my new niece."

"I know the two oldest boys with you are the chief's sons. Who is the little guy?" Kelly asked.

Heather didn't answer immediately. She looked from Kelly to Laura and then to where the boys had headed, before looking back at Kelly. "Umm, the woman Joe found last night?"

Kelly's eyes widened. "Is that the little boy who was with her?"

Heather nodded. "Yeah. He's sorta staying with Chris until they can contact someone from his family. Chris knew his maternal grandparents and mom, but unfortunately, they've all passed away. The grandparents owned a sailboat at the marina Chris used to live in. The little boy had been living with the woman who was killed. She was his mother's best friend and his guardian. Chris knew her through Christopher's mom, and she looked him up and stopped by to see him. She left Christopher at Marlow House and told Walt and Danielle she would be back in an hour. When she didn't return, they called the police."

"And you took him shopping?" Kelly asked.

"Since the boy's staying with Chris until they find his next of kin, I offered to take him shopping and pick up some things he needs. Evan and Eddy are helping. They took him over to the toy section."

"According to Carla, he's Chris's son," Laura said.

Heather rolled her eyes. "He's not Chris's."

Laura shrugged. "Yeah. Lily said the same thing. That Chris isn't his father."

"Did Carla actually say Christopher was Chris's son?" Heather asked. "Who told her that?"

Kelly shook her head. "No. She mentioned he looks like Chris."

"He's not Chris's son. Can you imagine for a moment he would abandon his son?"

"Maybe he didn't abandon him. It's possible he didn't know about him," Laura said.

"Well, can you imagine Chris learning he had a son and then claiming he isn't his? No. I don't think anyone who knows Chris could imagine that. Now, I really need to get going. I have a lot to buy. See you guys later." Heather walked away as Laura and Kelly said goodbye, but she stopped and turned back and added, "Please don't be spreading that story around town about Chris being his father. Not cool."

"Well, gee, we weren't actually spreading it around town," Laura said with a pout after Heather was out of earshot.

AFTER HEATHER and the boys finished at the drugstore, they went clothes and shoe shopping. Heather silently commended herself for thinking to ask Evan and Eddy to come along, considering how much help they proved to be when buying clothes and making Christopher feel comfortable. As a reward, she let them each pick out a new T-shirt.

"You guys were amazing," Heather told the boys when they finished clothes shopping. Evan and Christopher stood by her while Eddy loaded the purchases into the trunk of her car. "So tell me, where do you guys want to go to lunch? Wherever you want to go. As long as it's in Frederickport."

Evan climbed into the back seat with Christopher while Eddy took the passenger seat. As Heather got into the driver's side of the car, the brothers discussed restaurant choices while Evan would occasionally ask Christopher questions, such as, "What do you like to eat?"

TWO MEN SAT in a booth in Beach Taco, eating their lunch and talking with each other in hushed tones, not wanting others to overhear their conversation. They stopped talking when a young woman walked into the restaurant, three boys in tow. After the woman and her small entourage passed their table, on their way to the order counter, one man said to his companion, "That's what I imagine Wednesday from *The Addams Family* would look like all grown up."

The other man chuckled in response. But when he glanced back to the woman, who now stood at the counter placing her order, the boys turned from her, walking toward a booth facing them. When doing so, the youngest of the group turned in his direction and momentarily looked right in his face.

After the boy turned away, the man reached across the table and grabbed hold of his companion's hand just before it was about to pick up a tortilla chip.

The man being grabbed looked up with a frown. "What?"

He released hold of his companion's hand and whispered, "You know that thing we've been looking for since last night? It just walked in with Wednesday."

HEATHER ARRIVED at the booth with a basket of tortilla chips and salsa, and empty soda cups. Evan and Christopher sat on one side of the booth, with Eddy sitting on the other side.

"They'll bring us our food when it's done." Still standing, Heather set the chips and salsa on the table.

"You sit down. Evan and I can get the drinks." Eddy stood up and reached his hand out to Heather, waiting for her to hand him the soda cups. "Just tell me what you want."

Heather smiled at the teenager. "Why, thanks, Eddy."

When Eddy and Evan returned minutes later, Eddy scooted into the seat next to Heather and whispered to her, "Those guys sitting in the booth across from us. They keep staring at you."

Heather glanced over at the booth and saw two men. If they had been staring, they were no longer looking their way. The next moment, a server brought their food, and Heather didn't give the men much thought.

She had just finished one of her tacos when she noticed motion from the direction of the booth Eddy had mentioned earlier. Heather looked that way and saw the two men stand up. Heather wondered if they had just gone to church, since they both wore suits. She watched as they gathered up their trash and then dumped it in a nearby receptacle. Heather was about to look away, but the next moment, each man took out a pair of dark sunglasses and casually slipped them on as they sauntered toward the restaurant's door.

Heather let out a gasp. She grabbed her cellphone. Evan and Christopher were talking about something with each other and still eating and didn't notice Heather's reaction. Eddy noticed and looked to the door where the men had exited and back to Heather. He was about to ask her what was wrong, but she started talking on the phone. Not wanting to interrupt her, Eddy quietly waited for her to finish her phone call.

"I think I saw them," Heather said in a whisper on the phone.

"Who?" Brian asked from the other end of the line.

"Two men in suits, wearing sunglasses."

Heather didn't hear Brian's groan before he said, "I am assuming you're suggesting you saw the killers?"

"In Beach Taco. They were sitting right across from us."

"And because they are wearing suits...and sunglasses?"

"Who wears suits in Frederickport?" she asked.

"It is Sunday. And even when it isn't, Walt does sometimes. So does Adam. Hell, I've been known for wearing a suit."

"Yeah, I considered the church thing too. But then they put on sunglasses."

She could hear Brian chuckle. If she could have given him a smack, she would have, even though she had been trying to suppress her violent tendencies. After his chuckle, he said, "It's summer; who doesn't wear sunglasses at this time of year?"

Still clutching her cellphone to her ear, Heather slumped back in her seat. "I guess you're right. But Eddy said they were staring at me and Christopher when he and Evan were getting us our drinks."

"I imagine it was you they were looking at, not the boy. Heather, you tend to get people's attention."

"Why? Because I am a weirdo?"

Brian chuckled before saying, "That and the fact you're hot."

Heather rolled her eyes, which was totally wasted on Brian, since it wasn't a video call.

THIRTEEN

An hour later, Heather and the boys stood in the sporting goods section in the last store on Heather's list. Eddy helped pick out a tee-ball set, a baseball glove for Christopher, and then he and Evan helped Christopher pick out a few more things. Earlier, Heather had let each boy choose a set of Legos for themselves, and she'd considered buying Christopher a tablet yet opted instead for some books. Before going to the sporting goods section, she had asked Eddy to help pick out a video gaming set for Christopher with some appropriate games for a boy Christopher's age. She had to admit, buying stuff for kids on Chris's credit card was probably the most fun she'd had in a long time.

They ended up pushing two filled carts in the store. While heading to check out, they stopped for a moment, and Christopher held onto the side of one cart, stood on his tiptoes, and looked into the cart, his eyes wide. "Is that really all for me?"

"All but those two Lego sets." Heather pointed to the two sets Eddy and Evan had picked out.

"Is it my birthday?" Christopher asked.

"When is your birthday?" Evan asked.

Christopher shrugged. "I don't know. I haven't had one since Mom died."

"Do you have any of these toys at home?" Evan asked, assuming Christopher remembered his home he left before coming to Oregon.

Christopher shook his head. "No. I remember I had a lot of toys at my grandma's house when I lived there. But Mom said we didn't have room at Traci's house. Mom let me take one thing."

"What was that?" Evan asked.

"A dinosaur stuffed animal. I used to sleep with it." He sounded sad.

"Did you bring it?" Eddy asked.

Christopher shook his head. "Traci threw it away. She said it smelled."

"Did she buy you a new stuffed animal?" Heather asked.

Christopher shook his head no.

"Let's go over there," Heather said abruptly, leading the boys and carts toward another section of the store, where they sold stuffed animals. Once they arrived in the section, she looked at Christopher and said, "Pick something out. Something to replace your dinosaur."

Christopher's eyes widened, and he looked around excitedly, but when he glanced at the two older boys, he drew into himself. "No, I don't want one."

"Why not?" Heather asked.

"Stuffed animals are for babies."

Eddy looked at the younger boy and smiled. He reached out and rustled his hair. "No, they aren't. Who told you that? I have a favorite stuffed animal."

Christopher turned to the teenager, his eyes wide again. "You do?"

"Sure. So does Evan. So pick something out." Eddy smiled down at the boy.

"Really?" Christopher beamed.

Together, Evan and Christopher headed to check out all the stuffed animals, looking for the perfect one, while Heather stood with Eddy. She smiled over at the teenager. In a whisper she said, "Thanks, Eddy."

Eddy shrugged. "I could tell he wanted one."

"Do you really have a favorite stuffed animal at home?" she asked.

Eddy blushed and shrugged. "Maybe."

Twenty minutes later, Heather stood at the checkout stand with the boys when she noticed two men standing near the exit door, browsing through the magazine stand. They were the men from Beach Taco.

"Eddy, I have a favor to ask you," Heather whispered.

"Sure, what?"

"Those men who were at Beach Taco," she began.

"They're here," Eddy finished for her.

"You saw them too?"

"Yeah, when Evan was picking out a stuffed animal."

"Why didn't you say something?"

Eddy shrugged. "I didn't really think too much of it."

"They are over there by the magazine rack. One of them looks like he's reading, although not sure how he can see very well with those dark glasses on in the store."

"What's the favor?"

"When we leave, I'd like to see what kind of car they get into. I don't want them to know we're watching them," Heather whispered.

Eddy grinned. "Sort of like surveillance, like my dad does?"

Heather nodded. "Exactly."

As they moved through the checkout stand, she noticed the men shoving the magazines they had been reading back into the stand. They fairly rushed out the front door. Without being asked, Eddy sprinted to the door while Heather paid for the purchases.

"Where's Eddy going?" Evan asked as Heather took the receipt from the cashier.

"I asked him to check something for me."

When she reached the front door with the full carts, with Evan pushing one and Christopher by her side, Eddy was waiting just inside the door.

"I saw which car they're in," Eddy whispered.

Heather and the boys left the store. Once at her car, Heather took her time loading up the trunk with their purchases while Evan helped Christopher buckle up in his car seat. Eddy returned the carts for Heather while she got into the driver's seat. When he returned to the car and got in, he whispered, "They're still here."

Meanwhile, Evan and Christopher were oblivious to whatever Heather and Eddy discussed, as Evan was busy helping Christopher tear off the packaging from the Snoopy stuffed animal they had purchased.

Heather glanced briefly at the car but didn't stare. "Do you know what kind of car that is?"

"Yeah, it's like Uncle Bruce's. Even the same color."

"I'm going to sit here for a moment. Wait for them to leave." Heather then picked up her purse and opened it. Taking out a tube of lipstick, she repositioned her rearview mirror and looked into it, preparing to apply the lipstick, while glancing toward the parked car with the two men.

"Wow, is that black?" Eddy asked.

"I think it's called Death Kiss or something," Heather said before applying the lipstick.

After putting the cap back on the tube of lipstick, she returned it to her purse and took out her brush. While she was brushing her hair, Evan asked from the back seat, "Are we waiting for something?"

"Ahh, no, we're going," Heather said, glancing at Eddy and giving a shrug. The men remained sitting in their parked car.

When Heather drove out of the parking lot a few minutes later, Eddy, who focused his attention on the rearview mirror on the passenger side of the vehicle, whispered, "They just pulled out of their parking space." Heather took the next right, and when Eddy told her the men had taken the same right, she decided she didn't want to take Evan and Eddy back to their house. Instead, she drove to the police station. After they parked, Eddy turned around in his seat and watched the nearby road. The car that looked just like Uncle Bruce's drove by the police station.

EDDY AND HEATHER sat in the chief's office with Brian and the chief while Evan took Christopher into the lunchroom to play one game Heather had bought. Heather had just finished telling Brian and MacDonald about the two men from Beach Taco, with Eddy adding his version.

When Heather finished her telling, she looked at Brian and said, "You know how you said everyone wears sunglasses in the summer? Well, they don't normally wear them while standing in a store browsing through the magazine rack. And we're not talking about the lenses that get lighter when indoors. I'm talking *Men in Black* sunglasses."

"The fact you had Christopher with you is concerning," the chief said in a solemn voice.

Heather nodded. "Exactly. I don't think those men were looking at me in the restaurant. They were looking at Christopher. And according to Traci, those men who killed her wore suits and dark glasses."

Eddy's eyes widened. "Traci. Dad said that was the name of the woman who was killed. You talked to her ghost?"

Heather turned to Eddy and smiled. "Yeah, she dropped by my house this morning, and we had a little chat."

"Wow." Eddy slumped back in his chair and smiled.

"DID YOU GET EVERYTHING YOU NEEDED?" Lily asked her sister when she returned Sunday afternoon. "I thought you were picking up just a few things. You were gone a long time."

"Sorry. I wanted to take Kelly to lunch, to thank her for picking me up at the airport and for letting me stay with them. Where is everyone?" Laura set her purse on the coffee table and took a seat on the sofa next to her sister. She slipped off her shoes, and following her sister's example, she put her stockinged feet on the coffee table. Sadie had followed her into the living room from the front door and silently waited for a proper greeting, tail wagging. Laura obliged and ruffled the golden retriever's fur in a playful pet.

"I think we wore Mom out. She's upstairs taking a nap. Emily Ann is also taking a nap, and Ian and Dad took Connor down to the pier to get an ice-cream cone. So did you get everything you needed?"

"Yes, and while we were out, we saw—"

Lily cut her off. "Before I forget, your friend Dane called."

"Dane? What did he say?"

"That he was worried about you and has been trying to call you, but he didn't have your new number. He wanted to make sure you were okay. He asked for your new number."

"You didn't give it to him, did you?"

"No. You told me not to give out your number. But I told him I would tell you he called."

Laura let out a sigh of relief.

"So are you going to call him?"

Laura looked at her sister. "Did you tell him I'd call, or that you'd tell me he called?"

Lily considered the question. "I think I told him I'd tell you he called. I'm not sure. Are you calling him back?"

Laura frowned at Lily. "Why do you care?"

"One reason, if he calls again, I'm not sure what I should say."

"It's pretty easy. You have his number on your phone since he called you. Block his number, and you won't have to worry about him calling you again."

"Wow, Laura, what went on between you two? The last time I talked to you, you seemed crazy about this guy. It was all you ever talked about when we'd talk on the phone. And now, you're ghosting the guy. What did he do?"

"Who said he did anything?"

"I'm sorry, I don't mean to go all Mom on you. It's just that when you broke up with guys in the past, you always talked about it with me. I just want to know you're okay."

"I didn't break up with anyone. And I'm fine."

Laura stood up and slipped her shoes back on.

"Where are you going?"

"I'm going to walk down to the pier. See if Dad will buy me an ice-cream cone." Without saying another word, Laura turned, grabbed her purse from the coffee table, and headed for the front door.

FOURTEEN

Before coming outside, Danielle had changed her clothes and now wore a pair of denim shorts and a button-up cotton blouse. Instead of a braid, she had pulled her dark hair atop her head in a ponytail. She sat on the front porch swing, enjoying the warm sunshine of August and the gentle caress of the afternoon's sea breeze. Her sandals' outsoles gently pushed against the paver squares under the swing, maintaining the gentle rhythm of the soothing back and forth. She had brought a book outside with her, but it sat next to her on the swing seat with her cellphone. With all that had happened since yesterday, she couldn't focus on the book. Walt was upstairs in his office, working, while the twins were back down for a nap in the nursery, with the baby monitor on in Walt's office, should they wake.

Danielle's cellphone rang. She picked it up, looked at it to see who was calling, and brought it up to her ear after accepting the call. "Hey, Heather, how's the shopping going?"

"We're done. I'm at the police station right now, dropping off Evan and Eddy with their dad, and I was wondering, is Marie there?"

"Marie? No. Eva dropped by a little while ago, and Marie left with her. I think they're trying to find out if Traci's spirit has really moved on since this morning."

"What about Chris?"

"He's at his house. But he called me a few minutes ago. He was getting ready to come up here. He should be here in about ten minutes."

"What about Walt?"

"Why are you asking where everyone is?" Danielle asked.

"I think I might have run into Traci's killer."

Danielle's feet stopped pushing against the pavers, and the swing stopped moving. "What happened?"

"I get it sounds crazy, but when we were at Beach Taco, these guys were staring at me and Christopher. Eddy noticed. They were wearing suits and dark sunglasses."

Danielle started to say something, but Heather immediately cut her off. "I know what you're going to say. Brian already said it when I called him from Beach Taco the first time I saw them. But then there they were, over an hour later when we were leaving a store. They followed us after we left, so I drove directly to the police station."

"What are you going to do?"

"I'm waiting for Brian to finish something. He's going to follow me back to Marlow House, and then after Christopher and I are safely there, with Walt as security, Brian's going to look around town for their car. Check motels, restaurants. We didn't get a license plate number, but we have the make, model and color, so if he can find their car, he can at least run their license plate."

"Okay. Call me when you guys are leaving."

Heather promised to call, and they said goodbye. Danielle tossed the phone back on the seat next to her just as she heard Chris calling a hello from the sidewalk near the front gate. She glanced up and saw Chris walking her way, Hunny trotting along by his side.

"I just got off the phone with Heather. She told me something crazy."

Now in front of the swing, Chris picked up the book and cellphone next to Danielle and then sat down with her on the swing while saying, "You mean she's being Heather?"

Danielle absently took the phone and book from Chris and set them on her lap and then gave Hunny a welcoming pat. Chris's feet pushed against the pavers, and once again, the swing was in motion.

"I guess I should have said scary." Danielle then recounted her conversation with Heather.

"I'd be surprised if they were the killers. For one thing, Traci was murdered last night, and she saw the men this afternoon, still wearing their suits?"

"She never said they were the same suits."

Chris shrugged. "I understand why Heather is freaked. And I guess it makes sense for Brian to try tracking them down and running their plates."

"How about you? Did you find anything out?"

"A little." Chris sat back in the swing; his feet kept it moving back and forth. "I found some news articles and online obituaries for the Singers."

"That's Christopher's maternal grandparents?"

Chris nodded. "According to the obit I found on Bridget's dad, he died a year ago. While it didn't say how he died, I found a news article discussing Bridget's mother, who died six months ago."

"Wow, Bridget lost her mom six months after her dad?" Danielle shook her head.

"And then Bridget died three months later," Chris added.

"What did the article say about Bridget's mother?"

"The article was talking about Mrs. Singer's death and a pending lawsuit against her husband's company. Apparently, he was being sued and died from a heart attack before it went to court."

"How did she die?" Danielle asked.

"According to the article, an accidental overdose. Her doctor had put her on some antidepressants. She had been under a lot of stress since her husband's death, which I can understand. Her husband dies in the middle of a lawsuit involving their business, and from what I knew about Mrs. Singer, she wasn't involved in the business."

"Suicide?" Danielle asked.

Chris shrugged. "They called it an accidental overdose, but I wouldn't be surprised if it was really suicide. While I didn't find any articles on what happened in the lawsuit, I must assume they lost, and they lost big, which would explain why Bridget moved in with Traci. There might be more articles out there, and I'm not looking in the right place. There is a guy I'm calling tomorrow. I'll have him look into it more closely."

"Did you find out how Bridget died?"

Chris shook his head. "Like with her dad, I just found her obituary, and like his, there was no mention of the cause of death."

Danielle leaned back in the swing. "I'm surprised the Singers didn't have some sort of trust set up for their family to protect their assets. Businesses get sued all the time. They go bankrupt. But the family is typically protected."

"I didn't really know them that well. From what I picked up about them at the marina, he didn't come from money. Singer owned a construction company that he built from the bottom up, and from what I understand, his dad had worked in a factory. But if you met them, they liked to give the impression they came from generational wealth."

"What does that have to do with protecting his assets?" Danielle asked.

"Some people figure out how to make money, but not how to keep it."

"So what does this all mean?"

Chris let out a sigh. "Like I said, I'm going to turn this over to someone more skilled at digging than me. I'd like to see if Christopher has any family out there. I assume he has a father. But for some reason, Bridget wanted everyone to think it was me."

"Maybe for the Glandon money?"

Chris shook his head. "No one at the marina knew who I was. Not even Tad."

"Are you sure?"

"Even if they did, with DNA tests, you can't really pull that scam these days."

"True. And while DNA can prove you aren't his father, you can also use it to find his father. Have Christopher's DNA tested. It's entirely possible he has some relatives out there who will show up, which will lead you to the father."

"There is one thing that bothers me about that."

Danielle looked at Chris. "What?"

"Actually, I thought about having him tested last night, for that very reason. But then I got to wondering, maybe Bridget didn't name the real father because…he wasn't safe."

Danielle considered Chris's words for a moment. "Yeah, that is always a possibility."

"And once his DNA is in some database, who's to say the father won't find Christopher? And perhaps we don't want the sperm donor to find him."

Danielle let out a sigh. They were silent for a moment. Finally, Danielle asked, "Are you planning to keep Christopher until you find someone in his family acceptable to take him? And can you even do that? Won't CPS have something to say about that?"

"When I was at home, I called Mel. This isn't her specialty, but she has a friend—"

Danielle chuckled and, before he could finish, said, "Who has a friend?"

"Actually, her friend is the friend. Someone who works with CPS. He's going to call me. But for right now, the chief said there should not be a problem, considering Christopher's guardian left him in my charge, and if there is a problem, I could always claim to be his father. It's not like anyone is going to contest it."

"Seriously, you would do that?" Danielle asked.

"I can't let him go into foster care. And he's a sweet kid."

"Chris, taking in a stray kid is not the same as taking in a stray puppy. Didn't you say something like that to Heather?"

"It's not like I can't afford to hire whatever staff I need to take care of him."

"True, but a kid needs more than his own staff of domestic workers."

"I understand that. But I have to do whatever I can to keep him out of the foster care system. Some foster homes are good; unfortunately many aren't."

Danielle studied Chris for a moment. Finally, she nodded. "Okay. We'll be here to help, whatever you need."

THE GRAY SEDAN turned into the Seahorse Motel parking lot. After pulling into a space, the driver turned off the engine but did not get out of the car. Instead, he turned to the man in the passenger seat, waiting for him to finish the article he was reading. Ten minutes earlier they had stopped at a mini-mart, where they picked up the afternoon paper.

"Well, what does it say?" the driver asked.

"Not much. They're not naming her until they notify the next of kin. No mention of the kid." The man folded the newspaper and tossed it in the back of the car.

The driver unbuckled his seat belt. "Let's go check in. I need a shower and to get out of these clothes."

"I can't believe she turned into the police station." The passenger unhooked his seatbelt and opened the door.

The driver got out of the vehicle. "What is she doing with the kid? Who is she?"

"It's a small town. It shouldn't be too hard to find him."

An hour later, after checking into the Seahorse Motel, taking a shower, and slipping into more casual clothes, the men returned to their car. After getting into the vehicle and while putting on their seat belts, the passenger said, "According to the tracking device, she was on Beach Drive. And it looks like she was at that restaurant on the pier."

"Okay, let's go there first. See what we can find out." The driver slipped the key into the ignition and turned on the engine.

FIFTEEN

Carla's shift was about over when two men walked into the door of Pier Café on Sunday afternoon. Normally, she would tell the other server to get them, not wanting to take a new customer right when her shift was about to end. But she quickly changed her mind when she got a better look at the pair.

"Yummy," Carla muttered under her breath as she grabbed the water pitcher from the server station and started toward the booth the men had taken. She didn't know who they were, and she was familiar with all the local hot guys. Unfortunately, all the hot guys in Frederickport seem to be taken.

As the men sat down in the booth, they each removed their sunglasses and tossed them on the table. The taller man's dark blue polo shirt looked as if it had shrunk in the last wash, but considering how well it hugged his muscular shoulders and chest, she suspected it might have been a fashion choice.

The second man had brought in a rolled-up newspaper with him, which he set on the table next to his sunglasses. He wore a light blue, properly fitting, button-up shirt with his slacks. Carla thought they both looked fine. They were picking up the menus from the table when she reached them.

"How are you both doing today?" Carla asked as she flipped over the empty water glasses on the table and began filling them. Because of how the men held their menus, she got a clear view of their hands. Neither wore a ring. Carla smiled.

The man wearing the tight polo shirt smiled up at her. "At the moment, enjoying the view."

Carla grinned at the man. "So, aren't you sweet?" She set the water pitcher on the table.

"Purple's my favorite color," the man countered.

Carla's grin broadened as she preened, her right hand absently fluffing some of her purple hair. "Are you visiting Frederickport or passing through?"

"Up this way, checking out some possible real estate investments. We're staying at the Seahorse Motel tonight."

"But not sure how long we'll be staying now," the other man said as he picked up the newspaper, gave it a quick shake, and returned it to the table, today's major headline in clear view. He pointed to it.

Carla glanced down at the newspaper and cringed. She had read the article twenty minutes earlier after another customer had shown it to her. "Yeah, it's pretty scary."

"I wonder if they have any leads yet. Not exactly a headline I'd expect to find in a quaint little beach town on the Oregon coast," Tight Shirt said.

Without asking for permission, Carla sat down in the booth next to Tight Shirt. He scooted over, yet not enough where he and Carla weren't touching, which was totally fine with her.

"It's horrible," Carla said in a whisper. "The cop who found her is a friend of mine. They don't have any witnesses and no leads. I'm hoping whoever did it left town already. I hate the idea that some random person could simply pull up and shoot me while I'm sitting in my car!"

"That is chilling." To show his concern, Tight Shirt reached out and patted Carla's hand, letting his palm linger on her fingers a moment before pulling his hand away. She smiled over to him.

"Was she from here?" the other man asked.

Carla shook her head. "No. She stopped in here. I was one of the last people to see her alive. She had a little boy with her, and she told me they were passing through town on the way to see family. We got to talking, and it turned out we had a mutual friend. I guess she stopped to see him after she left here. When there, he agreed to look after the little boy for an hour. But when she didn't come back for the boy, he called the police. And that's who found her."

AFTER FOLLOWING Heather back to Marlow House, Brian was confident that if someone had been following Heather, they had driven away after driving past the police station. When he arrived at Marlow House, he found Chris there with Walt and Danielle. He stuck around for about twenty minutes, listening to what Chris had learned about the Singer family during his internet search. When Brian eventually left, he started searching for the car Heather described.

The chief couldn't exactly put out a bolo for the police to be on the lookout for the car Heather and the boys had seen. How would they explain that to Joe? Joe had found the victim, and he knew there had been no witnesses.

If Brian could find the car and the men, he could get their license plate number to run. If they were still in town, he would look first at the motels and restaurants. Since he was down the street from Pier Café, he stopped there first.

To Brian's surprise, he found the car described by Eddy parked in the pier parking lot. He knew it wasn't Bruce's car; this vehicle had California plates. Of course, it was entirely possible it wasn't the same car Heather had seen. There could be more than two cars like that in Frederickport. Brian took his cellphone from his pocket and snapped a photo of the car's license plate, and for good measure, snapped several more pictures of the automobile.

When Brian walked into Pier Café, he stood inside the entrance for a moment and glanced around. After scanning the room, he realized he knew everyone in the diner, all except for the two men sitting in a nearby booth. They weren't wearing suits, as Heather had described, but it was entirely possible they had changed clothes.

Brian spied the empty booth right next to them. Moments later, he was sitting in that booth. As he picked up a menu, Carla walked over to the men's table and handed them their checks. He heard her say, "I hope you boys have a nice visit in Frederickport."

"We've enjoyed it so far," one man said.

Brian held up the menu as if reading it yet looked over it and watched as the men each stood up. One pulled out his wallet from his back pocket, pulled out some bills, and tossed them on the table while Carla gathered up the dirty dishes. He heard Carla ask if he needed change, to which the man said no. Carla handed them each a pair of sunglasses from the table and picked up the newspaper, which one man said he didn't want, while the other man snatched it from her. Clearly, he did want it.

Brian watched and listened as Carla said goodbye again. She stood by their table, holding a small stack of dirty dishes, while they walked toward the exit door. Just as they were about to step from the restaurant, they both paused for a moment, then each slipped on their dark glasses and left the restaurant.

Brian looked over to Carla, who continued to watch the parting men. She gave a little sigh, turned back to the table, and then spied Brian, who sat in the next booth, silently observing her.

"Hi, Brian," she greeted.

"Afternoon, Carla." Brian flashed her a smile.

Carla dumped the dishes back on the table, walked over to Brian, and then plopped down in Brian's booth, sitting across the table from him on the opposite bench. "Why are the really hot guys just passing through?"

Brian arched his brows. "Gee, I'm not hot?"

Carla rolled her eyes and then plunked both elbows on the tabletop before resting her chin on balled fists. "You're taken."

Brian nodded toward the door the men had just exited. "Who were the guys?"

"Just some cuties passing through. They're staying at the Seahorse Motel."

"Passing through to where?"

Carla thought about it a moment and frowned. She sat up straighter, her chin no longer resting on a balled fist. "Now that I think about it, they didn't say too much about themselves, other than they're checking out property in the area and staying at the Seahorse Motel for the night. But then we got to talking about the murder." Carla shrugged.

Brian arched his brows. "Talking about what?"

Noticing the way Brian arched his brows, Carla repeated the eye roll. "Oh, put away your cop hat. That isn't your lone shooter. For one thing, there are two of them."

"Who said it was a lone shooter?"

Carla slumped back on the bench, crossing her arms over her chest. "It has to be. I don't see two really cute guys going around shooting strange women. That's something a psycho does. And I don't think shooters run in pairs."

"I was just curious. And you're probably right about it being a lone shooter," Brian lied.

Carla relaxed. "When I asked them if they were visiting Frederickport or only passing through, they told me they were up here looking at some real estate investments, but then they showed me the newspaper article on last night's murder, and I think that dampened their interest in our area. I guess I understand."

"Murder's not great for the property value."

"One of them said something funny after showing me the article." Carla giggled. "He said something about being shocked that something like that would happen in such a...how did he phrase that?...oh yes, a quaint little beach town on the Oregon Coast."

Brian arched his brows again. "Why is that funny?"

"The part about Frederickport being a quaint little beach town."

"It isn't quaint?"

"Yeah, if you define quaint as homicide central. Which I didn't tell them, by the way. I don't want to scare off the hot guys. But I have a feeling they won't be sticking around, not since they read about a killer on the loose."

"Homicide central?"

"Oh, come on, Brian, I don't think I could count all the murders in Frederickport in the last six years on both hands; I would need my toes. And if we counted the bodies found—most of whom were found by your girlfriend—"

Brian raised his right hand, showing Carla his palm, as if asking her to say no more, while resisting an urge to laugh. When she stopped talking, he asked, "Serious question. Why do you stay in Frederickport? What's keeping you here? You don't have family in town, and as you've told me on numerous occasions, we have a shortage of hot guys."

Carla looked at Brian as if he had said something incredibly stupid. She leaned toward him from across the table and said in a whisper, "And miss all that goes on around here? How boring would that be?"

SIXTEEN

W hen Brian arrived back at Marlow House late Sunday afternoon, he found Chris and Heather in the side yard, playing catch with Christopher, who proudly used his new baseball mitt. Walt and Danielle sat on the back porch, each holding a baby, as they watched the three playing ball, while Hunny raced alongside Christopher, waiting for her chance to retrieve any stray balls.

Chris and Heather didn't stop playing with Christopher when Brian walked into the yard by the front gate. Instead, they each shouted a quick hello to him while focusing most of their attention on their backyard play.

Brian strolled up to the patio, walking past the three playing ball, and joined Walt and Danielle. He sat down.

"Poor Chris," Walt said with a chuckle after Brian joined them.

"Poor Chris, what?" Brian asked.

"It's a little intimidating playing ball with Heather. That girl has some arm." Danielle chuckled.

Brian nodded in agreement. "She does."

"So did you find them?" Danielle asked.

"Yes, but I seriously doubt they're our guys."

Brian was about to explain what he had learned that afternoon, but paused to listen to Chris, who had just shouted, "Heather and I are going to take a little rest. Why don't you play ball with Hunny. I'll get you the tennis ball. I don't want you throwing that hard one for Hunny."

The next moment, Chris jogged over to the patio while Heather followed behind him at a slower pace. Christopher, who was now petting Hunny, failed to notice the tennis ball that had been sitting on the picnic table lift from the table and fly in Chris's direction. Chris stopped walking and held up his right hand. The tennis ball slowed down and landed in his open palm before his fingers closed around it.

Chris yelled, "Thanks, Walt," before turning back toward the yard and tossing Christopher the tennis ball. Heather strolled onto the patio, carrying Christopher's new baseball mitt and baseball. She placed them both on the picnic table and then walked over to Brian, Walt, and Danielle.

A FEW MINUTES LATER, the five adults sat on the back porch of Marlow House, with Danielle and Walt each holding a baby while Christopher threw the ball for Hunny.

"Why are you sure they aren't the killers?" Heather asked after Brian repeated what he had said to Walt and Danielle upon arriving.

"When I left here, the first place I checked was Pier Café. The car was there, and there were two men in the diner. While they weren't wearing suits, they had dark glasses, and they fit the description you gave us. After I left the diner, I went back to the station and ran the plates. The car is registered in California. We looked up the owner and his driver's license, and he looks like one of the men in the diner. He's a real estate agent in Eureka, California. And it tracks, because they told Carla they were here checking out investment property."

"A real estate agent?" Heather frowned.

Brian nodded. "From what Carla said, they told her they were in town looking for investment property. Yet, after seeing the article about the murder, they didn't seem as interested."

"I wonder if they are the same men," Heather said. "There might be more than two cars like that in town."

Brian pulled out his cellphone, opened his photo app, and handed it to Heather. "Are these the guys?"

Heather looked at the screen on Brian's cellphone. It looked like a picture taken from a real estate website. Heather handed the phone back to Brian. "It could be. I didn't get a good look at either of their faces because they were both wearing glasses. But it could be them."

"The one on the right, his name is Derrick Tyler. He has no record aside from a couple of minor traffic violations. And it looks like he's had his California real estate license for about five years. The other one is his brother, Kevin Tyler. I checked out their real estate page online. They call themselves Team Tyler. The brother has had his real estate license for the same amount of time, and he doesn't have a record either."

"I don't think they are the killers," Chris said.

"But they were following me. And they followed me to the police station," Heather argued.

"Heather, I doubt they were following you. This is a small town. Two guys come to town and drive around, checking out the area for investment property; not surprising you might run into them. Fred-erickport isn't exactly a big town," Chris reminded her. "And chances are, if Traci hadn't stopped by your house this morning and told you about how the killers wore suits and dark glasses, you wouldn't have noticed those two men even if they had been at Beach Taco, the store, or driven behind you to the police station."

"Eddy would still have noticed. He told me they were staring at Christopher and me, and he didn't hear what Traci had told me. At least not then," Heather grumbled.

"You know what I mean," Chris countered.

Heather let out a sigh and slumped back in her chair. "I suppose you're right. I'm just jumpy. And I guess I'm glad they are just real estate investors. I was a little freaked at the idea the killer might be looking for Christopher. I was going to ask Marie if she could stay with him until we figure this out. So what now?"

"I'm taking Christopher back to my house in a little while. I'll put Christopher in the guest room closest to mine. We don't need to keep camping out at Marlow House. And I don't want to spend another night on the couch. I'll need to get the stuff out of your car before I leave."

"No reason to do that. I'll drive over to your house when you're ready to go," Heather offered. "And I'd like to throw Christopher's new clothes in the wash when we get to your house."

Danielle looked at Brian. "Since that lead didn't go anywhere, do you have anything? If this is a random shooter, then it could happen again."

"I called the chief after I ran the plates," Brian said. "He'd already gone back to his house with Eddy and Evan. Since Traci was emphatic that there was no one who wanted to kill her, it's entirely possible this was a robbery. A crime of opportunity. Some guys turn down a lonely road, find a woman alone, and rob her."

"That's cold," Heather said. "They didn't even know if she had anything worth taking, much less worth killing for."

Brian shrugged and said, "And considering where we found her car, it's entirely possible whoever killed her was never in Frederickport."

Walt looked at Brian. "Why do you say that?"

"I suppose they could have been leaving town—or arriving. The road Traci was on is right off the highway, heading out of town. Maybe the men saw her turn down that road. They followed her. Figured she was alone. And after they shot her and took her wallet, they headed back out of town," Brian explained.

"But why bother moving the body?" Heather asked. "You said where she had obviously been killed—considering what Joe picked up. It's not like her body would be visible from the road."

"True, but moving the body could have delayed looking for her," Brian explained. "If we didn't know she was dead, and someone saw the car on the side of the road and stopped, they might assume she had simply broken down and she called someone to pick her up.

There would be no reason to call the police, not unless the person saw the car sitting along the side of the road for a long time. So it would give the killers more time to distance themselves from the area."

"Which probably means they are miles from here." Heather let out a sigh.

BRIAN WENT HOME to take a shower and change his clothes, while Heather followed Chris down to his house. Rather than move the car seat to Chris's car, Christopher rode with Heather. Brian planned to meet Heather at her house later.

Christopher helped Heather and Chris carry in the packages from her car and take them to the room he would be staying in. After they brought in all the packages, Christopher stood in the middle of the room and looked around. "How long am I staying here? When's Traci going to be back?"

Heather, who had just been gathering up the sacks with the clothes, stopped what she was doing and looked over to Chris.

Chris looked at Heather. "Heather, can I talk to Christopher alone for a few minutes?"

Heather smiled sadly at the confused boy looking up at Chris. She quickly snatched up all the bags with the clothes. "Sure. I'll take these out and get them in the laundry."

A few minutes later, Christopher and Chris sat on the side of the bed, with Hunny sitting between them. Considering how the boy seemed attached to the dog, in the same way he had responded to Max, Chris didn't balk when Hunny jumped up on the bed.

"She's not coming back, is she?" Christopher started the conversation.

"There has been an accident," Chris began.

The boy looked up at Chris, his eyes wide. "Is she okay?"

Chris smiled sadly and shook his head. "No. I'm afraid not."

"Is she dead?"

Chris nodded. "I'm so sorry."

"Why does everyone die?" the boy asked.

Chris took a deep breath. "It sometime feels like that. My mother died when I was very young, like you."

Christopher stared at Chris. "Did you live with your dad, then?"

Chris shook his head. "No. My father died before I was born."

"So you didn't have anyone either?"

"When I was about six, a nice couple adopted me. They became my new parents. And they were good to me. I was happy with them. I loved them. They loved me. But I remember being young like you before they adopted me. I was scared. Uncertain."

"Where are your parents now?"

Chris took another deep breath and smiled sadly. "My parents died."

"So everyone does die. My grandpa, grandma, mom, Traci, your parents." Christopher looked down at the pit bull, who rested her head on his lap. Christopher absently stroked the dog's back. "But I don't really remember much about my grandpa. But Mom used to talk about him."

"Remember how Traci's neighbor told you your mom is in Heaven, and you will see her someday?"

"Yes. After I die."

"I'm going to tell you a secret. Can you keep a secret?" Chris asked.

Christopher stared at Chris. "What kind of secret?"

"When Mrs. Brown said your mom is in Heaven now, and you would only see her again when you died, she was only half right."

"Mom didn't go to Heaven?"

Chris smiled at the boy. "No, your mom is in...what some call Heaven. What Mrs. Brown was wrong about, we don't always have to wait until we die to see our loved ones again. Sometimes, after people die, their spirits can visit us in our dreams. They often do this to let us know they're okay."

"Really?"

Chris nodded. "You met Evan and Eddy today. Their mom died."

"Evan told me."

"Did he also tell you his mother sometimes visits him in his dreams?"

Christopher's eyes widened. "She does?"

Chris nodded. "But that is the secret I want you to keep. You can talk to Evan about it, but don't tell other people."

"Why can't I tell anyone?"

"Some people don't believe it's true. But it is. I can't tell you how I know. But I do. And the only reason I'm telling you is because I don't want you to be afraid. I want you to understand that even though you are really sad right now, things are never as dark as you think they are. I need you to hold on to that thought. While your mom is not here with you right now, she is watching over you. But she had to move on, just like someday I will have to move on, or you will. But while we are here, on this side of Heaven, it's our job to do the best we can. Do you understand?"

SEVENTEEN

"I need some clean clothes," Derrick grumbled on Monday morning as he stood in front of the dresser mirror in their room at the Seahorse Motel. Leaning closer to the mirror, he tried rubbing a small food stain from his shirt's collar, using a damp washcloth from the motel's bathroom.

"It's not like we planned to be gone so long, or that we'd be taking a side trip to Oregon," Kevin said as he tossed his clothes into the open suitcase on the bed.

Derrick dropped the washcloth on the dresser and turned from the mirror. He faced his brother. "I think we need to get out of Oregon. If you hadn't been so quick to pull that trigger, we could have seen she didn't have the kid with her."

Kevin straightened his posture, no longer leaning over the suitcase. He glared at his brother. "Says the guy who hasn't the stomach to pull the trigger in the first place. It's done. One problem solved. We can still get the kid, and even if we don't, the problem could still be solved."

"Police are going to start asking questions of strangers in town. I'm surprised one didn't come knocking on the door last night. This is a small town. If they ask us why we're here, and if we give them the same story we gave that waitress, a cop is bound to ask us what property we're looking at—or what local agent we're working with."

"That's where my idea comes in."

Derrick groaned. "God save us your ideas…But go ahead. What is it?"

"First, I agree; we need to head home. But before we do, I say we stop by Marlow House. That's where the waitress said Lind dropped the kid."

"What, just show up and tell them we've come to pick up the boy Lind left there?"

"Hear me out."

AN HOUR LATER, they checked out of the motel, and instead of stopping at a restaurant for breakfast, they went through a drive-through and picked up a couple of breakfast burritos. They sat in the car in the parking lot as they ate their burritos, each careful not to drop food on their shirts. They needed to look professional, and neither one had another change of clean clothes.

"What happens if they take us up on our offer?" Derrick asked before taking a bite of his burrito.

"I told you, they aren't going to. I read all about the place last night on my phone. The owners are rich, and the place has been in their family for generations. No, they aren't going to sell. But someone who has money and has opened their home to strangers— as they have done, if those online articles are to be believed—are more likely to offer showing us around the place, even if they aren't interested in selling."

"What good does that do us?"

"For one thing, if we're questioned by cops why we're here, our story holds up. For another, while getting a tour of Marlow House, we can get a better idea if the boy is still there or not. And while touring the house, we can engage in small talk, which means one of us should mention the concerning article we read in yesterday's paper. Hopefully, they will be as chatty as the waitress."

Twenty minutes later, they pulled up in front of Marlow House and parked.

———

MARIE HAD FINISHED HELPING Danielle change the twins from their sleepers into clean clothes. They waited for Walt to help her carry both babies downstairs safely. While Danielle could have done it with Marie's help, Danielle knew Lily and might bring her parents and sister over this morning, and she didn't want to greet them with flying babies.

"So Evan is spending the day with you?" Marie asked.

"Yes. I imagine it's going to be easier for the chief when the boys go back to school in a couple of weeks. It's not hard with Eddy now that he is a teenager."

Marie scoffed.

Danielle frowned at Marie. "What?"

"Dear, I know what it's like to have teenage boys in the house. With my son, then Adam and his brother." Marie shook her head. "I would feel more comfortable leaving Evan home alone than a teenage boy."

Danielle chuckled. "Yeah, I can imagine Adam was a handful."

"He did have a knack for getting into trouble." Marie let out a sigh. "But I do love that boy."

"According to Heather, Eddy was really helpful with Christopher yesterday. Oh, and did I mention Christopher's spending the day with us too?"

Marie arched her brows. "You didn't mention that."

"Chris needs to go to the office, and he's trying to get a hold of some private investigator he's worked with before."

———

DOWNSTAIRS, Walt was just stepping out of the library when the doorbell rang. When he opened the door a few minutes later, he found two men, each wearing suits, standing on his front porch.

"Mr. Marlow?" one man asked.

"Yes? How can I help you?"

The man handed Walt a business card. Walt accepted the card, read it, and then the man said, "Hello, I'm Kevin Tyler, and this is my partner, Derrick Tyler." Both men held out their right hands to shake.

The moment Walt read the business card, he recognized the men's names, along with the name of the real estate brokerage from Eureka, California. They were the same men Heather believed had followed her and the boys yesterday; they were the men Brian had told them about the night before. But why had they stopped at Marlow House?

Curious, Walt tucked the business card in his shirt pocket, gave each man a perfunctory handshake, and then asked, "How may I help you?"

Kevin flashed Walt a smile. "Perhaps we can come inside for a moment?"

Walt returned the bright smile. "No."

Kevin looked momentarily taken aback but quickly rebounded. "I'm sorry. Is this a bad time?"

"What is this about?" Walt asked, his bright smile now gone.

"We're real estate agents from California," Derrick explained.

"Yes. I know that. I just read your card. We aren't looking for a real estate agent."

"We wanted to talk to you about Marlow House," Kevin said.

Walt arched his brows. "What about it?"

"Perhaps we can come inside and discuss it?" Kevin asked.

"Sir, you are the one who rang my doorbell. Please state your reason for being here, because I am a busy man."

"We want to buy Marlow House," Derrick blurted.

Walt smiled. "Is that all?"

"Like we said, we are in real estate. We've been looking for prop-erties that we can convert into a B and B. Not Airbnb, but the old-fashioned bed-and-breakfast. We found Marlow House online and recently learned that you're no longer operating it as a business

THE GHOST AND WEDNESDAY'S CHILD

because you just welcomed twins into your family—congratulations, by the way," Kevin explained.

"Thank you," Walt said, looking more like he was guarding the entrance to his home rather than preparing to invite them inside.

"And since your interests are now elsewhere, we wondered if you might consider selling your property. We understand it's been in your family for generations, and we'd want to continue calling it Marlow House, and preserve its current charm. And if you're not interested, we understand. This might seem all very sudden. But even if you don't feel you want to sell, we would appreciate it if you would spare us a few minutes to give us a tour since we are already here, and if you change your mind, you can contact us, and we would be better able to make our offer without having to come back up to look at the property."

"That's all?" Walt asked.

"Yes. Are you interested in discussing this more?" Kevin smiled.

"No. Not for sale. Have a nice day." Before Kevin or Derrick could say another word, Walt shut the door on them.

They could hear the deadbolt lock.

"That was a brilliant idea," Derrick grumbled. "We learned a lot, didn't we?"

Kevin turned from the door with Derrick and started back down the walk toward their car. "If nothing else, we've established a reason for being up here."

Inside the parlor of Marlow House, Walt stood out of view from the outside as he peered out the slit in the curtain. He watched the two men walking to their car. He took out his cellphone and placed a call.

"Hey, Walt. What's going on?" Adam Nichols asked when he answered Walt's call.

"I'm just curious. Do you know two real estate agents from Eureka, California, named Derrick and Kevin Tyler? They call themselves Team Tyler." Walt pulled out the card they had given him and read the name of the brokerage firm they worked for to Adam.

"No. Sorry, Walt. Never heard of them. Can I ask why?"

"They just knocked on my door and offered to buy Marlow House."

"Really? For how much?"

"They didn't say." Walt tucked the business card back in his shirt pocket.

"If they show up again, Walt, tell them they have to talk to your agent, and give them my number."

"But we don't want to sell."

"True. But maybe I can sell them something else."

Walt laughed. "Okay, I'll remember that."

DERRICK DROVE the car north on Beach Drive. They were several houses past Marlow House when Kevin shouted, "Quick, pull over!"

Derrick steered the car to the sidewalk and parked, the motor still running. He glared at his brother, who had just opened the glove compartment, pulled out a pair of binoculars, and was now turned in his seat, looking out the back car window. "What?"

"It's the kid. Look." Kevin handed his brother the pair of binoculars.

Turning in the driver's seat, Derrick looked through the binoculars, aiming them through the side window at a house they had just passed on the other side of the street. He saw a little blond boy picking flowers off a bush next to the sidewalk.

"It's him. Outside, alone," Derrick said.

"Let's get him."

Without having to be told twice, Derrick tossed the binoculars to his brother, put the car in drive, and made a U-turn. A moment later, he pulled up to the sidewalk, less than six feet from the boy. Derrick put the car in park, the motor still running, as Kevin swung open the car door. Their sudden appearance seemed to surprise the small boy, who looked up, his blue eyes open wide.

"Hey, Christopher," Kevin shouted.

Christopher frowned.

"Christopher, it's me. I've been looking for you. We've been so worried about you."

Hesitantly, Christopher stepped closer. "You know my name?"

Kevin smiled. "Of course I do. Don't you remember me? I'm Mrs. Brown's friend."

"You are?"

"Yes. Mrs. Brown's been worried about you. Traci told Mrs. Brown you two were coming up here, and when she didn't call her last night, she got worried. She told us you were up here, so I promised to check on you. Let me take you to her."

Kevin held out his hand, prepared to grab the boy as he took another step closer, when a dog, who had been concealed by the large flowering bush, burst out. Its muscular body nudged the boy back, away from the street, before putting itself between the child and the car, teeth bared, hair on the dog's back standing up. It looked as if the ferocious animal was about to lunge into the car, prepared to tear someone's throat out.

The car door slammed shut as Derrick stepped on the gas, racing down the street from the now barking dog.

Kevin's heart practically burst out of his chest. "Holy crap, that was a pit bull! Where did that come from?"

EIGHTEEN

Heather started late on her Monday morning run because she and Chris were not going into the office at the normal time. Chris wanted to make Christopher breakfast before taking him to Marlow House for the day. After finishing her run, Heather stood across the street from her house. She looked both ways, preparing to cross Beach Drive so she could go home, shower, and get ready for work. But she quickly stepped back from the sidewalk, away from the road, when she spied a car racing down the street in her direction. As it whizzed by, she recognized the men in its front seats.

Heather stood there a moment, and when they drove out of sight and she was fairly certain they weren't coming back, she raced across the street. Instead of going to her house, she ran up the road to Marlow House. Instead of going to Marlow House's front door, she entered by the side gate and headed for the kitchen door. She entered without knocking and found Danielle and Walt walking into the kitchen, each holding a baby, while Marie trailed along behind them. They froze when they saw Heather.

"Those guys who I thought were following me yesterday, they just raced down the street." Heather pointed toward the pier.

"What do you mean raced?" Danielle asked as she put Addison into one of the two baby swings already set up in the kitchen.

"Like they were at the drag races or being chased by the cops. If I hadn't been paying attention when I was about to cross the street, I could be on Marie's side right now."

"Interesting," Walt said as he fit Jack into the empty baby swing. "Right before you walked in, I was telling Danielle and Marie about the men who showed up at our door this morning."

Heather frowned. "Who?"

"The men you say raced down the street minutes ago. Although when I saw them, they were heading in the other direction."

"They were here?" Heather asked, still standing.

"You want a cup of coffee?" Danielle stood by the counter, pulling mugs from the overhead cabinet.

"Yes, please." Heather looked at Walt while Marie took a seat at the table. "Why were they here?"

"They said they wanted to make an offer to buy Marlow House." Walt took the cup of coffee Danielle poured, walked to the table, and set the mug in front of Heather. Heather sat down at the table next to Marie while Walt returned to the counter.

"They wanted to buy Marlow House?" Heather frowned.

Walt returned to the table with the sugar and cream set while Danielle walked to the table carrying two filled mugs of coffee. They both sat down. Danielle handed Walt his mug while Walt removed the lid from the cake pan on the center of the table, revealing a platter of Old Salts cinnamon rolls. Nearby, the twins' swings moved gently back and forth while tiny hands made little fists and waving motions.

Walt shrugged. "That's what they told me." He took a sip of his coffee.

"Brian said they were real estate agents, but that's weird, and why did they think it was a good idea to turn Beach Drive into a raceway?"

Walt elaborated on Team Tyler's visit that morning. As he finished his telling, the kitchen door opened, and Chris walked in holding Christopher's hand, with Hunny trailing behind him.

Christopher's other hand tightly gripped a bunch of freshly picked flowers from Chris's yard.

Normally, Chris would have enjoyed teasing Heather with a snarky comment, such as asking her why she was still in her running clothes and not dressed for work. Instead, he continued to hold the boy's hand while facing the three people and ghost who sat at the kitchen table.

"Something disturbing just happened," Chris said.

Heather looked at Chris. "Disturbing how?"

"This morning, as we were getting ready to come here, Christopher wanted to pick some flowers. He wanted to bring them to Danielle and Heather."

Both Danielle and Heather let out a low, "Aw," and flashed a smile at the boy before looking back at Chris.

"I ran inside to get something. I told Christopher to stay in the yard, and I didn't see a problem leaving him out there for a few minutes because Hunny was with him. And it's a good thing she was."

"What happened?" Danielle asked.

"I think someone tried to kidnap him."

Marie let out a gasp and then gave Chris her chair and took an imaginary one in the corner. Chris sat down, no longer holding the boy's hand. "I was getting ready to go outside when I hear Hunny barking like hell. I step on the front porch, and I see a gray sedan racing down the street."

While Chris explained what Christopher had told him about the departing car, Heather silently pulled the boy to her and offered him half of her cinnamon roll. She tore it in half, set it on a napkin, and set it before him. Christopher smiled up at Heather, and before taking the cinnamon roll, he gave her half the flowers while giving the other half to Danielle. Both women grinned at his gesture and mouthed, *Thank you*, while listening to what Chris was saying.

During the telling, Walt looked at Hunny; the two exchanged thoughts. When Chris finished recounting what Christopher had told him, Walt said, "I believe you're right." Chris, who noticed

Walt and Hunny staring at each other, knew intuitively Hunny had told Walt something.

"Those were the men I was telling you about. I was right," Heather said.

"Had you seen those men before, Christopher?" Danielle asked.

"I remember seeing them yesterday at lunch."

"Before that?" Danielle asked.

Christopher shook his head. "No. I don't think so."

The imaginary chair Marie had been sitting on vanished, and she now floated over the table. "I know what I need to do!"

Everyone looked at Marie except for Christopher, who had no idea the grandmotherly ghost floated over the table.

"I believe we may have found the killers. But even if Edward brought them in for questioning, they could simply say they saw a boy alone near the road and were worried about him. So unless they found the murder weapon on them, he would have to let them go. And I would be surprised if they still have the gun, considering there is a big ocean out there. Let me learn more about why they killed Traci and want Christopher. What kind of car did you say it was?"

Heather glanced at Christopher, who was busily eating his cinnamon roll. "That gray sedan about ran me off the road."

"That business card with their pictures on it would be helpful. I don't want to drive around in the wrong gray sedan."

Walt pulled the business card from his shirt pocket, and when he was sure Christopher wasn't looking his way, he sent it flying over the boy's head to Marie while Danielle jumped from the table and walked over to the back door, opening it while saying something about needing fresh air.

While Heather distracted Christopher from looking toward the now open back door with another cinnamon roll, Marie and the business card moved outside.

———

HEATHER HAD GONE HOME to get ready to go to work, although she didn't imagine she could focus on work today. As she got to her house, she spied the police chief driving up Beach Drive on his way to Marlow House with Evan.

―――――――

THE CHIEF SAT in the parlor with Walt, Danielle, and Chris, while Evan and Christopher were in the library playing with one of the Lego sets Heather had bought the day before. Chris had finished explaining to the chief what Christopher had told him.

"According to Hunny, she didn't have a good feeling about the men. One had his arm out toward Christopher, and she felt he was about to grab him."

"And Marie is with them now?" the chief asked.

The next moment, Marie popped into the parlor, her image hovering above the room. Danielle looked up. "I guess not. Marie is here."

"Found them!" Marie announced. "I'm going to stay with them, find out what I can find out. They just got on the highway, and I need to get back before they turn off some road and I can't find them again. And tell Edward I was right. They already threw the gun in the ocean. They dropped it off the end of the pier." Marie vanished.

"Well, that answers a couple of questions," Danielle said.

"Marie didn't find them?" the chief asked.

Danielle shook her head. "No. She found them. And it seems they are the killer."

―――――――

MARIE SAT in the back seat of Derrick's gray sedan as they traveled south down the highway. It had been a relatively boring trip thus far, aside from her discovering they had been the shooter. She had initially managed to get into the moving vehicle with the business card Walt had given her before Derrick rolled up all the windows so he could turn on the air conditioning. Said business card now lay on the floor of the back seat.

She had entered the car as the men were discussing getting out of Oregon, and then one of them said something about how they were glad they had dropped the gun off the end of the pier before eating at Pier Café. They had been afraid the local police might target visitors to town after the shooting, and if they searched the motel room or their car and found the gun, they would be linked to the shooting. Without the gun, they believed nothing linked them to Traci Lind.

Marie had left briefly to let the others know where she would be, and to tell them about the gun's fate. After she returned to the car, she found the two men untalkative and listening to music on the radio. From the photo on the business card, she knew the driver's name was Derrick, and the passenger was Kevin.

They had been driving for about thirty minutes when Kevin's cellphone rang. She watched as he looked at his phone.

"It's him."

Derrick sighed. "You might as well answer it and tell him we're on our way back."

Kevin nodded, swiped his finger over his cellphone's screen, and then put the phone to his ear.

"Hey. We're heading back…Yeah, we found where he is…No… It will not be a problem. No one knows. And with Lind gone, I don't see how anyone is going to find out…yeah…I know this isn't how you wanted us to handle it, but hey, it's the best we could do, and we needed to get out of there before they connected us to Lind, and you don't want that…Hold on…" He looked at his brother. "Are we going all the way to Brookings tonight?"

Derrick nodded. "That's my plan. I want to get as far away from Frederickport as possible. We can stay at the same place we stayed at coming up here."

Kevin turned his attention back to the phone call. "Yeah, he wants to get to Brookings. We'll stay in the same place…yeah… okay." He disconnected the call and tossed the phone on the console.

"So what was that all about?"

"He said it was probably best that we got out of there. He wants to see us right when we get back."

Marie wanted more information—whom were they talking to? But they went silent again. Hours passed. When they arrived in Brookings, they picked up takeout food and checked into a motel. As they ate dinner in their room, Marie popped back to Marlow House, updated them on the situation, and then returned to the motel.

The next morning, Marie was already sitting in the back seat of the sedan when the men got into the car. They each put on their seat belts, and then the driver put the key into the ignition and turned the key.

In the next moment, Marie found herself in the center of an explosion as the gray sedan blew up, sending everything around her flying in all directions while simultaneously engulfed in flames. Had she been a living person, the experience would have been both deadly and terrifying, yet she found it utterly fascinating.

NINETEEN

After her initial surprise at finding herself in the heart of an explosion, Marie's apparition floated upwards some twenty feet. She looked down and watched flames engulf the gray sedan. Random sounds like gunshots came from the burning massive ball of fire beneath her.

Glancing around, she saw parts of the gray sedan strewn across the parking lot. Some of the burning debris had landed on other vehicles. People rushed out of their motel rooms, and there was shouting and chaos.

Concerned over the close proximity of the initial explosion to the motel, and the possibility its fire might easily jump to the building and endanger lives, along with the possibility of nearby vehicles catching fire from the burning debris, Marie focused on the scene below.

Without considering what the gathering onlookers might think, she used her energy to nudge what was left of the gray sedan away from the building and away from other parked cars. She then used her energy to gather up the scattered and burning debris, sending them back to the original vehicle now consumed in flames.

When done with her task, she looked over at the gathering

crowd and heard sirens in the distance. She noticed most of the people in the crowd had their phones out and had been taking pictures. Unconcerned at what they might think, or what pictures or videos they might have captured, she felt relief that she had minimized the damage. The next moment she stood on the pavement some distance from the still burning debris. It was then she remembered the two men who had been with her in the car.

Fire engines and police cars barreled into the parking lot, and suddenly there were police officers directing the crowd. Marie looked toward the group of people and spied Kevin and Derrick standing among the onlookers, yet they weren't following the directions of the police; instead they stood still, staring not at the burning car, but at Marie.

Marie wondered briefly how they had gotten out of the vehicle before it exploded, but in the next moment, she had her answer when they both disappeared.

"THEY ARE DEAD," Marie announced when she appeared in Marlow House's living room on Tuesday morning. She found Walt, Danielle, Chris, and Heather sitting in the living room, talking to the chief, while the twins were each in a portable crib in the room, and by the sounds coming from the open doorway, Marie surmised Evan and Christopher were in the entry hall, rolling a ball for Hunny.

"Who is dead?" Heather said at the same time Danielle told the chief Marie had arrived.

"They got up this morning, ready to leave the motel. I was sitting in the back seat when they both got into the car. And then the next moment—kaboom!"

"Kaboom?" Walt asked.

"The car blew up!"

"What is Marie saying? Are the men still at the motel?" the chief asked.

"In a manner of speaking," Danielle muttered.

The chief frowned. "What's going on?"

"Marie just said their car blew up," Chris explained.

"I have to say, it was quite the experience." Marie took a seat on an imaginary chair and then told them about the morning. When finished, Danielle repeated Marie's words to the chief.

"Somebody blew up their car?" the chief muttered. "What motel were they at?"

Before Danielle could relay the answer Marie had just given to the chief, Heather was already on her cellphone. She looked up from her phone and announced, "It's all over Twitter. Check the hashtag *angel explosion*, all one word." The next moment everyone took out their cellphones, logged into Twitter, and started watching the videos taken within the last half hour.

"Angel explosion?" the chief asked.

"I suspect it has something to do with how that car seemed to just magically move away from the motel to protect others," Chris said. "Like an angel intervened."

"Cool how all the burning debris floats off the other cars back to the burning car," Heather said.

All but the chief looked at Marie for an explanation.

Marie shrugged. "I couldn't very well leave it like that and risk burning down the motel and hurting someone."

"Whoever came up with that hashtag, they have no idea how close they came to the truth," Danielle said with a chuckle.

"Did you just call me an angel?" Marie grinned at Danielle.

Heather set her phone down and looked at Marie. "So they just disappeared? You didn't get to talk to them?"

Marie shook her head. "To be honest, for a moment there, I thought they had somehow escaped the explosion."

"Why would you think that?" Danielle asked.

Marie turned to Danielle. "Because of how they looked. I would assume two people blown up like that would look—somewhat gruesome. After all, look at that poor woman they killed. She had a bullet wound in the center of her forehead. They looked rather alive—and put together—if you know what I mean."

"Could this mean they don't realize they were dead?" Heather asked.

Danielle shrugged. "Maybe, but when you first saw Traci, she didn't know she was dead, but you could see she had been shot."

"What are you all talking about?" the chief asked.

"Just the fact the Universe doesn't have clear-cut rules about some things," Heather grumbled.

They discussed the explosion a few more minutes before the chief glanced at his watch and said, "I need to get going. Traci Lind's brother arrived last night, and he's coming into the station to talk to me at ten. And with this new development, there are some things I need to do, including all of us getting our new story straight."

"New story?" Danielle asked.

The chief nodded. "While Joe and the rest have accepted my story about a tip regarding the murder weapon, I didn't mention the kidnap attempt because Marie was right. Had we brought them in, they would have spun it. I was hoping she'd come back with more we could use."

"And now?" Heather asked.

"Now I want to say Chris talked to me about yesterday's events. But the men had left town, and I was going to look into them—"

"And then you heard they blew up?" Chris finished for the chief.

The chief nodded. "Considering everything, the possible kidnap attempt, the gun, the explosion, and the fact Heather and Eddy believed they were following them the other day, they are obviously people of interest. I'll call the police in Brookings when I get to the office."

"I STILL CAN'T BELIEVE Heather was right all along," Brian told the chief later that morning as he sat in his office with him. "I thought she had an overactive imagination."

The chief shrugged. "I suspect people like Heather, Danielle, Chris, and even my son...they probably have sharper instincts, considering their sensitivity to spirits. Something was telling her to pay attention, that those men were the ones, and it wasn't simply because they were wearing suits and sunglasses."

"Now what?"

"Like I said, according to the Brookings police, it looks like someone put a bomb under the car, rigged to go off when the ignition turned on. Currently, they don't have any leads."

"I'm assuming they have security cameras on the property?"

"Not in that part of the parking lot."

"And no one saw anything?" Brian asked.

"If they did, no one has come forward. When I talked to the Brookings police this morning, they were still interviewing the motel guests. I'm calling them again this afternoon."

Brian let out a sigh and leaned back in his chair.

"But we know a little more about Christopher's mother and what happened to her money. Chris gave me this when I saw him this morning at Marlow House." The chief lifted a folder from his desk to show Brian before setting it back down.

"What is it?"

"It's what his private investigator came up with on Bridget's family so far."

Brian arched his brows. "And?"

"The Singers were in a lot of debt, living beyond their means. But the last straw was a lawsuit against his construction company. To save money, Singer had cut some corners, which led to a worker getting killed. I suspect the stress of the lawsuit and the potential criminal charges got to him. He had a heart attack, and six months later the wife died. She couldn't keep it together. They called it an accidental overdose, but it's possible it was really a suicide. The bank took their home within a month after Mrs. Singer's death. Which was right after Bridget wrote her will, giving Traci guardianship."

"So when Traci agreed to be Christopher's guardian, should something happen to Bridget, she probably assumed there would be plenty of money to support them?" Brian asked.

The chief nodded. "That's what it looks like. From what the investigator found out, it seems Bridget didn't realize her father's business was embroiled in a lawsuit, and even after her mother died, she had no clue what was going on. Apparently, it came as quite a shock to her, not only losing her mother, but to discover she was penniless."

"Wow. Did he find out what happened to Bridget?" Brian asked.

"She fell down the steps of her apartment building."

THE CHIEF WAS ALONE in his office when Traci's older brother, Kent Lind, showed up on time for his ten o'clock meeting with the chief. The two men shook hands, exchanged greetings, and the chief once again expressed his condolences.

"I went to the funeral home, arranged for Traci's cremation," Kent said as he took a seat across from the desk, facing the chief. "Is there any update?"

"Yesterday, we received a tip that someone had thrown what looked like a gun off the end of the pier." It wasn't a complete lie.

"And?"

"We recovered it, and it appears to be the revolver that killed your sister. Someone tried removing the serial numbers, yet they didn't do a good job."

"Do you know who it belonged to?"

"Yes, and no. Someone reported it stolen in Eureka, California, about a year ago."

"So you don't have any real leads?"

"Not exactly." The chief let out a sigh. "Yesterday morning, two real estate agents showed up at Marlow House."

"Marlow House?"

"It's a local bed-and-breakfast. The real estate agents claimed to be interested in purchasing the property, which isn't for sale. When they left Marlow House, they drove down the street and attempted to coerce Christopher Singer into their car."

"The boy my sister has been taking care of?"

The chief nodded. "Your sister left Christopher with Chris Johnson before she was killed. The boy was standing in Chris's yard when the men drove up. Fortunately, he was out there with Chris's very protective dog, and the dog scared them off."

"And what has any of this to do with the gun you found?"

"The men, who are indeed real estate agents, are also from Eureka, California, where the gun was stolen. The men are also brothers, and one of them is into competitive shooting. While the gun we found at the end of the pier didn't belong to him, he owns several firearms and knows how to use them."

"Have you talked to them yet? It sounds like they were trying to kidnap the boy."

"No, I can't talk to them. They left town right after they tried grabbing Christopher. They got as far as Brookings, Oregon. But their car blew up this morning, with both men inside. Someone had placed a bomb under their car. Neither man survived."

TWENTY

Kent Lind sat back in the chair and let out a sigh. He shook his head in disbelief. "None of this makes sense. Why would my sister leave Christopher with this Chris Johnson guy?"

"Ever heard of Chris Johnson before?"

Kent shook his head. "No. Traci never mentioned him."

"Chris met Bridget and your sister back in California before he moved up to Oregon."

"You said his name is Chris? Is he Christopher's father?" Kent asked.

The chief shook his head. "No. Although, it seems your sister believed he was. But according to Chris, he and Bridget were only acquaintances. He met Bridget when he lived on a sailboat down at the docks where the Singers kept their boat. And he met your sister through Bridget. Since a DNA test can easily verify what Chris says, I have no reason to doubt him."

"It wouldn't surprise me if Bridget lied to Traci."

"Why do you say that?"

Kent shrugged. "Past history."

"You didn't like Bridget?"

Kent looked at the chief and smiled. "Not really. Bridget used

Traci. She constantly got Traci to do things for her. Oh, I'm not talking about taking advantage of her financially, at least not until the end. Bridget had plenty of money back then, but she treated Traci like her personal assistant."

"What can you tell me about your sister agreeing to be Christopher's guardian?"

"After Bridget's mother died, Traci came to me, all excited that Bridget wanted to make her the executor of her estate should something happen to her, and to be Christopher's guardian. With the grandmother gone, Bridget wanted to make a new will. To be clear, Traci wasn't excited because of all the money she would have access to should Bridget die."

"You mean the money she assumed they had?" the chief interrupted.

Kent nodded. "Exactly. This was before Bridget moved in with her, right after her mother died, and before the bank swooped in and took everything. Traci certainly wanted nothing to happen to Bridget. But Bridget wanting her to be Christopher's guardian if something happened, Traci saw it as an honor. A sign of how much Bridget trusted her."

"How long were they friends?"

"Since high school. Back then, Traci lived with our dad and his wife. So I didn't really get to know Bridget, not until Traci moved in with me after she turned eighteen. Bridget was both boy crazy and spoiled. Everything was always about her."

"When Bridget lost everything, whose idea was it for her and Christopher to move in with your sister?"

"I'm not really sure. Bridget and her kid had already moved in when Traci told me about it. She said Bridget didn't have any family she could count on. I guess when they lost everything, whatever family Bridget had distanced themselves pretty quickly from it all. I always assumed they knew how spoiled Bridget had been all her life, and they were afraid if they took her and the kid in, they would end up supporting her like her parents had been doing. But that's just my guess. And my sister told me Bridget was her best friend, and she needed her."

"After Bridget's death, did anyone come forward from her family contesting the will, wanting custody of Christopher?"

Kent shook his head. "Not that Traci ever told me about."

"Do you know anything about Bridget's death?"

Kent shifted in his chair as if trying to get comfortable. "Bridget fell down the stairs of their apartment. Traci had agreed to babysit the kid so Bridget could go clubbing. That night, Bridget wore some ridiculously high heels, tripped going down the stairs, landed on the concrete. She laid there for a couple of hours before another tenant found her. It was pretty awful."

"If she fell down the stairs and was not found immediately, I have to assume she hadn't gone clubbing with a date. I'm surprised she could afford that. What kind of a job did she have?"

Kent let out a snort. "Bridget never tried looking for a job. But she had some expensive jewelry that she kept, and the courts couldn't take it since it belonged to her, not her parents. My sister paid the rent and bought the food, but Bridget's money, what she got from pawning her jewelry, she used to fund her social life."

"Her social life?"

"That night Bridget fell down the stairs, it wasn't the first night she went out and left Traci babysitting. Traci told me Bridget went clubbing to find a rich husband. And once she found one, all her money problems would be solved. After her death, Traci sold what was left of the jewelry, which wasn't much, because Bridget had been selling off her jewelry to buy new clothes and shoes. Like the pair that killed her."

"Do you have any idea who might have killed your sister? Was there anyone who expressed an interest in Christopher?" the chief asked. "Maybe someone Bridget met while clubbing? Someone she brought back to their apartment?"

Kent considered the question for a moment before shaking his head. "No. According to Traci, Bridget never brought any guys to their apartment. I have to give her credit for that, not exposing her son to a string of men. And until you told me about someone trying to grab the boy, I assumed this was a random act of violence by a stranger. I can't think of anyone who would want to hurt my sister.

And to be honest, she had a small circle of friends. And ever since Mr. Singer died, most of those friends Bridget and Traci stopped seeing. I know this because when I attended Bridget's funeral, many of the girls who had been friends with my sister came up to me and mentioned they hadn't seen much of Bridget or Traci since Bridget's father died."

"And Traci never mentioned anyone who showed any sort of interest in Christopher?"

"No. But she started complaining about how she hadn't signed up for this."

"You mean raising Bridget's son?"

Kent nodded. "Yes. A few months back, she had to take Christopher to the doctor. She used up a chunk of the money she had from the jewelry she'd sold to pay for the visit and some tests. Raising a kid is expensive. I told her she needed to apply for government assistance. It wasn't the first time I told her that. But the last time I did, a couple of weeks ago, she told me she was going to find Christopher's father instead. He needed to take responsibility. I assumed she meant she was having Christopher's DNA tested and would try tracking his father's family down. You see, right after Bridget died, I had asked Traci about Christopher's father, and she claimed Bridget never told her. And she never mentioned this Chris dude. She also never told me she was driving to Oregon. I had no idea she had come up here."

"Do you know who Mrs. Brown is?"

"You mean Traci's next-door neighbor?"

"Yes."

"Sure. Nice lady. Widow, she would watch Christopher for Traci sometimes after Bridget died."

"Did you know her very well?"

Kent shook his head. "Not really. I've only met her a couple of times."

Not ten minutes after Kent finally said goodbye and left the police station, an unexpected call came in for Chief MacDonald from the very person he and Kent had been discussing minutes earlier—Mrs. Brown.

She first introduced herself to MacDonald, explaining she was the next-door neighbor to Traci Lind. "I can't believe this has happened. Traci's brother contacted our landlord, told him what happened, and that he would be making arrangements to clean out her apartment, but first he was going up there to bring her home. I ran into the landlord when he was coming out of her apartment. He told me he needed to check to make sure her apartment was okay, and he explained what happened. This is horrible. There was no mention of Christopher. Is the boy okay? He wasn't hurt, was he?"

"Christopher is safe. He wasn't with Ms. Lind when she was killed."

"Oh, thank God!"

"I'm glad you called, Mrs. Brown. Christopher has mentioned you. He said you would sometimes watch him."

"Yes. It was hard on Traci, working and watching the boy after Bridget died. Bridget didn't work, so she could stay home with her son. And after she died, I'm afraid Traci struggled to pay for childcare."

"I wanted to ask you about some of your friends that Christopher mentioned."

"Friends?" Mrs. Brown asked.

"Yes. Kevin and Derrick Tyler?"

"Who?"

"They are brothers. Real estate agents from Eureka, California."

"I don't know anyone from Eureka. And I don't know a…what did you say their names are again?"

"Kevin and Derrick Tyler."

"I don't know any Derrick. While I know a couple of Kevins, none have the last name Tyler, and they aren't real estate agents, or live in Eureka. You must have misunderstood Christopher."

"Can you tell me what friends of yours you have introduced to Christopher?"

"Let me think…just my grandkids and daughter when they come over. That's really all."

"Mrs. Brown, now with Christopher's guardian gone, do you

know of anyone who might step forward to be his guardian—or who wants to be?"

There was silence on the phone for about half a minute. Finally, Mrs. Brown said, "Oh dear, that poor child. I didn't really know Bridget's extended family, and none of them seemed involved in her life. Although two of Bridget's cousins stopped by to see Traci and Christopher, but she had already left on her trip, so she missed them. I know nothing about his father. While I love the dear child, I'm certainly not in any position to care for him full time. I just turned eighty."

Five minutes later, Brian looked into the chief's office just as he was getting off the phone. The chief hung up and waved Brian in.

"I'm going to lunch and wondered how the meeting with Lind's brother went."

"Okay, but no new leads. However, I just had a call from Mrs. Brown."

Brian walked all the way into the office and sat down in a chair facing the chief. "The one who is supposedly friends with the Tylers?"

"She claimed not to know them. And if she had been behind the kidnapping, she didn't act like someone eager to assume custody of the boy."

TWENTY-ONE

"We would have come over sooner," Tammy Miller told Danielle on Tuesday afternoon as she stood by the baby swings that were now set up in the living room. She watched the gurgling antics of Addison and Jack as they kicked their little stockinged feet and waved tiny hands while rocking back and forth in a steady and slow rhythm. Tammy glanced over at the boys playing in the corner and added in a whisper, "But Lily told us about your young houseguest."

As she looked over to the three boys rummaging through the pile of toy trucks, blocks, and random toys, they reminded her of stair steps, with her grandson, Connor, being the youngest, one month shy of his second birthday. Lily had told her Christopher was four, but she thought he looked older. Evan was the oldest, and Tammy couldn't recall his age, but she thought Lily had told her he was ten or eleven, but he also looked older, being a tall boy, and he was obviously good with the younger children.

"We've been watching him during the day, but he's staying with Chris," Danielle explained. "Evan's been keeping him entertained, which has been a big help."

"That Evan seems like a sweet boy." Tammy turned her attention back to the twins. "They are adorable! I can't decide who they look like. But they have their father's blue eyes."

Danielle smiled. "While my parents didn't have blue eyes, both my grandmothers did, so I figured it was always possible one of those recessive genes might have made its way to me, and I guess we have the answer now." Danielle smiled down at her babies.

"Well, they are beautiful."

Laura, who had been walking around the room carrying her niece, made her way over to Tammy and Danielle, while Walt and Gene stood with Lily on the other side of the room, engaged in their own conversation.

"How long will he be staying with Chris?" Laura asked Danielle in a low voice.

Danielle glanced over at the boys and back at Laura and Tammy. "Until they can find a next of kin who can take him, or they can make another arrangement. Mel put Chris in touch with an attorney who works with child protective services, and they're working all that out."

Lily walked up to the three women and interrupted the conversation by asking, "Why don't we take the boys outside, and they can play ball? Evan told me about that tee-ball set Heather got for Christopher. And it's such a beautiful day, I'd like to be outside."

Danielle glanced briefly at the twins and said, "Why don't you guys take the boys out there, and Walt and I will join you in a little bit. I think those two are getting hungry."

TAMMY, Gene, Laura, and Lily sat on Marlow House's patio set, with Tammy holding her granddaughter, while they watch the boys playing in the side yard, with Hunny and Sadie standing close by, eyeing the balls. Evan had set up the tee-ball stand with a ball. He handed Connor a plastic bat, and the two older boys laughed good-naturedly as the toddler repeatedly swung the bat. Connor managed to hit the stand several times without tipping it over, and on his last swing, the bat connected with the ball, sending it flying off the stand. The two older boys cheered and applauded the toddler, who dropped the bat and ran with the dogs to get the ball he'd sent flying off the stand.

On the patio the adults laughed at the boys, with Gene commenting on how good the older boys were being with Connor. Lily's cellphone buzzed, and she looked at it. Danielle had sent her a text message.

"Laura, help me for a minute." Lily stood up. Laura stood and followed Lily into the kitchen. They returned a few minutes later carrying a plate of cookies, napkins, and a pitcher of lemonade and a stack of plastic cups.

"You making yourself at home?" Gene teased.

Lily flashed her father a smile. "Dani sent a text message a minute ago. I'm only following instructions." After Lily finished organizing the refreshments on the patio table, she looked out to the yard and noticed how Sadie and Hunny kept trying to grab the ball from the boys. She called the dogs to her and put them both in the house before locking the dog door.

THE TWO MEN peered over the fence and spied the three boys playing in the side yard. The smallest had just hit a ball with a bat, and now he sat some distance between the tee-ball stand and the other two boys. He had spied the two dogs and was relieved when a woman put them in the house.

They watched as the taller boy set another ball on the tee-ball stand before walking over to where the younger boy sat. It was the boy now standing at the tee-ball stand, bat in hand, who interested the men. They didn't care about the other two boys, only the boy holding the bat.

"We could grab him before they could do anything," one man told his companion. He nodded to the adults sitting on the patio. They appeared to be eating and drinking something and not paying close attention to the boys, while the two other boys sat between the patio and the boy they wanted—who was the closest one to them, maybe six feet away, with only the fence separating them.

"YOU CAN DO IT, CHRISTOPHER!" Evan shouted from where he stood with Connor. Just as Christopher swung the bat, something caught Evan's attention. He spied two men walking through the fence to Christopher, whose bat had just grazed the ball, sending it off the stand onto the ground and rolling a few feet away.

Evan's eyes widened at the sight. They were the two men who had followed them on Sunday. His father had told him they murdered that woman. They had also tried to kidnap Christopher. While Evan had heard they died in the explosion, he would have known they were dead without hearing about their car blowing up, considering they had just walked through the fence—without opening it. Evan knew the taller one was Kevin, and the shorter one was Derrick. He'd heard they were brothers.

Christopher had just picked up the ball and set it back onto the stand when the two men reached him. One grabbed at his arm, but his hands went through the boy, and then the next moment the other man tried.

"Stay here, Connor," Evan ordered before marching over to Christopher and the two ghosts. Christopher, who was oblivious to the two ghosts trying to grab him, set the ball back onto the stand and took another swing, this time sending the ball a significant distance away from him.

Christopher ran after the ball, with the two men on his heels. But both Christopher and the two men stopped in their tracks when Evan shouted, "Stop! Don't move!" They all looked at Evan.

"Christopher, please get your ball and go take Connor up on the patio. I need to do something."

By Evan's serious tone, Christopher didn't question the older boy but ran to retrieve his ball and then to Connor while Evan stepped in front of the two men, hands now on hips as he faced them both.

"Oh, brave little boy," one sneered. "You think you can handle us both?"

"Since you couldn't even pick up a four-year-old, I'm pretty sure I can," Evan snapped back, sounding sassier than normal. Just last week, Evan had been at the beach with Eddy, playing Frisbee, when his brother had gone into the public bathroom, leaving Evan on the beach alone, when an older boy showed up and started bullying Evan, trying to take the Frisbee. Eddy had returned before the confrontation got violent, but it had left Evan frustrated, wishing he had handled the bully on his own, which was why he funneled that frustration into this current situation. When alive, these two men had been far more dangerous than the bully at the beach trying to take his Frisbee. Yet as ghosts, they were no match for Evan MacDonald. At the moment, Evan felt a little like Superman.

Glaring at Evan, Kevin backhanded him, sending his right hand through Evan's face—literally. Evan didn't flinch. Kevin pulled back his hand and stared at it. While doing so, Derrick tried slapping Evan, but like his brother, he inflicted no damage, and the boy only smiled at him.

Evan repeated a script he had always imagined saying to some ghost of a dangerous man he might someday encounter, whom he needed answers from. He just did not know he would use it so soon. "You are Kevin and Derrick Tyler, and unless you want to live for an eternity with regret, you will listen to what I have to say."

"How do you know our names?" Kevin demanded.

"Why did you kill that woman?" Evan asked.

"I don't know what you're talking about." Derrick looked around nervously.

Evan glared at the two ghosts, his hands still on his hips. "And why did you try taking Christopher?"

Snow fell from above. The two ghosts looked up at the clear blue sky, confused. "Is that snow?" Kevin asked.

Evan groaned. "Aw, come on, Eva. I wanted to do this."

In the next moment, Eva and Marie materialized, with Marie standing on Evan's right, and Eva on his left.

"Sorry, dear, but we saw you, and we really need to speak to these two," Marie told Evan.

Derrick pointed at Marie and exclaimed, "That's the woman we saw!"

WALT AND DANIELLE walked onto the back patio, each carrying a baby. They found their guests—at least the adults—sitting on the patio furniture. But instead of visiting with each other, they stared off toward the street, no one talking, while Christopher and Connor stood silently next to Lily.

"What's going on?" Danielle asked.

Laura pointed out across the yard. When Walt and Danielle looked in the direction Laura pointed, they didn't see what Laura and the others did. They saw Evan standing with Marie and Eva while talking to the ghosts of Kevin and Derrick Tyler. Walt and Danielle exchanged quick glances, both understanding that all their friends saw was Evan standing in the yard, seemingly talking to himself.

The next moment, Sadie and Hunny rushed out of the doggie door after just discovering Walt had unlocked it before coming outside. Both dogs raced past the people on the patio and toward Evan and the ghosts, both barking. Right before Sadie and Hunny reached Evan and the ghosts, Kevin and Derrick, and then Marie and Eva, vanished. The next moment, Marie appeared by Walt and Danielle's side and said, "It's our killer's ghosts. Eva and I are going to look for them." Marie vanished again.

Walt and Danielle knew that from their friends' perspective, the dogs had just been barking furiously at the fence before suddenly stopping and sitting by Evan's side.

"What is over there?" Tammy asked. "For a moment, I thought Evan was talking to himself."

"I did too," Laura said with a chuckle. "I was wondering about that kid."

"By the way those dogs were barking, something was obviously there," Gene said.

"He told me to bring Connor over here. He sounded kinda serious," Christopher told them.

Walt handed Lily his son. "Take Jack. I'll go see what's going on out there."

"I have a good idea," Lily muttered under her breath as she took the baby and watched as Walt sprinted across the yard to Evan and the dogs.

TWENTY-TWO

"A chipmunk," Walt said when he reached Evan. Hunny and Sadie greeted Walt.

Evan frowned. "What?"

Walt glanced to the patio and back at Evan while petting both dogs. "They saw you talking to them. But they couldn't see *them*. If you know what I mean."

Evan glanced briefly to the patio and spied Lily's family staring at him. He cringed and looked back at Walt. "You saw?"

Walt nodded. "When they ask who you were talking to, say it was a chipmunk on the fence, and you started talking to it."

"Sounds kinda lame."

Walt chuckled. "Have another idea? Do you want to tell them you were talking to ghosts?"

Evan looked to the patio again and back at Walt. He shrugged. "I guess a chipmunk isn't as nuts as a ghost. And it explains Sadie and Hunny barking."

Walt smiled. "Exactly." He put his arm around the boy's shoulder and started back toward the house with him while asking, "Did you find out why they did it?"

"No. The dogs scared them off."

When they reached the patio, Laura asked Evan, "Who were you talking to?"

Evan shrugged. "A chipmunk."

Laura smiled. "You were talking to a chipmunk?"

"Why not?" Danielle asked. "I talk to Max all the time."

Laura frowned at Danielle and looked back at Evan and asked, "You sent Christopher over here with Connor. I guess we assumed there was something else by the fence."

Evan stared at Laura for a minute and shrugged before saying, "Not sure what you mean."

"You told me to get Connor and go to the patio," Christopher reminded him.

"It's probably because Evan noticed Lily brought cookies out," Danielle suggested. "But the chipmunk distracted him."

Evan grinned. "Yeah, Danielle makes the best cookies."

"I'M DYING to find out, Dani. Who was Evan really talking to?" Lily asked Danielle when she followed her into the house ten minutes later. Danielle carried Addison, who needed a diaper change. Danielle told her what she had seen, but since she hadn't talked to Walt or Evan yet, without the others around, she had no idea what Evan had learned from the two ghosts.

"Are you sure they were the two who blew up in the car?" Lily asked as they walked into the living room.

"That's what Marie said." Danielle watched as Lily pulled a changing pad from Danielle's nearby diaper bag and placed it on the sofa. Danielle sat down on the sofa cushion and laid Addison on the pad.

Lily handed Danielle the wipes and a diaper from the diaper bag while saying, "I wonder if the killers told them why they did it."

Danielle shrugged. "No clue. But I'm curious too."

Walt walked into the living room carrying Jack. "This one needs a change."

Danielle looked up briefly. "Are you alone?" She looked back to

Addison, gave her a kissy smiley face, and finished changing her diaper.

Walt glanced behind him to the doorway and looked back into the room. "No one followed me in here."

"So what did Evan find out?" Lily asked.

"Our ghosts don't realize they're dead." Walt handed Danielle Jack before picking up a squirming Addison from the sofa. "Although they might now."

"What makes you think they didn't realize they were dead?" Lily asked.

"Evan said they kept grabbing at Christopher, which I assume was another failed kidnap attempt."

"THEY OBVIOUSLY DON'T KNOW they're dead," Eva said. She stood with Marie on the rooftop of Marlow House, surveying the neighborhood, looking for the ghosts of the Tyler brothers. "Which isn't surprising, considering they weren't expecting their car to explode, and I don't imagine there was much left of their bodies. And often it's seeing one's body after leaving it that helps a spirit accept the reality of death."

"They recognized me from the explosion site, but why did they come here? I'd expect them to return to California, where they're from."

"Tells me they've come here because of unfinished business."

Marie wrinkled her nose. "Considering what they did when they were alive, it was nasty business."

"We need to find them before the Universe snatches them up. That's if we want to learn who is behind all this."

Marie nodded. "I imagine whoever is behind this is the same one who blew them up, believing they had outlived their usefulness. Which is concerning on many levels, because does that mean they'll send someone else to get Christopher? And why?"

"I suggest we start by following their footsteps from the last time they were in Frederickport when they were alive."

"We can start at Pier Café. I understand they went there."

"BINGO," Marie said when she and Eva arrived at Pier Café a moment later. The two spirits stood just inside the front entrance. They spied Derrick and Kevin sitting in a booth on the other side of the restaurant, trying to get Carla's attention. Neither Tyler brother seemed to notice Eva and Marie's entrance.

"Seeing us again might scare them off," Marie said. "When they recognized me back at Marlow House, the way they looked at me, I suspect they might have vanished even if Hunny and Sadie hadn't run out and scared them off."

"Let's step outside before they notice us. I have an idea."

The next moment, Eva and Marie stood outside on the pier.

"What's your idea?" Marie asked.

"I'd like to get in costume. Assume a role." The next moment Eva was no longer dressed as a woman from the early 1900s, but instead wore denims and a midriff blouse, her long hair down past her shoulders.

Marie startled at the transformation. "Oh my, I wouldn't recognize you. You look like you could be one of Danielle's friends."

"I am one of Danielle's friends."

"I meant one of her living friends." Marie looked Eva up and down. "That blouse is a little…umm…revealing. And I didn't know you had a belly-button ring."

Eva looked down at her exposed belly button and smiled. "I never did. But it is rather fun, don't you think? And I suspect this costume won't scare them off, but encourage them to stick around, which will give me time to tell them what we need to."

"Oh my."

"Now let's do you." With her right hand, Eva motioned toward Marie's torso.

"What do you mean?"

"For starters, let's shave some years off. Don't you want to be twenty again? Just for a while?" Eva's eyes twinkled mischievously.

Marie laughed. "Oh, I see what you're doing! I think I remember how to do this." The next moment Marie looked as she had looked in her twenties. "Since I don't have a mirror—and couldn't use one anyway, how do I look?"

"Ahh, I remember that young girl." Eva grinned. "This is how I remember you from back when I'd drop in to see how you were doing. Now do the clothes. You don't want to dress like a little old lady."

"IS the waitress ever coming over here?" Derrick grumbled.

"Calm down. She'll be over here in a minute. You just said you weren't hungry, and to be honest, neither am I."

Derrick frowned at his brother. "Then why are we in here again?"

"For one thing, we need to remember where we parked our car. And we need to figure out what in the hell is going on. I'd rather do it while sitting down." Kevin started to say something else but stopped talking and looked toward the entrance of the diner. "Wow, look at what just walked in."

Derrick turned in the direction his brother stared. Two attractive young women had just walked into the diner.

"Where have you been all my life?" Kevin muttered.

"Which one?" Derrick asked with a chuckle.

"Either, but both would be better."

They laughed and then stopped laughing when the two women looked directly at them and then walked past an empty table and continued walking in their direction.

"MAYBE YOU SHOULD TELL me the plan before we get to their table," Marie whispered.

"I'm taking a page from Heather's book."

Marie stopped walking for a moment and looked at Eva. "From

Heather's book?"

Eva grinned. "I do love that girl's imagination. Like when you convinced some people she was a witch. I believe she could be an actor."

"You want us to pretend we're witches?"

"No, dear, I'm going to be psychic."

Moments later, they reached Kevin and Derrick's booth. "Why don't you boys scoot over and make some room for us ladies?" Eva purred.

Speechless, the two brothers, who sat across from each other in the booth, each scooted over on their bench seats, making room for the two women.

Marie and Eva smiled at the men and sat down. "I'm Eva, and this is Marie."

"Hello, ladies," Kevin said, his smile wide. "I'm Kevin, and this is my brother, Derrick."

Eva smiled at Kevin and said in a low voice, "I don't want to scare you two off."

Kevin laughed. "Why would we be afraid of two pretty ladies like you?"

"You see, we've come to tell you something, and I'm afraid when you hear what I have to say, you might just—well, disappear. And if you do that, I suspect it will be something you regret for eternity."

Derrick smiled at Eva. "For eternity?"

"If you only knew," Marie muttered.

"This is going to sound crazy, but please listen. We saw you coming in here…and well…please don't laugh…but I'm a psychic. I had a premonition. And I feel compelled to warn you."

"A premonition?" Kevin grinned. He crossed his arms and leaned back in the booth, studying Eva. "So tell me."

"First, let me say this; if you leave before I finish telling you everything, I promise you there will come a time when you want to talk to me about this. Just remember, you can find me at the local cemetery. Just ask around for Eva."

Kevin chuckled. "Oh brother. I got to hear this."

Frowning, Derrick glanced from Eva to Marie and back to Eva, yet said nothing.

"I suspect all of us have done things that other people consider bad to varying degrees. And when our lives are over, we have to atone for those discretions. Of course, if the bad thing is something like forgetting to return a library book, it's not the same thing as, let's say…killing someone."

Kevin frowned at Eva. "What are you talking about?"

"I thought you said you were a psychic. Are you some sort of religious nut out to save souls?" Derrick asked with a snort.

Eva shrugged. "Considering you murdered Traci Lind and tried to kidnap Christopher Singer, you may need some saving."

Marie cringed, expecting both ghosts to disappear again. Instead, Kevin glared at Eva and asked, "Who the hell are you?"

"Someone who is trying to help you. And if you'd like to save your soul, or at least minimize what you'll face, I suggest you start by telling us who sent you here and why."

HEATHER AND CHRIS walked into Pier Café on Tuesday afternoon. They had left the office early, and before picking up Christopher at Marlow House, they wanted to get something to eat, as they had both skipped lunch, and they knew Danielle had probably kept Christopher well fed all day.

They were about six feet inside the entrance when Heather froze in her tracks and grabbed Chris's wrist, pulling him to a stop. "They're here. The Tyler brothers," Heather hissed under her breath as she nodded toward the booth.

Chris looked across the diner and frowned. "Where?"

"In that booth, with those two women."

Chris tugged his wrist from Heather's grip. "The Tylers are ghosts now. And those women are obviously having a conversation with them. You're a little jumpy, which I get, considering everything."

"No. It's them. But who are they with?"

TWENTY-THREE

The four people in the booth who caught Heather's attention continued talking amongst themselves, seemingly oblivious to the people around them. Reluctantly, Chris followed Heather to the booth next to the four, convinced the two men weren't the dead Tyler brothers. He couldn't fathom their ghosts had not only returned to Frederickport from California but had hooked up with the ghosts of two attractive women—or two random mediums. Ghosts only conversed with other ghosts or mediums and, of course, some animals. If they were the ghosts of Traci's killers, Chris felt the women would more likely be mediums as opposed to ghosts, because he didn't understand why four ghosts would hang around at a restaurant, chatting, when at any minute a group of customers could come and sit down on them. From what Chris had learned over the years, ghosts found it exceedingly annoying when a living being passed through their apparition.

Chris sat down in the booth and was surprised when Heather sat next to him as opposed to sitting across from him. She gave him a little nudge with her hip for him to move down the bench. Chris soon realized why Heather sat next to him. In the booth behind them sat the men who Heather believed were the ghosts of the Tyler brothers. If she wanted to eavesdrop on their conversation—which Chris assumed she did—she was closer on this side of the booth, and with their backs to the four, they remained somewhat incognito.

Chris picked up two menus from the end of the table and handed one to Heather. They quietly looked at the menu. He didn't think Heather was actually reading hers but instead trying to overhear what was being said. Unless her ears were better than his, he doubted Heather overheard anything, because the woman sitting on the other side of the booth seemed to be doing most of the talking.

"I can't hear anything," Heather whispered to Chris.

"It's not them, anyway. They probably went back to California or maybe are wandering around confused in Brookings. Why would they come back here?"

Heather's cellphone vibrated. Still holding the menu with one hand, she picked up her cellphone from where she had set it on the table moments earlier. After reading the text she received from Danielle, she handed her phone to Chris and said, "You're wrong."

With a frown, Chris took the cellphone from Heather and read the text message—*We had unexpected visitors in the backyard a little while ago. Tyler bros.*

Chris stared at the message a moment and then glanced briefly behind him. He set the phone on the table and then whispered, "If it's them, who are the women? Ghosts or mediums?"

Heather closed her menu and set it on the table. She picked up her purse, opened it, and removed a tube of lipstick and a compact mirror.

"What are you doing?" Chris asked. He then watched Heather remove the cap from her lipstick, flip open the mirror, and look into it. Just as she was about to apply the lipstick, she froze. Staring into the mirror, she tilted it from side to side.

Heather lowered the mirror without putting on lipstick, turned to Chris, and handed him the mirror. "Look."

Chris looked into the mirror, aiming over his shoulder. The booth behind them was empty.

"Well, hi, guys." Carla's sudden appearance startled both Chris and Heather. They looked up at Carla, Chris still holding the small mirror while Heather held a tube of lipstick.

"Umm…Hi." While still looking at Carla, Heather slipped the cap back on her lipstick and dropped it in her purse.

But Carla's attention was on Chris, not Heather. She cocked her head to the side as she studied Chris. "Do you have something in your eye?"

Chris flashed Carla a weak smile, then looked back into the mirror and, with his free hand, swiped the corner of one eye with a thumb. "Yeah. But I got it." He handed the mirror back to Heather, who muttered thanks before dropping it in her purse.

Carla, who stood over them, holding a pitcher of water, glanced across the table of their booth to the empty bench and then looked back at Chris and Heather. "Are you waiting for someone? Do you want to wait to order?"

Heather grabbed her purse and phone, scooted out of the booth next to Chris, and stood up. "Umm, no. We just got a message that they aren't coming." Heather lied. She moved to the other side of the booth and sat down, now facing Chris and the booth behind him—the booth that looked empty when viewing from the mirror, but from her current perspective, four people sat there.

Chris hadn't moved back to the center of the bench since Heather's departure, and Carla took the opportunity to sit where Heather had been sitting moments earlier. Now sitting next to Chris, Carla grabbed one of the empty glasses on the table and began filling it with water. "Do they have any leads on who killed your friend?"

"I haven't heard." Chris wondered if the entire town was talking about the woman who visited him at Marlow House right before her murder.

Carla filled a second glass with water and set the pitcher on the table and looked at Chris. "I'm sorry about your friend."

"Yeah, me too." Chris picked up one glass of water and took a sip.

"Oh, you won't believe what else happened this week," Carla said, her voice a little louder than it had been a moment earlier.

"What's that?" Heather asked.

"When I was on my break, I was surfing on my phone, and a hashtag was trending on Twitter. *Angel explosion* sounded interesting. So I looked."

Heather and Chris exchanged quick glances but said nothing and looked back to Carla, who continued with her story.

"A car freaking exploded at some motel in Brookings. Someone put a bomb on it. The videos were crazy, because it looked like some invisible force picked up the burning debris and moved it away from the motel. But the really freaky thing, I met the guy who owns the car!"

Chris frowned. "You did?"

"He came in here the other day. He's a real estate agent from California. I don't know if he was in the car when it exploded. They showed his picture on a video I watched. I guess they're trying to find him. Just because he owns the car doesn't mean he was in it when it exploded. So I called the police in Brookings after I read that post and told them I recognized the guy, and that he had been in here with another dude, said they were staying at the Seahorse Motel. I wonder if he was killed in the explosion."

Heather looked past Chris and Carla and figured that not only was it the Tyler brothers who had been sitting in the next booth, they had probably just overheard what Carla had said, because they just vanished, leaving behind the two female ghosts.

"That is wild," Heather muttered, now staring at the ghost with the long straight hair who looked back at her. There was something eerily familiar about the ghost.

"Crazy world." Chris picked up his menu. "But we should probably get our order in, busy day. I'll have the burger."

After they put in their order and Carla left their booth, Heather leaned across the table and whispered, "I think they overheard Carla. They're gone."

Chris arched his brows. "Why are you whispering?"

Heather leaned back and shrugged. "They're gone, but the women ghosts...oops, they left too." Heather stared at the now empty booth behind Chris.

The next moment Chris and Heather startled when the two women ghosts appeared in their booth, with the long-haired ghost with the belly ring sitting next to Chris and the other one sitting next to Heather.

Heather stared across the booth at the ghost sitting next to Chris. The ghost smiled at her. Heather's eyes widened before blurting, "Eva?"

Chris looked from the ghost next to him to the one across the table. He immediately recognized the mischievous smile on the ghost sitting next to Heather.

In the next moment, the two ghosts laughed as they transformed back into the versions of themselves most familiar to Chris and Heather.

"What are you guys doing?" Heather demanded.

Before they could answer, Carla returned to the table with the beverages they had ordered. Eva eyed Carla, prepared to move should the server decide to sit down again. She turned her attention back to Heather and Chris after the server left the table.

"We saw them at Marlow House," Eva explained. "But before we could talk to them, they vanished."

"Danielle sent Heather a text message about that," Chris said.

Heather looked from Eva back to Marie. "Was the new look your attempt to seduce the information from them? Can you seduce ghosts?"

"We didn't want them to take off like they did at Marlow House." Eva explained.

"Did you learn anything? Who was behind the killing? Do they know who blew them up?" Chris asked.

Eva let out a sigh. "Unfortunately, I hadn't quite gotten to the *surprise, you are dead* part. I was just getting to it, wanting to ease them into the idea and hopefully make them more amenable to giving us information, when Carla sat down. I'm fairly certain they now understand they're dead. And by their reaction, not happy about it."

"Whoever is?" Marie asked.

"So you got nothing? Dang, does this mean they've moved on?" Heather grumbled.

"While they didn't tell us anything, it doesn't mean they've moved on. And before they disappeared, I told them where to find me when they're ready to talk," Eva said.

"In Danielle's text message, did she mention they tried grabbing Christopher again?" Marie asked.

"No," Chris and Heather said at the same time.

Marie nodded before looking across the table at Chris. "Which makes me wonder, are you certain no one in Bridget's life knew you are really Chris Glandon?"

Chris shrugged. "Aside from her parents and Traci, I didn't really know anyone from Bridget's personal life away from the marina. And I can't imagine how they would have found out. I suppose anything is possible. But why?"

Marie shrugged. "Think about it. Bridget knew you weren't the boy's father, but she obviously told some people you were—such as Traci. Who else besides Traci read that statement Bridget made about you being his father? Perhaps someone she knows wanted to find out more about you. It's possible they were initially trying to help her. And if they discovered your true identity, well, a son of Chris Glandon is vulnerable to kidnapping."

"Heck, even the son of Chris Johnson might be," Heather added. "If Chris wasn't a Glandon, the outside world sees him as having access to a lot of money, even if they don't realize it's his."

Chris let out a sigh. "I hate to say it. But I think you're probably right. I was hoping to find someone from Bridget's family who would provide a loving and stable home for him. I worried Bridget refused to name the real father because he might be someone dangerous. But it's also dangerous if people believe I'm his father."

"You talk as if you will never have children," Eva said.

"If Chris Glandon has children someday, he understands that means spending millions for that child's security. It's not the money that is the problem for me; it's the child's quality of life. I understand the risks I take for myself by using an alias instead of spending a fortune on security. I often worry about my friends—there was already one kidnapping attempt." Chris looked from Eva to Marie. "And I suppose, if it weren't for the special company I keep that provides its own level of safety, I would become that recluse the world believes Chris Glandon is."

TWENTY-FOUR

Emily Ann, who had been resting contently in her grandmother's arms, began to squirm and root for a nipple. Lily, who sat next to her mother on Marlow House's back patio, looked over at her daughter and said, "We should probably get going. I need to feed her and put her down for a nap. And I want Connor to take a bath before dinner."

Her family quickly obliged. Gene and Laura stood, while Lily took Emily Ann from Tammy's arms. Walt and Danielle, each holding an infant, remained sitting but thanked them for coming over. As they all said their goodbyes, Chris and Heather walked in the back gate. Hunny and Sadie ran to welcome the pair, while Laura looked at Chris and realized she no longer harbored any romantic interest in the man.

But after the greetings with the new arrivals, and the goodbyes to all, Lily and her family walked across the street to Lily's house. Ian came downstairs from his office when they arrived home. After saying hello to their son-in-law, Tammy and Gene headed upstairs to wash up and rest before dinner, and Laura excused herself to use the bathroom. While alone with his wife and children in the living room, Lily, while nursing her daughter, quickly filled Ian in on what had happened over at Marlow House.

When Laura walked back into the room a few minutes later, Ian suddenly remembered something and said, "Laura, a letter arrived for you this afternoon."

Laura frowned at Ian. "A letter from who?"

Ian shrugged. "I have no idea. I put it on the end of the breakfast bar."

"Thank you." Laura turned and headed to the kitchen to retrieve the letter. When she came back to the living room a moment later, she opened the envelope and removed its contents. After unfolding the sheet of paper, she stopped walking and stared silently as she read the letter.

"Who's it from?" Lily asked from the sofa as she nursed Emily Ann while Connor played with some nearby toys on the floor. Ian sat next to her on the sofa, and Sadie napped on the floor.

Laura didn't answer immediately. After a moment, she looked up from what she had been reading and folded the sheet of paper in half before slipping it back into the envelope. "Just junk mail. I'm going to walk to the pier." Without waiting for a response, Laura folded the envelope, tucked it into the back pocket of her denim pants, turned, and left the living room, heading to the front door.

"Who puts junk mail in their pocket?" Lily whispered.

"Apparently your sister."

Lily turned to Ian. "Who was it from?"

"I don't go around opening our guest's mail."

Lily rolled her eyes. "You didn't look at the return address?"

"It didn't have a return address. Just a postmark. From New York."

"New York? Who does Laura know from New York?" Lily frowned.

———

LATE TUESDAY AFTERNOON, police chief MacDonald had already left his office, preparing to leave the police station, when they told him he had a call from a Mrs. Brown regarding the Traci Lind case. The chief returned to his office, took the seat behind his desk, and answered the call.

"Chief MacDonald, I thought I'd better call you. Remember when I mentioned Bridget's cousins who stopped by the apartment after Traci and Christopher left for Oregon?"

"Yes. What about them?"

"They're Derrick and Kevin Tyler. The real estate agents you asked me about."

The chief sat up straighter at the desk, holding the phone to his ear. "They are?"

"Yes, and I think they're dead. I was watching the news this afternoon, and a segment came on about a car exploding in Brookings, Oregon. They said the owner of the vehicle was a Realtor from Eureka. Authorities believe the Realtor and his brother may have been in the car when it exploded. They showed pictures of the two men, asking anyone who had seen them in the last few weeks to contact the authorities in Brookings. I recognized them. They were here, at the apartment building, last Wednesday. I told you about it."

"And you knew them as Bridget's cousins?" the chief asked.

"I can't say I knew them. I only met them that one time. Last Wednesday I was leaving my apartment early in the morning, going to my daughter's house. I met them as I was going down the stairs; they were coming up. I was a little startled; that stairwell only leads to my apartment and Traci's. I asked them if I could help them. They told me they were Bridget Singer's cousins, and they were coming to see Traci and Christopher."

"They didn't tell you their names?"

"No. And I didn't bother asking. Bridget once told me her only cousins were two brothers who were a little older than her, which could describe the men on the stairwell. She mentioned it once when we were talking about her family after her mother died."

"So they went up to the apartment?"

"No. I told them Traci wasn't there. She and Christopher had just left that morning to take a car trip up the coast. I told them they had just missed her."

"Did they just leave? Did they say anything?"

"They asked me where Traci and Christopher were going. If they were visiting her family or going on a trip with friends. I told them it was just the two of them. They were driving up to Oregon, and from what Traci told me, it was more of a spur-of-the-moment trip. They were going up the coast, exploring. Traci mentioned something about taking Christopher to see the Sea Lion Caves."

"Was there anything else?"

"No. Not that I remember. They thanked me and just left."

"Did Bridget tell you anything about these cousins aside from what you already mentioned?"

"Only that they weren't close. They hadn't even gone to her mother's funeral. That's how she happened to mention it."

"Did she mention what side of the family?" he asked.

"I believe it was her mother's side of the family. From what Bridget told me, her mother only had one sister, who died a few years before Bridget's mom."

"Thank you, Mrs. Brown. I appreciate you calling."

When the chief got off the phone, he called Danielle to tell her he would be a little late picking up Evan, as he needed to call the Brookings Police Department. He had already been told about Evan encountering the Tyler brothers' ghosts that afternoon, but before they got off the phone, Danielle quickly mentioned Chris and Heather, along with Eva and Marie, had run into their ghosts again at Pier Café, but they'd learned nothing that would help in the case, and she would tell him more about it when she saw him.

LATER THAT AFTERNOON, the chief sat in the kitchen with Walt, Danielle, Heather, and Evan. Marie was upstairs with the twins in the nursery. Chris had already picked up Christopher and taken him to his house for the night.

"How is the boy doing?" the chief asked.

"He's quiet. Well behaved." Danielle looked at Evan. "He seems to talk more to Evan."

They all looked at Evan, who looked at his father.

"What do you guys talk about?" the chief asked.

"Just stuff. Christopher talks about his mom sometimes, and how Traci said they were going to find his dad. He wonders if Chris is looking for his father, and if that's who he's going to live with. He said it was really nice of Chris to buy him the tee-ball set and the other stuff."

"Does he seem real sad, depressed, quiet?" MacDonald asked.

Evan shrugged. "I haven't seen him cry."

"Yeah, from what Chris said, he hasn't seen him cry either, not even when he heard about Traci's death," Danielle said. "I would best describe him as stoic. And mature for his age. He doesn't talk like I expect someone his age to talk."

"That poor boy has had a lot of losses in his young life. His grandparents, who he lived with. Not long after, his grandmother, his mother, and now Traci." The chief shook his head at the profound sadness of the situation and then told them about his phone conversation with Mrs. Brown.

He then told them about his call to the authorities in Brookings. "I explained the Tylers were persons of interest in a case here, and I asked them what they knew about the brothers. They are fairly certain they were the ones in the explosion, but until the forensics comes back, they're not one hundred percent sure. Derrick Tyler and Kevin Tyler are the ones who checked into the motel in Brookings last night, and that was their car that exploded. After running a background check on them, they discovered they worked for a real estate agent in Eureka, California."

"Which is what they told me," Walt said.

The chief gave Walt a nod and then continued, "They called Tyler's broker in Eureka, a Kyle King. King owns the real estate company they work for, and he's the broker there. From what King said, the Tylers have been wanting to invest in some property along the coast. And since property along the coast in Oregon is not as expensive as California, they took some time off and took a trip up to Oregon."

"Does that mean their offer to Walt was serious?" Heather asked.

"I have no idea. But the broker said he spoke to the Tylers yesterday afternoon. They'd told him they were heading back and planned to be in the office tomorrow morning. They had mentioned they'd looked at some properties in Oregon, but they didn't say where in Oregon they looked. Since this supposed business trip was personal business, I can understand why he hadn't bothered to ask them where they had been or why they hadn't shared their itinerary with him."

"Are they really Bridget's cousins?" Danielle asked.

"That's what they told Mrs. Brown. We're looking into it."

TWENTY-FIVE

C arla had been complaining to the busboy about having to work the breakfast shift, since she'd worked an extra shift the previous day. But she stopped her complaining when a man walked into Pier Café. She had never seen him before. If she had, she would have remembered. The old cliché *tall, dark and handsome* popped into her head when she got a clear view of his face. He stood a few feet from the *Seat Yourself* sign by the entrance. He glanced around as if looking for somewhere to sit. The man looked more appropriately dressed for a nightclub than a little diner on the pier for breakfast. After glancing around the restaurant, the man walked to the counter and sat down.

Carla smiled. *He's alone.*

"Good morning," Carla cheerfully greeted the man a few minutes later, coffeepot in hand. "Can I start you off with some fresh coffee?" With her free hand, she flipped the clean empty mug over on the counter near him.

Not looking at Carla, he said with a British accent, "I'd love some." He leaned back on the counter stool and glanced around the diner as if looking for someone while she filled his cup with coffee.

"You are obviously not from around here." Carla set the coffeepot on the counter.

He turned back to face her and smiled. "This is my first trip to Oregon."

"Are you here on vacation? Visiting family? Business?"

"I'm planning to surprise a good friend of mine." He reached for the sugar and added some to his coffee.

"Oh, how nice." *I hope it's not a woman*, she thought.

He looked up at Carla and said, "Her name's Laura Miller. She's the one who suggested this restaurant."

Carla's heart sank. Drat. *Why are the hot guys always taken?* she asked herself. Forcing a smile, she said, "I know Laura."

"You do?" His smile brightened.

"In fact, she came in yesterday afternoon, right before the dinner rush. Although, it wasn't much of a rush." Carla absently handed him a menu.

He accepted the menu. "Do me a favor; if you run into Laura before I do, don't mention me. That would spoil the surprise. I didn't want to go to her sister's house this early, so I decided I'd have some breakfast first."

"Well, I doubt you would have found her at her sister's house this early, anyway."

He arched his brows. "I wouldn't?"

Carla picked up the coffeepot. "No. Laura isn't staying with her sister. She's staying at Kelly's house."

"Kelly? Laura has mentioned her, but I can't remember who she is."

"She's one of Laura's girlfriends, who happens to be her sister's sister-in-law. The last time I saw Laura, she was here for Kelly and Joe's wedding. Laura was Kelly's maid of honor."

LATER THAT MORNING, Kent Lind stopped by police chief MacDonald's office to see if there had been any progress in the case. The two men shook hands as Kent explained why he had dropped by. When the handshake ended, the chief motioned to a chair for Kent. After both men sat down, the chief said, "While we have a few new leads, I'm afraid I'm not at liberty to discuss them yet. But we are doing everything possible to find your sister's killer."

"I understand. And there is someone you might want to call." Kent stood up, pulled a slip of paper from his pants pocket, leaned across the desk, and handed the paper to the chief.

The chief picked up the piece of paper, looked at it, and then looked back at Kent. "Who is it?"

Kent sat back in his chair. "Elena Sanchez. She was a friend of Bridget and Traci's from high school. Traci hadn't talked to Elena in a long time. But I got a call from Elena this morning. She heard about Traci's death. They had all once been good friends. She asked about Christopher and who he was going to live with. I told her I had no idea. She asked about his father, and when I told her Bridget never told Traci his identity…well, call her and talk to her yourself."

The chief leaned forward, resting his elbows on his desktop. "She knows who his father is?"

"She knows some things about the father. Not sure if it will help. But you might want to talk to her yourself. She told me it would be okay if I gave you her number. It's her cellphone, and she suggested you FaceTime her, if possible, for a video call. Frankly, I got the impression she is uncomfortable talking about this with a faceless stranger on the phone. A video call would make her more comfortable."

"I'll call her." The chief set the note on his desk. "When are you planning to head home?"

"Earlier this morning I talked to the mortuary, and they told me Traci's body will be cremated tomorrow. I'll pick her ashes up early Friday morning and then drive to the airport." Kent paused for a moment, let out a deep breath and then said, "This is all surreal. I can't wrap my head around the fact I'm taking home my baby sister's ashes."

"Are you planning on having a memorial service? I understand your mother lives in Hawaii, and your father lives in Florida."

Kent frowned at the comment and tilted his head slightly as he stared across the desk at the chief. "I don't remember telling you that. Oh, I guess you probably did a background check on Traci's family before you called. I imagine that's how you got my number. I never asked."

"Yes, that's how," the chief lied. In truth, it had been Traci's ghost who had passed that bit of information on to Heather, along with her brother's phone number.

"But yeah, Mom still lives in Hawaii, and Dad's in Florida. I called both parents before I came up here, telling them what had happened. They didn't really say much, and frankly, I haven't made any plans beyond taking my sister home."

About fifteen minutes later, Kent said his goodbyes and promised to contact the chief if he learned anything that might help in the investigation; the chief promised to keep him informed of any updates in the case.

Again alone in his office, the chief picked up the note Kent had given him, looked at it, then set it on the desk so he could read the number. He picked up his cellphone and made a video call to Elena Sanchez.

"I still can't process someone actually murdered her," Elena said not long after the chief introduced himself and his reason for calling. As the chief could see, she was an attractive woman in her mid-twenties with long black hair.

"Her brother just left my office," the chief began.

"Oh, Kent, my heart breaks for him. They were always so close."

"He mentioned you might know who Christopher's father is."

Elena let out a visible sigh. "I wish I did. Traci didn't. I asked her about it at Bridget's funeral."

"I was under the impression you had information about the father?" The chief wondered why Kent had suggested he call Elena.

"I do…sort of. I don't know who he is, but I know some things about him. About six months after Christopher was born, Bridget came over to my apartment to hang out. She had just stopped breastfeeding, and it was her first chance to go anywhere for any length of time, while her mom stayed with the baby. It was just her and I. Traci wasn't there. Bridget got pretty drunk. The whole motherhood thing was really getting to her. She started talking about her baby daddy. It was probably a crappy thing for me to do, but I asked who it was. I figured she was drunk and might tell me."

"But she didn't?"

"She giggled and said something like you could never guess if you tried. Then she said something that really surprised me. She claimed to have told her parents who the father was. I assumed she hadn't told them. I always figured if her father knew, he would be getting out his shotgun. She started giggling some more and said her parents thought Christopher's father was some loser who lived on a boat, and they had no clue he was really this rich dude. Richer than her father."

"Really?"

Elena nodded. "I said, if he was so rich, what was the problem? Why not marry the dude? I guess I shouldn't have said that. The next minute she started crying, like really ugly sobs."

"Did she say anything else?"

"Not really."

"And you never talked about it again?"

Elena shook her head. "No. But I didn't see her much after that. Honestly, it was probably because of her parents. They weren't thrilled with me because she ended up staying at my place that night, and when I took her home in the morning, she had a major hangover."

"Do you think she ever told anyone else about the father?"

Elena shrugged. "It's possible. I still see a lot of the girls we used to hang with back in high school, but none of them have ever said anything about it. But most of them sorta lost touch with Bridget after Christopher was born. And Traci, well, to be honest, while I considered her a friend, the truth was, she was always more Bridget's friend. If Bridget told anyone who the father was, I would expect her to tell Traci. After all, she told her parents. But like I said, when I asked Traci at the funeral about it, she swore she had no idea who Christopher's father was."

TWENTY-SIX

On Wednesday afternoon, police chief MacDonald and Brian Henderson met Chris and Heather for lunch, along with Walt and Danielle, at Pier Café. The chief and Brian arrived last.

"Where are the babies?" the chief asked as he sat down at the table.

"Joanne offered to watch them while we came to lunch," Danielle said.

"And Marie insisted on staying to keep an eye on things. Of course, Joanne doesn't know that." Walt chuckled.

"Doesn't Marie trust Joanne?" Brian asked, now sitting next to Heather.

"I doubt Marie one hundred percent trusts any of us to watch the babies," Heather answered for Walt. They all laughed.

Carla interrupted the conversation when she showed up at the table with a pitcher of water. She immediately asked the same question the chief had asked about the twins. After giving the answer, without adding the part about Marie also watching over them, Carla took their orders.

"Is Christopher with Joanne too?" Brian asked after Carla had left the table to put in their orders.

"No, he's spending the day at Lily's," Danielle said.

"Aren't her parents visiting?" Brian asked.

"Yes, but they're pretty much just hanging out at her house. It's kind of hard to run around and do stuff with a toddler and newborn. And Tammy is enjoying spending time with the grandbabies and visiting with her daughters. Lily suggested Christopher come over and spend the day and play with Connor," Danielle said.

"Those two boys may be a couple of years apart, but they get along well," Walt said.

"Evan had a good time yesterday. While he enjoyed helping the younger boys play tee-ball, I suspect the highlight was coming face-to-face with our killers," the chief said.

"Thankfully, it was just their ghosts," Heather muttered.

The chief nodded in agreement.

"Christopher going isn't only a play date. Lily offered to play some games with the boys to assess Christopher's skills. From what I understand, Christopher has never attended preschool, and we don't know if Bridget or Traci worked with him," Chris explained. "But he seems much older than his age, and I'm not just talking about his size. Lily agrees he is very mature, and she wants to know if he knows his letters and numbers."

"Lily is putting on her teacher's cap? Does this mean she misses teaching?" the chief asked.

"I don't think she misses it exactly, but she always loved teaching," Danielle said.

Brian looked at Chris. "School starts in a couple of weeks. Are you going to enroll him?"

"He's not old enough for kindergarten," Chris said. "I know he looks like he could be in second grade, but he just turned four this past June. Technically, I'm his foster parent until we hopefully find a family member who will provide him with a loving home. Not sure how long that will take, but it's one reason Lily offered to work with him. If we enroll him in a preschool, I'd like to find one that best suits his needs."

Carla interrupted their conversation when she returned to the table with some beverages. When she left the table, Danielle said,

"Chief, you mentioned on the phone Traci's brother came in this morning."

"Yes. He came in to say goodbye, but he also gave me a number to call." The chief recounted his visit with Kent and told them about the video call with Elena Sanchez.

When the chief finished recounting his morning conversations, Danielle said, "That sounds like Bridget described Chris. A guy who lives on a boat and is richer than her father."

Chris put up his right hand to stop Danielle from continuing. "Hey, I am not Christopher's father. Bridget and I, well, we never. Ever."

"I'm not saying you're the father, but it's almost like Bridget had convinced herself you are," Danielle countered.

Heather nodded. "Danielle has a point. She named the kid after you. She had that document written up declaring you are his dad. And he even looks like you, which makes me wonder if she hooked up with some guy who looks like you. Intentional, or does she just have a type?"

Walt looked at Chris. "I suppose it is a good thing there are DNA tests these days because it wouldn't be looking good for you."

"Yeah, well, I am not his father." Chris slumped back in his seat. "And if I was, I certainly would never deny it."

They all went silent for a moment. Finally, Danielle said, "Walt is right in the sense that these days you can't get away with claiming someone is the father if he isn't. At least not for long. But let's say Bridget found out your true identity, and she created some fantasy that you were the dad."

"She obviously told Traci, yet Traci's ghost had no clue who Chris really is," Heather said.

Danielle nodded. "True. But let's say Bridget discovered Chris's true identity after she told her parents and Traci he was the father. Think about it; if Mr. Singer found out someone with Chris's money fathered his grandchild, wouldn't he send his lawyers after him to set up his daughter financially? Especially considering his money problems."

"So you're saying, once Bridget found out who Chris really was, she hid that information from her parents and Traci, for fear they would confront him and find out she lied to them?" Brian asked.

Danielle nodded. "Exactly. But who's to say she didn't get drunk with someone else, like the woman the chief talked to today, and Bridget started talking about how the baby daddy was really rich. And if that someone figured out who she was talking about, perhaps even came across that document when visiting her in the apartment that stated Chris was the father, well, that might be an incentive for…"

"Kidnapping," Brian finished for her.

"Does this mean the Tyler brothers are really Bridget's cousins?" Heather asked. "If someone thought Chris was really the father, and learned his true identity, wouldn't they need to be close to Bridget to find that out? Like, cousins?"

"That's possible," Danielle said.

"But there is one thing about this I don't understand," Heather said.

"What?" Brian asked.

"What was the point of Bridget making that signed affidavit about Chris being the father? She knew he wasn't. A DNA test would disprove it. What was the point?" Heather asked.

They all considered Heather's question. Finally, Walt said, "When we are young, we think we're immortal. I once thought that way. I suspect when Bridget wrote that affidavit, its purpose was to convince someone in her life—like her parents—that Chris was the father, because she didn't want to tell them who it really was. And when Bridget asked Traci to be Christopher's guardian if something happened to her, I doubt she ever thought Traci would ever need to step into those shoes. "

KELLY MORELLI SAT at the computer in her home office, rereading her daily blog before posting. She glanced at the time in the upper right-hand corner of her computer monitor. It was almost two o'clock.

Kelly turned her attention back to her blog, when she heard the front doorbell ring. With a frown, she glanced at the doorway leading to the hall. She wasn't used to people ringing her doorbell. She didn't get many houseguests. Her parents never stopped by. They expected her to go to their house or to Ian and Lily's. The same was true for her brother. When was the last time he had stopped by? She couldn't recall Lily ever just stopping by, either. Kelly then thought of Laura. Had Laura borrowed Lily's car and come back early? Why hadn't she called first?

"Well, you're never going to find out who's at the front door if you don't get off your butt," Kelly said aloud as she stood up from her desk and headed to the front door.

She was about five feet from the front door when the bell rang again.

"Okay, okay, I'm coming," Kelly muttered. A few moments later, she swung open the front door, fully expecting to find Laura standing on the front porch. Instead of Laura, there stood a tall, well-dressed man who looked to be in his thirties.

He flashed her a smile, his dark eyes reminding her of Adam's. "Hello, are you Kelly?"

Kelly frowned. She had never seen this man before. Was it someone who read her blog? she wondered.

She answered his question with a question. "How can I help you?"

"I'm here to see Laura."

"Umm...Laura?" Kelly frowned.

"This is the Morelli house, right? You're Kelly?"

"Umm, yes."

"I'm a friend of Laura's, and I heard she was staying with you."

"Oh. Hello. And you are?"

He flashed her another smile while he tried looking around her as if Laura might be standing in the entry hall behind Kelly.

"Laura's here, isn't she?"

"No. She's not."

"I thought she was staying with you."

"She is, but she's over at her sister's. And you are?"

He flashed her another smile. "Do me a favor; don't tell Laura I stopped by. I want to surprise her." Without saying another word, he turned from the door and started down the walk. She remained standing inside the open doorway as he walked toward his car. She was about to go back into the house and shut the door when he turned around again and said, "Remember, don't tell her I was here."

A few minutes later, Kelly stood in her living room, looking out the front window, and watched as the man drove away. When his car was no longer in view, she rushed back to her office and picked up her cellphone and called Laura.

"Hey, Kelly. Finished with your blog?"

"Laura, a guy just stopped by, looking for you."

"What guy?"

"I don't know. He wouldn't tell me his name. Said he wanted to surprise you. I wasn't supposed to tell you he stopped by. As you can see, I didn't exactly keep that a secret. Of course, I never agreed to it."

"What did he look like?"

"Umm, tall, good looking, dark hair. His eyes reminded me of Adam's. More black than brown. He was a slick dresser, could give Walt a run for his money. Oh, and he had a sexy Brit accent."

"It can't be..." Laura fairly groaned.

"Who is this guy?"

"Someone I don't want to see."

"I'm really sorry, Laura. I assumed you had told him you were staying with me. And when you weren't here, I said you were at your sister's. So if he knows where your sister lives, then he is probably heading over there."

"Oh, crap."

TWENTY-SEVEN

K yle King sat behind the desk in his office on Wednesday afternoon. He had just gotten off the phone when a knock came at his open doorway. He glanced up to see one of his agents, Griff Paulson, standing outside the office door. Kyle motioned for him to come into his office.

"Have you found out anything else?" Griff asked, now standing in front of Kyle's desk.

"I assume you're talking about Derrick and Kevin?"

"Yes."

"I just got off the phone with the police. It's still not official. They say it will take some time to identify the bodies, if they even can. But it was Derrick's car. And both he and Kevin checked into that motel on Monday night, and no one has seen them since Monday evening. I may have been the last one to talk to them aside from whoever checked them into the motel. They called to tell me they'd be in the office today."

"Damn." Griff took a seat on a chair facing the desk and leaned back, looking across the desk to Kyle. "Is it true someone put a bomb on their car?"

Kyle shrugged. "That's what the police say. But if someone put a bomb on their car, why? It must have been some sort of mix-up."

"Mix-up?" Griff asked incredulously.

"Obviously, if someone put a bomb on the car, they intended to kill someone. I meant I don't think they intended to kill Derrick and Kevin. I told the police they need to take a closer look at the other people staying at that motel, because once the assassin figures out they blew up the wrong people, they'll try again."

"Why were they even in Oregon?"

"Kevin and Derrick talked about buying some investment property. Kevin wanted to buy property near the beach, but with the prices in California, he didn't feel they could afford it, so Derrick suggested checking out the prices in Oregon. At least, that's what they told me when they let me know they'd be gone for at least a week. But from what they said when I last talked to them, it didn't sound like they found anything they wanted to make an offer on."

"Is there anything I can do? You need help cleaning out their desks, checking on any of their clients?" Griff offered.

"Thanks, but I have it covered."

———

AFTER GRIFF LEFT Kyle's office, he went to what they called the up-room. It was down the hall from the front entrance of the real estate office. The room's glass wall separated it from the hallway, enabling whoever was in the room to see into the hall, and in turn, allowed those walking down the hallway to see who was in the up-room. The up-room was where the agents met with walk-in clients, and when not used for clients, agents often gathered there for coffee and conversation.

When Griff stepped into the up-room, there were three agents, Linda McGee, Julie Jameson, and Tim Peake, sitting at the lone banquet table in the center of the room, each with a cup of coffee. As soon as Griff entered the room, Linda asked, "What did he say?"

"They still haven't positively identified the remains. But it was Derrick's car." Griff recounted his conversation with Kyle.

When Griff finished, Tim said, "Maybe the bomb was intended for them. Some pissed-off husband?"

"Tim, that is awful!" Julie scolded.

"He's not wrong," Linda said. "Those two were players. And I'm not sure what money they were going to use to buy investment property. I can't remember the last time either of them had a closing."

"Even so, it's horrible someone killed them," Julie said.

For the next ten minutes they discussed their murdered colleagues, but when an attractive, well-dressed woman walked pass the window that looked out into the hallway, Julie, the newest agent of the four, who had only been working for the brokerage for two months, asked, "Who's that?"

They all turned to the window and saw the woman walking down the hallway from the direction of the entrance toward the private offices beyond the up-room.

"That's Kyle's mommy." Tim snickered.

Linda rolled her eyes and countered, "Stepmom. Kyle Sr.'s wife." They all understood Kyle Sr. had been Kyle's father and the founder of the real estate company. After his sudden death from a heart attack the previous year, Kyle took over his father's real estate company. He had already been its designated broker.

"I can't remember the last time I've seen her in here," Griff said.

"Isn't she an owner, too?" Julie asked.

Griff shook his head. "Nope. From what I understand, Kyle inherited the real estate company. His stepmother owns no part of it."

"Wow, wonder how she feels about that," Julie muttered.

"I don't think she cares. Her first husband was worth a fortune, and when he died, she was set up for life. I heard Kyle senior and she had a prenup before they were married, more for her benefit than his," Griff said.

ROSALYN KING HAD STOPPED COLORING her hair in her late forties, and now at fifty-three, she had gone completely gray, yet it looked more platinum blond than elderly blue. Instead of cutting it short like her mother at her age, she wore it shoulder length. Rosalyn prided herself on being impeccably groomed, and her friends often sought fashion advice from her because she had a unique knack for selecting the perfect color or style to complement a specific skin tone or body shape. Hers was trim and tall, the trim from her dedication to yoga classes, and her height to genetics.

She didn't knock at the door to her stepson's office, she simply walked in. The office had previously belonged to her husband. She found her stepson sitting at the desk. He looked up in surprise when he saw who had just walked in.

"Rosalyn, I didn't think you were coming back for another week." He stood up, walked around his desk, and gave her a perfunctory kiss on the cheek before she sat down. When she did, he asked, "Can I get you something to drink? Coffee, tea, water?"

"Thank you, no. I'm fine."

Kyle returned to his desk and sat down. "I had no idea you were back in town. How was San Clemente?"

"It was fine."

Kyle frowned as he studied her face. "Is something wrong?"

"Yes. I need to talk to you." She stood up, walked to the open door, shut it, and then returned to the chair and sat down, once again facing her stepson.

Kyle arched his brows. "This sounds serious."

"It is. I need your help."

"DOES SHE LIVE IN EUREKA? I've never seen her before," Julie asked. Everyone else had left the up-room except for her and Griff, who had just finished his coffee.

"She has a house here and one in San Clemente. The one in San Clemente belonged to her first husband. She goes back and forth between the two houses."

Julie let out a sigh. "Must be nice. I'd like to be able to afford property in San Clemente."

"The story goes—and you didn't hear it from me because they frown on office gossip. We may technically be self-employed, but trust me, they can fire us." Griff gave a snort. "Mrs. King's first husband was considerably older than her and loaded. I think they were married about two years when he died of a heart attack."

"Isn't that how her second husband died?"

Griff chuckled. "Yeah, there's been some gossip over that, too. Anyway, she and her first husband had a son together, and after the old dude died, she inherited everything. Nothing was left to their son in his will. Of course, the kid was just a baby at the time. I suppose that's why she had Kyle's dad sign a prenup before the I do's, to protect her son's inheritance."

"I can understand that."

"When I first started selling real estate here, I had a client who had known Mrs. King's first husband. He was a chatty dude. The friend, not the husband. The husband was already dead." Griff chuckled, finding himself amusing. "From what he told me, her first husband might have been old, but he was a player. He had been married two times before her. No kids. But apparently, he had been fooling around with the upstairs maid while courting wifey three."

"Upstairs maid?"

Griff gave a snort. "Well, I made that part up. But she did work for him. Anyway, he got her pregnant, paid her off, the would-be missus found out, and to show how much he loved her, he had the new will written so none of his offspring could come back and claim it. I suspect there might have been a few more out there that she didn't know about. Anyway, that was what I was told. So no idea if it's true."

"Sounds like a poorly written soap opera. Where does her son live?"

"He doesn't. He died a while back."

"From a heart attack?"

Griff let out another snort.

"No."

ROSALYN HAD BEEN in Kyle's office for over fifteen minutes, and she had been doing most of the talking. He sat quietly, listening. Finally, when she was done, Kyle let out a sigh and said, "Damn, Rosalyn, that's a lot to take in."

She nodded in agreement. "I know."

"What are you planning to do? You said you had a favor to ask me."

"I want to go to Frederickport. But I don't want to go alone. Would you please go with me?"

"Why would you want to go to Frederickport? What is the point?"

"Do you really have to ask me that?"

Kyle let out another sigh. "What do you plan to do when you get there?"

She shrugged. "I'm not really sure."

Kyle leaned forward and rested his elbows on the desktop. He studied Rosalyn for a moment before saying, "Perhaps you should think about it for a while. What is the rush?"

She shook her head. "No. If you don't want to go, I'll go myself."

"I didn't say I won't go. But...well...why don't you let me go instead?"

She smiled at him and cocked her head slightly. "And when you get there, what are you going to do?"

He considered the question for a moment and then shook his head. "Honestly, I don't know. But you don't have a plan either. I just don't think we need to rush into this."

"I'm going with or without you. I just was hoping I wouldn't have to go alone."

Kyle let out a deep breath and leaned back in his chair. "Okay, when did you want to leave?"

"I'd love to go now, but I understand that's not possible. You need to find someone to cover for you."

"And you just got back from San Clemente," he reminded her.

"I actually got home Monday night."

"There are other ways to handle this type of situation. And considering everything, it might be best if you let me find someone to take care of this for you."

She shook her head. "No. I need to do this myself. We need to keep it in the family."

"Okay. If that's how you want to handle it, I'll go with you." Kyle looked at the computer monitor on his desk and grabbed his mouse. A few swipes later, he was looking at his calendar on the monitor. He looked back to his stepmother. "If you're determined to do this, I can change a few appointments. How long do you expect us to be gone?"

Rosalyn smiled. "Thank you, Kyle. I knew I could count on you."

TWENTY-EIGHT

W hen Walt and Danielle returned to Marlow House on Wednesday, they updated Marie on what the chief had learned, along with their theory. The theory being the Tyler brothers had targeted Christopher because they believed Chris Glandon was the boy's father.

They also theorized the Tyler brothers had been working with someone else, and that accomplice had decided the brothers had become a liability. Because of that, they had arranged the hit. If the person—or people—responsible for blowing up Derrick Tyler's car was behind the kidnap attempt, that meant they were now responsible for three murders, and until the police apprehended the wannabe kidnappers, Christopher and those around him were at risk. Marie offered to stay close to Christopher until they discovered who the Tyler brothers had been working with.

Before Marie went across the street to the Bartleys' house to watch over Christopher, Danielle had given Lily a call and quickly filled her in on what they had learned and told her Marie would be there shortly.

Marie had been at the Bartleys' house for about an hour, feeling a bit like a peeping Tom as she listened to Tammy visit with her daughters in the living room while the boys played Legos with Grandpa Gene in the nearby hallway. Sadie napped under the dining room table, and Ian had retreated to his upstairs office to do some work, but Marie suspected he just wanted some quiet time away from the in-laws.

Laura's cellphone rang, and several moments later Marie heard her say, "Hey, Kelly. Finished with your blog?" The tone of Laura's conversation quickly changed, catching Marie's attention. Marie noticed how Laura moved from the recliner into the kitchen, away from her mother and sister, to finish her phone call. Tammy and Lily, whose attention had been on the baby in Tammy's lap, failed to notice Laura's mood change when she returned to the living room a few minutes later. Instead of sitting back on the recliner, Laura walked to the front window and silently looked outside, paying no attention to her sister and mother, who continued their discussion on the nearby sofa.

Laura had been standing at the window for about five minutes when Lily asked, "Laura, what are you looking at?"

Laura turned to face her mother and sister. "Umm, Mom, I'd like to talk to Lily alone. Lily, can we go to Connor's room and talk?"

Marie had to give Tammy credit. She didn't seem hurt or offended that Laura wanted to talk to Lily alone. And while Tammy might respect Laura's privacy, Marie was simply too nosey. She followed the sisters into Connor's bedroom, and when Laura shut the bedroom door behind them, Marie took a seat on Connor's bed. Unfortunately, she had to move quickly when Lily sat in the same spot while Laura remained standing.

"What is going on?" Lily asked.

"Remember how I said I lost my phone and got a new number?"

"Yeah."

Laura began pacing back and forth in front of the bed as she talked. "I didn't exactly lose it. I kinda tossed it on a moving train before I left for the airport to come back to the US. When I arrived in New York, one of the first things I did after checking into the hotel, I bought a new cellphone."

"You what? Why would you do that?"

Laura stopped pacing, faced her sister, and gave a shrug. "I know. It was probably silly. But…well…I sorta wanted to get away from someone. And I figured, if I had a new phone, with a new number, it would be harder for him to find me."

"You're talking about Dane?"

"Yeah. He became…umm…sorta intense."

"Intense? As in violent?" The pitch of Lily's voice rose.

Laura shook her head. "No. Never violent. Nothing like that. While he was a great guy, I realized about a month ago, I didn't want to stay in Europe as long as I initially planned and certainly not forever. To be honest, I got homesick. I can't fall in love with someone who lives in London. I realized I needed to end our relationship before I got too serious. He was already getting serious."

"Okay, but I still don't get why you needed to get rid of your phone."

"Neither do I," Marie said to deaf ears.

"About three weeks ago, I told him I was preparing to leave London and continue with my travels. He immediately suggested he join me. I didn't want to do that because traveling through Europe with some guy I am already attracted to sounded like a good way to fall in love. And why set myself up for all that heartbreak?"

"Doesn't this guy have a job?" Lily asked.

"That was going to be my question," Marie muttered.

"Yes. He works remotely, so he can work anywhere. But his roots are in London, and there is no future in that."

Lily frowned. "I'm still not following the reason for ditching the phone."

"Not long after I told him I was planning to leave London, he asked to see my phone. He's sort of a tech guy, and whenever I had a problem with my phone, he would help me. I didn't think about it when he asked. I just unlocked it and handed it to him. A few minutes later, he hands it back to me and says now he'll feel better with me traveling through Europe by myself. Apparently, he did something to my phone, allowing him to track my location."

"Ian did that on my phone, which I thought was sweet. But if I was just dating a guy, it would be kinda creepy. Especially if he didn't ask first."

"Exactly!"

"While I can understand the creep factor, why didn't you change the settings on your phone after he left? Why get rid of your phone?"

Laura let out a sigh. "His job often takes him to other countries in Europe, which is kinda like going to another state in the US, distance-wise. He told me he wanted to join me. He could still work, and there would be stops he'd need to make for business, but we'd see Europe together with him as my guide. I told him—as nicely as I could—that while I had really enjoyed our time together, I would eventually be going back to the States, and I didn't see the point in making it harder for me to leave by spending more time with him and possibly falling in love. At first, he seemed to understand, but then I overheard a conversation between him and one of his friends."

"What kind of conversation?" Lily asked.

"He planned to surprise me during my travels. By tracking my phone, he'd know where I was, and he could just show up. *Like, surprise! I'm here!*" Laura rolled her eyes.

"Again, why not change your phone settings?"

"First, you need to understand that when I told him I wanted to travel alone, and that we didn't have a future, I was very clear that when I left London, that would be a final goodbye. But, well, he was kind of persistent and sort of love-bombing me. And I needed to figure out some way to make a clean break. Frankly, I was sorta afraid I might fall in love, and then everything would be so complicated."

"Sounds complicated now," Marie muttered.

"So I returned to the States, and I never told him my plans. He saw me off at the train station, and fortunately he had a meeting for work, so it wasn't like he was going to see me actually get on the train. After he left, I sat next to a nice lady carrying a large bag, and we got into a conversation. When she wasn't looking, I sorta dropped my phone in her purse and then checked into a motel. I had to make a reservation to come back to the States, and I found out I couldn't get a flight back for a few days. Which was a bummer, because I no longer had a phone."

"You're not serious?"

Laura shrugged. "Seemed like a good idea. And I knew the battery on my phone would run out in about two hours, so it wasn't like he was going to show up at the little old lady's motel and demand to know why she had my phone."

"Oh, Laura…"

"Your sister is a little ditzy," Marie said to deaf ears.

Laura smiled sheepishly. "And that letter I got. It was from him. Somehow, he must have figured out that I came back to the States and never got on that train."

"Laura, Ian read the postmark on that letter, and it was New York, not London. He's in New York."

"No. Actually, he's in Frederickport. Kelly just called. He showed up at her place, looking for me."

"How did he find out you were at Kelly's?"

Laura shrugged.

"What did the letter say?"

"He said he hoped the letter would get to me. That we needed to talk."

"You said he was a great guy, but Laura, that sounds kinda creepy."

"He's not creepy. Maybe he tries too hard sometimes, but he's a good guy. I just don't want to live in London, and I think it's a bad idea to get close to someone you could fall in love with if you can't be with them. And I didn't want to come back to the States and have him as my pen pal."

"I'm sorry, Laura, but that is one of the most harebrained things I've ever heard."

"It certainly is," Marie muttered in agreement.

Laura sat on the bed next to Lily. "I know. And it didn't work, anyway."

A knock came at Connor's bedroom door, and the next minute it opened without waiting for someone to say *come in.* Gene popped his head into the bedroom and said, "Your mother told me you were in here sharing secrets. Reminds me of when you two were kids."

"Tell Mom we'll be out in a minute," Lily said.

"That's not why I'm here. A young man is here to see Laura. Says he's a friend of hers." Gene looked at Laura and added, "He's waiting in the living room with your mother. By his accent, I suspect you met him when you were in London. He says his name is Dane Carslaw."

TWENTY-NINE

Laura and Lily stepped out into the hallway from Connor's bedroom with their father, and Laura said, "I'm going to the bathroom real quick. I'll meet you in the living room." She rushed into the nearby bathroom and shut the door behind her.

Marie arrived in the living room before Lily and Gene. She discovered Ian had since come down from his upstairs office and now sat on a recliner holding his daughter, while a man Marie assumed was Dane Carslaw sat on the sofa next to Tammy.

The three adults were involved in what sounded like a lively and friendly discussion, which included intermittent laughter. Marie wondered if Dane had just told a funny story about how he'd stalked Laura across the Atlantic Ocean, or perhaps Tammy had shared a funny anecdote from Laura's childhood.

Sadie sat on the floor next to Ian's recliner; her chin—which, technically, was not actually a chin—rested on Ian's knee. Without moving her head, her gaze shifted from the stranger on the sofa to the infant on Ian's lap and back to the stranger.

Curious about the visitor, Connor had abandoned his Legos and now stood next to his father, on the opposite side of the recliner from Sadie. Christopher had remained in the hallway, quietly playing Legos by himself.

The chatter stopped when Lily and Gene stepped into the living room. Dane stood up and smiled at Gene and Lily. "You must be Laura's sister, Lily," Dane said with exuberance. He walked over to her and extended his hand. When she accepted his handshake, he said, "You and your sister could almost be twins. I'm Dane Carslaw, a friend of your sister's."

"Nice to meet you, Dane. My sister should be out in a moment." Lily glanced from the recliner to the sofa, where Dane had been sitting. She motioned to the recliner, urging him to take a seat there.

They had all sat down, with Lily on the sofa next to her mother, and Dane sitting in the recliner next to Ian, when Laura stepped into the room a few minutes later. Marie now understood the real reason for Laura ducking into the hall bathroom. She had combed her hair, and Marie suspected Lily must keep makeup in that bathroom considering Laura looked as if she had applied blush, lipstick, and some concealer to cover up the dark circles Marie had noticed when they first went into Connor's bedroom. Dane stood and immediately greeted Laura, offering a hug, which she accepted. He kissed her cheek, and when the hug ended, Marie thought Laura looked uncomfortable, while Dane looked like a man whose true love had accepted his proposal.

Marie would have loved to have stayed and eavesdropped on their conversation, but motion from the hallway, where Christopher silently played with Legos, caught her attention. She moved to the hallway and found two men standing over Christopher. Christopher seemed oblivious to their presence, which wasn't surprising, considering they weren't living men, but ghosts, the ghosts of Derrick and Kevin Tyler.

"You!" Marie gasped.

The two ghosts, who had been standing behind Christopher, looked up.

"You were there when our car exploded," Kevin accused. "And that was you in the yard of Marlow House."

"Yes. It was. I assume you now realize you're dead?" Marie asked.

Instead of answering, the brothers exchanged nervous glances and looked as if they were preparing to disappear again.

"Please don't leave," Marie blurted. "I can help you."

"What are you? An angel or something? Can you bring us back to life?" Derrick asked.

Marie smiled. "That's the second time this week I've been mistaken for an angel. But no, I don't have the power to bring you back to life."

Derrick took a step back, away from Marie. "A demon?"

Marie rolled her eyes. "Heavens no. I'm a ghost, like you two."

"We're ghosts?" Derrick asked.

"What did you think you were? Certainly not angels, considering your behavior during your last days."

"What do you know about us?" Kevin demanded.

"That one of you shot Traci Lind, although I'm not sure which one. Yet it doesn't really matter who actually pulled the trigger. You're both responsible for her death, and that will be held against you. And you tried to abduct Christopher here. I suspect there are other crimes in your past. Before you move on, mitigate the damage before you have to—as they say—face the music."

"Move on where?" Derrick asked.

"You wouldn't believe how many ask that question." Marie chuckled. "While we don't stay indefinitely on this plane, because our spirit moves on in its journey, it doesn't mean each of our journeys after leaving this place is the same. If you move on with too much baggage, well, it can be an arduous journey. Uncomfortable."

"What do you mean, too much baggage?" Kevin asked.

"Murdering Traci, well, that's some baggage you'll need to carry with you on your journey, and from what I understand, you will be required to…umm…let's just say there will be some sort of penance."

"Are you saying there is a hell? Are we going to hell?" Derrick choked out.

Marie shrugged. "I can't say it's a hell, exactly. I know, or at least I have been told, it can be unpleasant and not something a spirit wants to endure. But if you can shake off some of that baggage before you move on, it can mitigate the consequences to some degree."

"Maybe you're wrong. We met someone; she said her name is Eva. She said—"

Marie interrupted Kevin's sentence and said, "—that she could help you. That if you wanted help, you could find her at the cemetery."

"How do you know that?" Kevin asked.

Tempted to transform into a younger image of herself, Marie decided not to, fearing it would spook the ghosts—a phrase that always made her giggle—and they might disappear again. Instead, she said, "Eva is a friend of mine. She was trying to help you in the same way I'm trying to help you now."

"I still don't understand how you can help us," Derrick said. "You already said you can't bring us back to life."

"While I don't have the power to pardon you for the crimes you've committed in your last lifetime, I know that if you refuse to share information that might prevent someone else from being hurt, then that will be another strike against you, and your punishment more severe. So why don't you tell me who wants you to kidnap Christopher? And is it because they believe Chris Glandon is his father?"

Kevin frowned. "Who's Chris Glandon?"

"Chris Johnson, then."

Kevin shrugged. "We didn't try taking the kid because we wanted some ransom."

"If you weren't trying to kidnap him, why did it look like you were trying to take him?"

"We were going to drown the kid. Toss him off the pier," Derrick blurted.

"You were what?" Marie gasped.

Before the brothers could answer Marie, the hallway ceiling

above them opened up with a roar, revealing not the new second floor of the house but a vast, dark ominous space filled with gray clouds, and from it emerged a tornado vortex with a rapidly rotating column of air extending from above and moving toward Kevin and Derrick, who stood as if frozen, their eyes wide and mouths agape as they watched the lower tip of the vortex reach out to them.

The next moment, screams of agony came from the brothers, whose apparitions morphed and contorted as the vortex consumed their energy, sending them swirling round and round until it changed directions and returned to the dark cavity from which it came. The next moment, the ceiling above Marie and Christopher closed and then looked as it had ten minutes earlier, off-white paint over drywall, and the only sound Marie heard was the conversation coming from the living room.

Marie looked down at Christopher, the child oblivious to what had just taken place several feet from where he played. She could hear him humming softly as his right hand gently pushed along a Lego truck he had just built.

The next moment Marie stood in the cemetery where Eva had told her she would be at, should the ghosts of the Tyler brothers come looking for her.

"Oh, Marie, you scared me!" Eva laughed.

Marie's serious expression dampened Eva's jocularity.

"Come back to Lily's house right now. Meet me in the down-stairs hallway. I can't leave Christopher alone. He's in danger." The next moment, Marie vanished.

Eva blinked in surprise, glanced around, muttered, "Oh my," and then vanished.

EVA AND MARIE sat together on the floor in the hallway at the Bartley house. Connor had returned to the hallway to play, and when he saw Marie, he wanted her to make his Lego toy fly, but she quickly convinced him to play with Christopher. She and Eva moved farther down the hall towards Lily and Ian's bedroom, because Marie didn't want Connor to listen to their conversation, but she wanted to be close enough to monitor Christopher.

Marie had just finished telling Eva about her visit with the Tyler brothers, along with the now debunked theory that someone wanted to kidnap Christopher so they could demand a ransom from Chris Glandon.

"It sounds like those two got sucked up like those nasty spirits who tried hijacking the body of Lily's cousin," Eva noted.

"It was actually the husband of Lily's cousin, but yes. I thought the same thing."

"While murder is a nasty business, attempting to harm an innocent child, that is another level," Eva said.

"Agreed. But why would anyone want to hurt that boy?" Marie glanced down the hallway to Christopher.

"I wish the Universe had not been in such a hurry." Eva let out a sigh. "And they said they didn't plan to extort Chris?"

"They didn't even know who he was. No, they said they intended to throw the poor boy in the ocean."

They stopped talking when a man Eva had never seen before came down the hallway from the living room, walked into the bathroom, and closed the door behind him.

"Who's that? Nice-looking man," Eva asked.

"Watch Christopher. I'll be right back." The next moment, Marie's apparition vanished from the hallway and reappeared in the middle of the living room. Sadie perked up when she saw her, her tail wagging, but Marie quickly asked Sadie to be still. She wanted to listen to what was being said.

"He is so nice," Tammy told Laura. "Why didn't you tell us about him?"

"Well, there are lots of people I met on my trip. I just didn't get around to telling you about him yet," Laura said.

"It doesn't seem like he's just a person you met on your trip." Ian snickered. "He obviously came all the way from London to see you again."

"Why didn't you tell him you were coming back to the States?"

Gene asked. "Poor guy, sounded like he thought something had happened to you."

The sound of a door shutting in the hallway drifted to the living room.

"Can we please talk about this later, after he leaves," Laura whispered.

THIRTY

It was late Thursday morning, and Danielle hadn't gotten dressed yet. It had been a rough night. The twins had woken up more than normal and couldn't seem to get enough milk. She might have been more concerned had she not read about what some called the four-month nursing crisis in one of her baby books, and the twins had recently turned four months. According to the book, it was a normal development phase, which included the baby signaling to the mother to produce more milk, which was why they kept waking her up and demanding to nurse more frequently.

Still wearing her fleece pajama bottoms and T-shirt, Danielle sat curled up on the sofa with her stockinged feet tucked under her as she sipped a cup of coffee and looked down at her husband and babies. Walt lounged nearby on a quilt spread over a portion of the living room floor with the twins. Leaning against one elbow, he cheered on Addison as she tried lifting her head while Jack quietly studied his tiny fingers.

Snowflakes fell from the ceiling. Together Walt and Danielle said, "Good morning, Eva." A moment later the snowflakes disappeared, and Eva stood between the sofa and recliners.

"You look comfy," Eva told Danielle before glancing over to

Walt and giving him and the babies a smile. "Oh my, they are growing so fast."

Danielle glanced to the babies and back to Eva. "They just turned four months."

Eva's apparition moved to a recliner and appeared to sit down. "I thought I'd drop in and check how you were doing now that you don't have Marie to help you."

"We're doing fine. Have you seen Marie this morning?" Marie had stayed with Christopher the previous evening over at Chris's house. They had all decided the safest place to keep Christopher during the daytime, until they learned more, was at the Glandon Foundation Headquarters, where Chris had recently increased security.

Heather had taken another shopping trip the previous evening with Brian. When they returned to the Glandon Foundation Headquarters, it looked as if Heather was converting one of the spare rooms into a preschool.

"When I last saw her, she was taking a walk along the beach in front of the foundation offices, with Heather, Christopher and Hunny. And I have a feeling that the room they set up for Christopher might eventually become childcare space for Chris's employees," Eva said.

Danielle arched her brows. "Really?"

"I overheard Heather talking to Chris about it, and he seemed interested. But he wanted to wait until we learn who was behind all this. He doesn't want to put any other children in jeopardy."

"That's understandable," Walt said.

"The main reason I'm here, Marie is dying to find out what is going on with Laura and that handsome man who followed her here from London."

"Dying?" Walt snorted, earning a hush from Eva before she turned her attention back to Danielle.

"Ahh, that Dane dude." Danielle chuckled. "I guess he stayed for dinner. Charmed Tammy and Gene, and even Ian seemed to like him. Lily told me he's staying at the Seahorse Motel. I'm not sure for how long."

"From what Marie told me, Laura left London without telling him she was returning home, and went so far as to get another phone number so she wouldn't see him again. Is she upset he followed her here? I recall a few enamored fans who would show up uninvited to my dressing room or backstage, bringing me gifts, and often it was more frightening than flattering."

"That's what Lily initially thought. She was concerned her sister had some stalker, which I guess she does. But Lily also suspects this might just be Laura being Laura."

"What does that mean, exactly?" Walt asked. "I overheard Lily saying that to you. But I didn't catch the rest of the conversation."

Danielle looked over at Walt. "I guess Laura has a habit of sabotaging relationships. On one hand, she talks like she wants to find someone, settle down, start a family. But considering Laura's relationship history, Lily wonders if her sister only says she wants those things because that's what people expect. Which is sad, not because she might not want those things, but sad if she feels she has to conform to other people's expectations. I understand getting married and having kids is not for everyone. And that should be okay."

"Heather insists she doesn't want marriage and children. And when I look back on my life, I don't think I ever wanted that either. Even when I married that loser husband of mine," Eva mused.

"I suspect Laura isn't really sure what she wants. And from what Lily says, it sounds like whenever she gets close to a guy, she does something to blow it up."

"Or they try to blow her up," Walt snarked.

Danielle looked over at Walt and nodded. "Yeah, Lily thinks that might also be the problem. She worries that traumatized her sister more than we realized, and now, when Laura has feelings for someone, she gets even more skittish."

"So is he planning on staying in Frederickport for long? Will Laura be seeing him when he's here? These are important questions Marie needs answers to," Eva said.

Danielle shrugged. "Like I said, I'm not really sure how long he's going to stay, but according to Lily, he and Laura are meeting

Joe and Kelly for breakfast at Pier Café this morning. So I guess she's planning to see him while he's here."

DANE HAD OFFERED to pick Laura up for breakfast, but she told him she would just drive over to Pier Café with Kelly and Joe, since she was staying with them, anyway. Before leaving for the restaurant, Dane stopped by the office of the Seahorse Motel. He wanted to tell the person at the front desk about the leaky faucet in the bathroom and ask them if someone could look at it while he was out. It had been difficult for him to fall asleep the previous night with the persistent dripping. At one point, he'd considered calling down to the office, but he didn't imagine they would have anyone around that time of night who could fix it.

When he arrived in the office, there were two people standing at the desk, checking in. Their backs were to him, but he could tell it was a man and woman. When they turned around a few minutes later, the woman looked directly at him. Dane froze.

The woman flashed him a smile—the type of smile one gives a stranger—not an invitation or hidden agenda, a simple smile forgotten as fast as it was given. She turned to her companion, and the two walked away, chatting amongst themselves, forgetting the man who stood behind them in line, waiting for his turn.

"Can I help you?" the man behind the registration desk asked Dane.

Dane, whose attention was still on the pair who had just stepped outside, did not respond to the question. But when asked a second time, Dane turned around and approached the desk.

He explained his problem with the leaky faucet while occasionally glancing toward the doorway where the couple had just gone through. After being told they would send someone to his room before noon, he thanked them, turned to leave, and then glanced down at the floor. He frowned when he saw what looked like a credit card peeking out from beneath one of his shoes. Dane moved his right foot, reached down, and picked up the credit card. He looked at it, and after reading the name on the card, he thought for a moment that his heart had stopped.

Gripping the corner of the card with a now shaking hand, he glanced back to the door. He had been right. The woman standing just a few feet from him was Rosalyn King.

"Is there something else?" the man behind the counter asked.

Pulled from his private thoughts, Dane looked at the man, cleared his throat, and then handed him the credit card. "This was on the floor."

The man took the card from Dane and looked at it. "Oh, it must have fallen out of her wallet. That's who just checked in. I'll call her room and let her know we have her card. Thank you."

Dane smiled dully, turned from the man, and headed for the door. *What are the chances I would run into her here?* Once outside, he headed toward his rental car, which he had parked right in front of his room. He was about five feet from his car when he glanced over to the motel room next to his, its window inches from the door of his motel room.

Through the window, he saw the man and woman who had just checked in. The man was opening the window, letting in the fresh air. He turned to face the woman—Rosalyn King. The two stood there talking, but Dane couldn't hear their words.

On impulse, instead of getting into his car, Dane walked to his motel room. Once at the door, instead of going inside his room, he leaned against the building, listening to the conversation coming from the nearby open window.

"All I know, Traci dropped the boy off at a place that used to be a bed-and-breakfast. It's called Marlow House. The person she left him with was somebody both she and Bridget knew before Christopher was born. I'm not sure how he's connected with Marlow House, if he works there or lives there. Apparently, the authorities are aware Traci was Christopher's guardian, and this person she left him with is some random friend. I don't know why they haven't put the boy in foster care," came a woman's voice.

"What do you want to do?"

"We start with finding out where they have him."

"Considering everything, we need to be careful who we ask questions of. After all, they're investigating a murder," said the man.

"That has nothing to do with us."

"But still. Considering everything, and you are a wealthy woman, Rosalyn, we need to be careful."

"Careful how?"

"They could easily extort you for money if the wrong person finds out about this. And it is possible we've come up here for nothing."

"I understand what you're saying."

"I'm going to the car, get my suitcase, and put it in my room. Then I'll go to the front office, pick up your credit card. I'll come back here; we can then get something to eat. I'd rather plan our next move on a full stomach. I'm starving."

"Thank you, Kyle. I can't believe it fell out of my wallet like that."

"Be grateful someone found it right away. I'll be back in a minute."

Upon hearing those words, Dane quickly unlocked his room and slipped inside. Once inside, he looked out through the peephole. He waited until the man who had been with Rosalyn was out in the parking lot before opening the door again and stepping back outside.

Dane walked to his car as if he hadn't moments earlier been eavesdropping on his neighbor. He saw the man's car parked next to his, and he was currently taking a suitcase out of its trunk. Dane gave the man a casual hello, got into the driver's side of his vehicle, pulled the car door shut, leaned back in his seat, and took a deep breath.

He sat in the car a moment, making no attempt to put on his seat belt. Instead, he tried wrapping his head around the fact Rosalyn King would be sleeping in the room next door. It wasn't that he had ever met the woman before. But he knew who she was. He had been stalking her online since college.

THIRTY-ONE

"So how long is your friend staying in Frederickport?" Joe asked Laura. He sat with her and Kelly in a booth at Pier Café, waiting for Dane to join them. Carla had filled their mugs with coffee and didn't stay to take their orders after being told they were waiting for someone else to arrive.

Laura absently fiddled with her coffee cup while glancing over at the front door of the restaurant. Dane was late; it wasn't like him. She wondered if after seeing her last night, he had decided it had been a mistake to come. Had he returned to London without saying goodbye, as she had done to him?

Laura looked to Joe. "He didn't say. I didn't really get to talk to him alone yesterday. Mom asked him to join us for dinner. He stayed and left before Kelly got there to pick me up. Said he had jet lag and wanted to go to bed early. Other than agreeing to meet here for breakfast, we really didn't discuss his plans."

"Oh, there he is," Kelly said. Joe and Laura looked to the front door and saw Dane standing inside the entrance, looking around for their table. When he looked their way, Laura gave him a wave. He flashed her a smile and started walking toward them.

Joe stood up when Dane reached their booth. The two men

shook hands, and Laura made introductions. Joe sat down, and Dane sat across from him in the booth on the bench next to Laura.

"Sorry for being late. I had to stop at the front office of the motel before coming over here to report a problem. I didn't realize it would take so long."

"Laura said you're staying at the Seahorse Motel. I hope it is nothing major," Kelly said.

"Just a leaky bathroom sink." Before he could elaborate, Carla showed up at the table.

Coffee pot in hand, Carla smiled down at Dane. "I hope the surprise went well."

"She agreed to have breakfast with me." Dane grinned back at Carla.

Both Laura and Kelly arched their brows. "You two have already met?" Laura asked.

"I stopped in here yesterday to get something to eat," Dane said, flashing Carla a smile.

Carla motioned to his mug. "You want coffee?"

Dane reached for the clean mug in front of him and flipped it over. "Please."

"After you look at the menu, I'll come back and take your order." Carla filled the cup with coffee and left the table as Laura handed Dane a menu.

"I figured you'd rather have tea," Kelly said as Dane reached for his coffee.

"They drink coffee in the morning all the time over there," Laura said.

Dane looked at Joe. "Laura mentioned you're a police officer."

"She told you about us?" Kelly asked, sounding surprised, forgetting for a moment that Dane had stopped by her house the previous day, looking for Laura, which suggested Laura had probably mentioned them to Dane.

Dane smiled at Kelly. "Yes. She told me how her sister's sister-in-law was her close friend, that she had recently been in their wedding, and that Joe was in the local police department."

"Gossiping about us," Kelly teased Laura, to which Laura rolled her eyes.

Dane turned his attention back to Joe. "Where I'm from, it's more uncommon for a police officer to carry a gun than carry one. Do most police here find they use theirs?"

"While I can't speak for most police, there have been times I needed one."

"Frederickport seems like this quiet little quaint town. But they have had more than their share of crime. Last week, a woman was found murdered. It was on a road on the edge of town. Poor Joe here, he found her." Laura shivered at the thought.

"Oh, that's horrible." Dane looked at Joe. "Have they arrested the killer?"

Joe shook his head. "No. It's still an open case."

"There was an article in this morning's newspaper about the murder," Laura said. "They showed a picture of her. Her name was Traci Lind. She was only twenty-two. So sad."

Dane, who was about to take a sip of his coffee, froze for a moment. He set his mug back on the table without taking a sip. "What did you say her name was?"

"Traci Lind."

"What makes it worse, she was the guardian for a little boy." Laura paused a moment before saying, "Actually, you sort of met him yesterday. Christopher, the little boy who was at my sister's house, playing with my nephew."

"What do you mean she was his guardian?" Dane asked.

"Christopher's mother died about three months ago," Laura explained. "Traci, the one who was murdered, she was the boy's guardian. Apparently, Traci stopped by Marlow House—that's the house across the street from my sister's that I told you about—to see Chris, and he agreed to watch the boy for an hour. When she didn't come back, Chris called the police."

"Who is Chris?" Dane asked.

Laura shrugged. "Just a friend of ours."

"He lives at Marlow House? I remember you telling me you

stayed at Marlow House; it's a bed-and-breakfast or something?" Dane asked.

Laura shook her head. "They aren't operating as a B and B right now. And no, Chris doesn't live there. He lives down the street."

"According to my brother, Chris has agreed to take care of Christopher until they can locate some family. Chris grew up in foster care, and he didn't want the boy to bounce around from one foster care home to another while trying to locate someone from his family," Kelly explained.

Carla returned to the table to take their order. Dane, who had not looked at the menu yet, quickly looked through his as the others gave their orders. When Carla finally left the table, Joe asked, "Is this your first trip to America?"

"The first one I remember," Dane said.

"You were here before, but don't remember?" Kelly asked.

Dane turned to Kelly. "I was pretty young the first time. But I've been meaning to come back. And Laura gave me a reason." Dane flashed Laura a smile and looked back at Joe and Kelly. "Before I was born, my mother traveled a lot. She made several trips to the US and even lived here for a couple of years after she finished college."

"Does your mother also live in London?" Kelly asked.

Dane shook his head. "No. My mother passed away right before I started college."

"Oh, I'm sorry. Does your dad live in London?" Kelly asked.

"I'm afraid my father is gone, too. It's just me."

The conversation shifted to Laura's time in Europe, and then Carla brought their food and refilled their coffee cups. The discussion over breakfast was light and superficial, and when they finished eating, Joe explained he needed to go to work. Carla took away their dirty plates, and Joe and Kelly said their goodbyes, while Laura and Dane remained behind, each with a fresh cup of coffee.

"Look at us, finally alone," Dane said. He remained sitting next to Laura, the bench seat across from them now empty.

Laura absently fiddled with the rim of her coffee cup, her eyes looking down at the table and not at Dane. "I guess you deserve an explanation."

"I'm not sure I deserve anything. I suppose I might be the one who owes you an explanation." Dane let out a sigh. "And an apology."

Laura looked at Dane with a frown. "Apology?"

Dane leaned back on the bench and stretched out his long legs under the table. "Last night, when I returned to the motel, I started thinking of my mother and what she might tell me if she were here right now. I don't think she would be happy with me."

"Your mother? What do you mean?"

"Like you know, my father died when I was very young, and the only parent I had was my mother. When I started showing interest in girls, she sat me down and told me I needed to treat girls with respect, and if one told me no, I needed to accept that and move on. I shouldn't assume she was being coy and really meant yes. And now, here I am, years later, following a woman across the globe after she not only said no, but I ignored the fact that she had gone out of her way to avoid me." His gaze met Laura's. "Last night, when we were talking about your trip and your mother mentioned you'd lost your cellphone right before getting on the plane and had to get a new one, well, the only reason someone gets a new phone number when they get a new phone is because there is someone who had their old one they don't want to hear from anymore."

"It wasn't that I didn't want to hear from you." She didn't sound convincing.

"Initially, I just wanted to make sure you were okay. I was getting worried when you seemed to just disappear. I didn't think of it as stalking at the time. It wasn't until last night, after seeing you and realizing you hadn't told your parents about me, that, well, I should have paid attention to you when you said there was no future for us. I apologize, and I think I should go back to London as soon as possible."

"Why do you have to leave so soon?"

Dane frowned at Laura. "You don't want me to leave?"

Laura shook her head. "No. Now that you're here, I don't want you to just leave. I'm sorry I ghosted you like I did. But, well, I was afraid."

"Afraid of what?"

Laura looked into Dane's eyes. "Of how I was feeling about you. And then you wanted to join me on my travels. When I talked you out of that, I overheard you telling Raj how you planned to surprise me when I was in Paris. I can't fall in love with you."

"Why? Would that have been so bad?" he asked softly.

Laura shook her head. "I haven't been playing games with you. But I know I don't want to live in London. The UK is great, and maybe I'll go back and visit again someday. But I know now, I don't want to be away from home that long again. My family's here. I want to be part of Connor's and Emily Ann's lives, and I don't want to do that over video chat. Mom and Dad aren't getting younger, and I don't want to be so far from them if they need me. I understand your home is in London, but mine is here. That's why I left. I was homesick, and I was afraid I was falling in love with you, and that would complicate everything. But now that you're here, I...I don't want you to just leave."

Dane started to say something but then froze when he spied something across the diner toward the entrance. Laura turned to where he looked and saw an attractive gray-haired woman and a younger man walking to a table. Laura turned back to Dane and studied his odd expression. "What is it?"

Still looking at the couple, Dane shook his head and then looked at Laura, his expression serious. "I won't leave unless you ask me to, and I promise to respect your decision. But I have a favor to ask you."

Laura frowned. "What?"

"Remember that friend of yours you told me about, the police chief?"

Laura nodded. "Yeah, police chief MacDonald. He's a good friend of my sister's. Why?"

"I think I need to talk to him."

"I don't understand."

"I'll explain on the drive to the police station. But we should probably leave now."

THIRTY-TWO

Police chief MacDonald sat alone at the desk in his office, sorting through a stack of mail, when a knock came from the open doorway. He looked up to see Laura Miller and a man standing in the hall, looking into his office. While he had never seen the man before, the chief had a pretty good idea who he was, considering he had talked to Joe minutes earlier.

"Laura, come on in," the chief called out, waving them into his office.

"Hi, Chief," Laura greeted as she and the man approached his desk.

"I hope you will excuse me for not standing up." He flashed them both a smile.

"How is that knee, Chief?" Laura asked.

"Doing pretty good. Joe told me you were in town and staying with him and Kelly." The chief turned to look at the man by Laura's side. "He also told me he and Kelly had breakfast with you and a friend from London. Can I assume this is the friend?"

Laura smiled. "Police chief MacDonald, this is my friend Dane. Dane Carslaw."

Dane extended his hand, leaned across the desk, and briefly

shook the chief's now extended hand. When the handshake ended, Laura said, "Dane needs to tell you something. It's about your murder investigation."

The chief arched his brows, then motioned to the nearby chairs for them to sit down. When they did, he told Dane, "You have my curiosity. From what Joe told me, you just arrived in the States from London. I can't imagine what you might have to say regarding our murder investigation. But I'm listening."

"It might be nothing," Dane began. "But I'm staying at the Seahorse Motel. This morning, before I met Laura and the others for breakfast, I had to stop in at the front office. A couple was checking in. The woman dropped her credit card. I noticed it after she left with her companion. I picked it up and handed it to the person at the front desk. When I did, I noticed her name. Rosalyn King." It wasn't a complete lie. While he already knew her name, seeing it on her credit card confirmed that. But neither Laura nor the chief needed to know about his connection to Rosalyn. It didn't matter to anyone but him.

The chief frowned. "And this has something to do with our case?"

"After I left the office, I needed to stop by my motel room before leaving for the restaurant. I noticed the woman and her companion had gone into the room next door to mine. Her window is very close to my door."

The chief nodded. "I'm familiar with the layout of the Seahorse."

"I walked to my room, and before I walked in, I stopped to look at my phone." It was a lie, but Dane couldn't come up with another reason for eavesdropping without coming right out and telling them about his connection to Rosalyn.

The phone rang. The chief put his hand up, signaling for Dane to hold that thought, and then he answered the call. When he got off the phone a moment later, he said, "Go on."

"They had opened the window, and I overheard their conversation. I didn't think much of it at the time. The woman mentioned something about Marlow House. I remembered Laura saying that's where she stayed the last time she was in town. I suppose that's why I started listening to their conversation. They said something about a woman who had been murdered. And they mentioned her name was Traci."

"I can understand Marlow House being a topic of conversation for visitors. It's pretty well known. And everyone is talking about the murder, and since her name was just in the newspaper—"

"It wasn't just that," Dane interrupted. "They talked about a boy named Christopher and that they needed to find him. He warned her they had to be careful because of the murder investigation. She told him that didn't concern them, and then he said something about having to be careful because she could be blackmailed."

The chief frowned. "Really? Did you mention any of this to Joe when you were talking about the case at breakfast?"

Dane shook his head. "No."

"I'm curious, why are you telling me now?" the chief asked.

"The couple walked into the diner after we finished breakfast. Joe and Kelly were already gone. Seeing them again, remembering what I had overheard, along with what Laura and her friends told me, I thought I needed to say something. It's not that I suddenly wondered if they had something to do with the murder, but when I thought about what they had said, I wondered if they might know something that would help you find the murderer. Something they don't even realize. It was obvious they wanted to see the boy. I couldn't not say something."

The chief let out a sigh, gave a nod, and said, "Thank you. I appreciate you coming in."

"If you talk to them, can you please not tell them who told you this?" Dane asked.

"It would be awful awkward for him, Chief," Laura said. "After all, they're staying in the room right next to him."

"She is. The man she's with is staying in the room on the other side of her," Dane corrected.

"So they're not a couple?" the chief asked.

"No. He's her stepson."

The chief frowned. "You overheard that, too?"

Laura looked at Dane. "You didn't tell me that."

Dane shrugged. "I assumed that was her stepson. It was just something they said. Perhaps I misunderstood. But they're not staying in the same room."

AN HOUR LATER, Heather led police chief MacDonald and his sons, Evan and Eddy, out to the back terrace of what was once the Gusarov Estate. It overlooked the ocean, with a stretch of lawn separating the beach from the terrace, and fencing on both sides of the property, which now belonged to the Glandon Foundation. Armed guards patrolled the perimeter of the property, yet the chief did not notice them immediately.

His attention was first drawn to the people sitting on the terrace's patio set. There were Walt and Danielle, each holding a baby, Chris, who stood up when the chief stepped onto the terrace, and Christopher, who was running up from the lawn upon seeing the arrival of Evan and Eddy. Hunny trailed behind him. While the chief couldn't see her, he understood Marie was also with the group, something that Evan was currently telling his brother.

There was a second table on the terrace; this one held platters of sandwiches, cookies, fruit and other finger foods, along with pitchers of lemonade, iced tea, clean cups, luncheon plates, and napkins.

While the chief exchanged greetings with his friends, Christopher told Evan and Eddy, "I set up the tee-ball set."

"Why don't you boys have something to eat before you play," Heather said, motioning to the table of food. She looked at the chief and added, "Help yourself."

"Thanks, Heather." The chief glanced over to the boys, who were each filling plates with food, and said, "Christopher, before you go play, I'd like to show you something."

Several minutes later, the chief sat at the table with his friends, a plate of food sitting near him, when Christopher walked up to him, carrying a plate of food.

"We're going to eat on the grass," Christopher announced. "Heather put a blanket down there. Like a picnic."

The chief smiled at the boy. "I want to show you something first." The next minute, he pulled a folded piece of paper from his shirt's pocket and unfolded it. He handed it to Christopher. "Have you ever seen either of these people before?"

Christopher looked at the picture for a moment and then shook his head. "No."

"Okay." The chief refolded the paper and slipped it back in his pocket. "You boys can go down to the grass if you want. Eat, play ball. Have fun."

"What did you show them?" Chris asked after all the adults were seated at the table and the boys, with Hunny following them, walked down to the grass area.

"The couple at the motel," the chief explained.

"Where did you get the picture?" Heather asked.

"Probably online," Chris answered for the chief, who gave a nod of confirmation.

"What did you find out?" Danielle asked.

The chief picked up a strawberry from his plate. "I called Sam, and he was kind enough to give me the information on the two guests. Which proved damn interesting." He took a bite of the strawberry.

"How so?" Walt asked.

The chief tossed what was left of his strawberry back on his plate and absently wiped his fingers on a napkin. "After Sam gave me the information, I did a little digging online. Laura's friend was right. The man with the woman is indeed her stepson. And the man, it just so happens, he owns the real estate company the Tylers worked for."

Chris stared at the chief. "You're kidding?"

"No." The chief picked up his sandwich and took a bite.

"Did they say anything to Sam about why they're here?" Danielle asked.

After swallowing his bite, the chief said, "According to Sam, when they were checking in, one of his other guests was waiting to talk to him. I assume it was Laura's friend. Sam was more focused on getting them checked in so he could see what his other guest wanted, so there was no small talk."

"Sounds like they were fairly chatty when they went back to their room," Walt said.

Marie, who had been quietly listening, said, "I should go over there."

The mediums looked at Marie. "You mean the motel?" Danielle asked.

"Wherever those two are," Marie said.

Heather looked at the chief. "Marie wants to do some eaves-dropping on our real estate dude and his stepmom. Where's his dad, by the way?"

"The stepmother is a widow, and her husband, who started the real estate company, left it to his son. From what I found online, she inherited nothing from her husband aside from their Eureka home."

"Does this mean she has to be nice to the stepson or he might kick her out on the street?" Heather asked.

"Like I said, she got the house. But even if she hadn't, she wouldn't need to worry about money. From what I found out, she inherited a fortune from her first husband."

"Enough of this," Marie blurted. The folded-up picture floated up from the chief's shirt pocket. Startled at the movement by his chest, the chief leaned back and watched as the paper floated across the table, away from him.

"Tell the chief I just want to see what the people look like. I don't want to go over there and spy on the wrong couple." The paper unfolded and hung in the air for a few moments. Marie vanished, and the paper floated down to the table.

THIRTY-THREE

Marie surmised Rosalyn King had returned to her motel room after having breakfast at Pier Café to take a nap, considering she found the woman, fully dressed, sleeping on the bed, while her stepson was in his motel room, talking on his cellphone, engaged in what sounded like real estate talk, reminding her of similar phone conversations she had overheard Adam engaged in while eavesdropping on him.

Confident these were indeed the people Laura's friend had overheard, since they looked like the people in the picture, Marie looked around each motel room, hoping to find something to explain the motivation behind the killer's actions. But she found nothing.

Marie had been at the motel for about twenty minutes and considered returning to the foundation headquarters when Rosalyn woke up. Marie watched as the woman sat up, stretched, got out of bed, and walked to the bathroom. Rosalyn returned to the room a few minutes later. It was obvious she had combed her hair and touched up her makeup. Rosalyn sat on the side of the bed, picked up the motel phone, and dialed her stepson's room.

Marie listened to Rosalyn's side of the phone conversation. "I just woke up...yeah, I feel much better. I'm too old to go hours without sleep." Rosalyn gave a short laugh. "I know what I want to do. That waitress said Christopher was still with that friend of Traci's. Chris Johnson. He has the boy with him at work. It's called the Glandon Foundation. I found the address."

"THEY'RE COMING HERE," Marie announced when she reappeared on the terrace of the Glandon Foundation Headquarters. Heather told the chief of Marie's presence and what she had said, and then the mediums listened as Marie told them what she had witnessed at the motel.

"The stepson did not want to come over here," Marie said. "He tried talking her out of it, but she was insistent. Apparently, the waitress, who I assume was Carla, was more than helpful and told her Chris Johnson lived down the street. Someone really needs to have a talk with Carla about not being so gabby."

"What are they going to do?" Heather asked.

"According to what the Tyler brothers claimed, the people behind this want that poor child dead. But I don't believe they are intending to come over here to hurt him."

Heather repeated Marie's words, and the chief asked, "Why do you say that?"

"Because when I was over there, I went through their rooms and their car, and they don't have a gun with them. And no bombs. I've become rather an authority on what a bomb looks like." Marie wasn't referring to the bomb that blew up the Tylers, but the one she'd exploded when she saved Laura.

"How did you know what car was theirs?" Heather asked.

"For one thing, the Seahorse has those little cards with the room number on it that the guests have to put on their dashboard."

KYLE PULLED his car up across the street from the Glandon Foundation and parked. He turned off the ignition and looked over at Rosalyn, who sat in the passenger seat. "There it is. You saw it. What now?"

"Stay here," Rosalyn said as she unbuckled her seatbelt.

"What are you doing?"

"Just stay here. I'll be right back." Rosalyn got out of the car, slammed the door behind her, and crossed the street. When she reached the sidewalk on the other side of the street, she approached the front entrance gate of the Glandon Foundation Headquarters. She glanced around, surveying the area; there was no person in sight. The entire property appeared to be surrounded by a wrought-iron fence. On one side of the property was a second gate leading to a driveway, while the gate she stood by led to the front door.

Rosalyn opened the gate. It was unlocked. She stepped onto the property of the Glandon Foundation Headquarters. Instead of staying on the walkway leading to the front door, she stepped onto the lawn and started to walk around the side of the house that led down to the ocean.

"Stop right there," a man's voice demanded.

Rosalyn twirled around and found herself face-to-face with two men, one pointing a gun in her direction.

"Where did you come from?" Rosalyn's attention fixed on the gun pointing at her.

"You are on private property," one man said.

"We'll take it from here," another male voice called out.

The man holding the gun lowered the weapon to his side.

Rosalyn turned toward the new voice and watched as two new men approached her. They came from the side of the house leading from the back of the property that faced the ocean. One man was dressed in some sort of uniform, but it was the other man who caught her attention. She stared at the second man, her eyes wide.

The two men who had initially approached her remained silently at her side as the other two men grew closer. When they were about six feet from her, they stopped, and the one not wearing the uniform said, "My name is Chris Johnson. I'm in charge of the Glandon Foundation. Can you please explain why you're on our property?"

Rosalyn stared at Chris for a moment and then finally stammered, "Did you say Chris Johnson?"

Chris nodded. "And you are?"

To everyone's surprise, Rosalyn broke into tears and shook her head. "I shouldn't be here. This is all a mistake." Now sobbing, she said, "I'm sorry I trespassed. I meant no harm. I just want to go home." She turned from the men as if planning to flee, but they detained her. When she turned toward the street, looking for Kyle to come and rescue her, she saw two police cars parked by his car, while Kyle stood outside the vehicle, his back to her, and the palms of his hands pressed against the car as one officer searched him.

INSTEAD OF ASKING Rosalyn King why she had trespassed, paramedics were called and forced to medicate her, as she sobbed inconsolably. An ambulance was called. Her stepson did not intervene, but silently watched from the sidelines and passively allowed the police officers to usher him into the back of one of their vehicles. Once Kyle was alone in the back seat of the police car, he looked out the door window and watched as they loaded Rosalyn into the ambulance. He smiled.

BRIAN HENDERSON SAT across the table from Kyle King in the interrogation room. Rosalyn King had been taken to the hospital after her emotional breakdown, while Kyle had been brought to the police station. In the adjacent room, Chris, Joe, and the police chief watched the interrogation through the one-way mirror.

"He doesn't seem overly concerned his mother was taken to the hospital. He hasn't even asked about her," Joe noted.

"Stepmother," the chief corrected. "But you're right."

"Why were you and your stepmother at the Glandon Foundation?" Brian asked.

"Rosalyn heard about the Glandon Foundation, and she was curious to see what it looked like."

"And why did she break down like that?"

Kyle looked Brian in the eyes. "To start with, one of your people pointed a gun at her. I imagine being surrounded by four men, and one being armed, would be terrifying for any woman. But she meant no harm. She was just curious. Perhaps she pushed sightseeing by daring to walk across the lawn. Would they have greeted her the same way had she walked up to the front door? I didn't see any no-trespassing signs. I would really like to go see her, make sure she's alright. Rosalyn's a fragile woman, and this was obviously too much for her. You people have unnecessarily terrorized my stepmother, and we will be talking to our attorney. Can I go now?"

"What is your relationship with Derrick and Kevin Tyler?" Brian asked.

Kyle stared at Brian. After a moment, he said, "I own a real estate company, and they used to work for me."

"Until someone murdered them."

Kyle frowned at Brian. "What does that have to do with any of this?"

"Why were they in Frederickport?"

Kyle shrugged. "Were they? I didn't realize that. They told me they came up to Oregon to look for investment property, but they never mentioned they came to Frederickport. Not sure what any of this has to do with my stepmother innocently trespassing."

"The Tyler brothers are persons of interest in a murder that took place in Frederickport while they were here."

Kyle shook his head. "That's ridiculous. Why would either of them murder anyone? And they were just up here looking for property. Who would they kill?"

"Do you know a woman named Traci Lind?"

"Not that I recall. I meet many people in my line of business."

"I have a witness who claims he overheard you and your stepmother discussing Traci Lind. She was the woman who was murdered."

Kyle stared at Brian for a moment without responding. Finally, he let out a breath and smiled. "We read a newspaper article about the murder after we came up here. And we naturally discussed it. After all, we were surprised to read something like that would happen in a little town like this. One of us may have mentioned the victim's name after reading the article, but it's not like I'm going to remember the name even an hour later. And I didn't know Kevin and Derrick stopped in Frederickport when they were here."

"Why were you looking for Christopher Singer?"

Kyle frowned. "Who?"

"The child who someone overheard you and your stepmother talking about needing to find."

Kyle shrugged. "I don't know what you're talking about."

"The child who was at the Glandon Foundation."

"I didn't see any child. Like I said, I have no idea what you're talking about."

"Why are you here?"

"Rosalyn wanted to get away, take a car trip, and she asked me to go with her."

"Why did she want to come to Frederickport?"

Kyle shrugged. "I'm not sure she wanted to come to Frederickport in particular. She just wanted to travel up the Oregon coast while the weather was still nice. We ended up here. I suppose in the same way Derrick and Kevin did."

In the other room, they continued to listen to Brian's interrogation. Finally, the chief said, "We don't really have anything to hold him on; we're going to have to let him go."

"What about his stepmother?" Chris asked.

"They're holding her overnight for observation. Considering what they gave her to help her calm down, I don't know when she can talk," the chief said.

THIRTY-FOUR

Not long after the police took Rosalyn and Kyle away, Eva showed up at the foundation headquarters. After much discussion, Marie agreed to stay close to Christopher until the danger passed, and Eva would keep a close eye on Kyle and Rosalyn. Eva soon learned Rosalyn wouldn't be causing any trouble for the night, as she was sleeping at the hospital. Eva arrived at the police station as Kyle was getting into a police car.

"Where are they taking him?" Eva whispered to Chris, who stood alone by his car in the parking lot, his attention on Kyle.

Chris looked at Eva and smiled. "You surprised me. No snowflakes."

"It seems all too serious for snowflakes. Where is he going?"

Chris and Eva looked back to the police car with Kyle. It drove out of the parking lot and down the street.

"They're taking him back to his car. The chief said they have nothing to keep him on." Chris let out a sigh.

"Well, I stopped at the hospital. His companion won't be going anywhere tonight. So I guess I'll stick with him. See what I can find out."

"Thanks, Eva."

Eva smiled at Chris before disappearing.

WHEN KYLE GOT into his car ten minutes later, he failed to see Eva sitting in his passenger seat. She had arrived at the car before him after leaving the police station. As they drove back to the motel, Kyle muttered aloud to himself, "This might work out after all... maybe I can commit Rosalyn...we need to get the hell out of here...never want to see this place again."

Eva frowned at his words. She wished she could ask him questions, but even if he could suddenly hear her words, it would probably cause him to crash into a tree, sending him over to her side. *Which might actually help*, Eva told herself.

Once at the motel, Kyle headed to his motel room. He kicked off his shoes and grabbed the TV remote and a stack of takeout menus someone had left on the dresser. Plopping down on the bed, he shoved all the pillows against the headboard behind him, leaned back, turned on the TV, and looked through the menus.

Simultaneously channel surfing and glancing over the takeout menus, Kyle eventually tossed the menus on the mattress next to him and started watching a movie on the television. After fifteen minutes of observing Kyle stare at the television, Eva drifted to the window and looked outside. She spied Laura's friend, who had just parked his car and was walking up to his motel room.

Eva glanced over at Kyle, who seemed engrossed in the movie. "Well, you're not going anywhere. I'll be back in a minute." The next moment, Eva stood outside the door of Kyle's motel room. She looked over at Laura's friend as he approached the door to his motel room.

"He is handsome." Eva followed Dane into his motel room. When he went into the bathroom, she stayed in the living room, sitting at the small table in the room's corner. A laptop computer sat on the table.

Sound from the bathroom made Eva look up. Dane entered the room and walked over to the table. He sat down, fortunately not in her chair, but the one next to it. He opened the lid to the laptop.

Looking over his shoulder, she stared down at the computer screen as his fingers clicked away on the keyboard. He was looking at his email. She understood what he was doing because she had observed Heather checking emails countless times when she was at work, and Eva had once asked her what she was doing. Dane closed his email and opened another window.

Eva frowned when a picture of Rosalyn King appeared on the screen. She knew it was Rosalyn because she had seen her sleeping at the hospital, plus the picture looked very much like the woman in the picture the chief had shown everyone.

Dane didn't have just one picture of Rosalyn on his computer, he had numerous photos of her. He clicked through the pictures, one after another. Eva frowned. In some pictures, Rosalyn was with an older man who looked very much like her stepson. A few pictures were of Rosalyn and her stepson. But the pictures that captured Eva's full attention were the ones of Rosalyn with a man who had an uncanny resemblance to Chris.

"WHAT ROOM IS ROSALYN KING IN?" Kyle asked on Friday morning. He stood at the window of the admittance desk at the hospital.

The woman at the admittance window looked down at a pad of paper on her desk and then looked back up at Kyle and asked, "And you are?"

"I'm her son," Kyle said.

"Do you have some ID?" the woman asked.

Gruffly removing his wallet from his pocket, Kyle removed his driver's license and handed it to the woman.

The woman behind the desk looked at the license a moment and handed it back to Kyle and smiled. "I have a note here that Mrs. King wants to see her stepson when he comes in. She gave his name as Kyle King, which apparently is you." The woman flashed him another smile. "Mrs. King is much better this morning than when she was admitted yesterday. I'm sure her doctor can tell you more. She's in room 210."

"I'M SO sorry for all this," Rosalyn told Kyle. She sat up in the hospital bed, still wearing the hospital gown they had given her. Moments earlier, she had finished explaining why she had gotten so upset yesterday. He sat by her bedside, holding one of her hands.

"There is nothing to be sorry for." Kyle patted the hand he held.

"We should never have come. I should have listened to you; let you look into it. I made such a fool of myself, practically got you arrested."

"I didn't get arrested. They asked me some questions, and I understand why you got upset. You've been through a lot the last couple of years. We need to put this behind us."

"I want to go home now," she said.

"Let me talk to the doctor. If they release you today, we can head home first thing in the morning."

"Can't we leave today?"

Kyle smiled at Rosalyn and gave her another pat.

"I would love to. But my experiences with hospitals, they take forever to discharge patients. And we aren't even sure they'll let you go home today. But I'm going to talk to your doctor."

A knock came at the door. Kyle and Rosalyn looked to the open doorway and saw police chief MacDonald, whom they had met yesterday, standing at the doorway. Although Rosalyn didn't know his name, she recognized his face and uniform.

The chief stepped into the room. "I need to speak to Mrs. King for a moment."

Letting go of Rosalyn's hand, Kyle stood up. "My mother is in no shape to talk to anyone right now."

Rosalyn spoke up. "I want to talk to him."

Kyle started to argue with her, but she cut him off. A minute later, Kyle begrudgingly left the room, yet stood in the hallway, just outside the open doorway. The chief, now standing in the hospital room, turned to the open door, closed it, and then turned back to the hospital bed. He walked over to Rosalyn and introduced himself.

"I'm police chief MacDonald."

"My, the police chief. Not just a regular officer. I guess I really messed up." Rosalyn glanced over to the now closed door. She looked back to the chief and said with a sad voice, "I think that's the first time Kyle has ever called me his mother."

"I have some questions for you."

"I imagine you do. Please, sit down. That way, I don't have to keep looking up." She flashed him a smile.

The chief sat on the chair Kyle had been in moments earlier. "What can you tell me about Derrick and Kevin Tyler?"

Rosalyn frowned at the chief. "Are you talking about the men whose car was bombed?"

"Did you know them?"

"Yes. Not that we were friends or anything. They worked for my husband and then my stepson. But I don't know why you're asking me."

"They had been staying in Frederickport before someone put a bomb on their car."

Rosalyn gasped. "Oh my. I don't think Kyle knows that, or he would have said something to me."

"He claims he didn't know."

"I doubt he did. On our trip up here, he told me what happened. I'd been at my place in San Clemente and had just returned to Eureka. I hadn't seen the news, so I hadn't heard about it. On our ride up here, he told me what happened. He thinks the bomber meant to kill someone else who was staying at that motel, because there would be no reason to kill Kevin or Derrick."

"Why did you want to come to Frederickport?"

Rosalyn stared at the chief for a moment before answering. Finally, she said, "I imagine what you really want to ask me; why did I break down yesterday? To be honest, I don't even remember all of it—I mean, after I...well, lost it."

"You seem rather calm now."

Rosalyn smiled sadly. "It's probably some of the drugs they've given me. When I get home—when they let me out of here—I suspect I'll have some serious work with my therapist."

"You still haven't told me why you came, or why you reacted how you did."

Rosalyn looked the chief directly in his eyes. "I thought I saw a ghost. Have you ever seen a ghost, Chief MacDonald?"

MacDonald did his best to suppress a smile at the unexpected question. He wanted to say *you have no idea*, but instead he said, "No."

"It wasn't a ghost. But for a moment there, it was like looking at my son, Peter."

The chief remembered, after doing a background check of Rosalyn King, that she had a son from her first marriage who had died in a snowboarding accident about four years ago. "You had a son who died?" It sounded like a question, yet it was more a statement.

"Yes, and that man, Chris Johnson, he looks eerily like my dead son."

The chief frowned. "And that's why you got so upset? Because he resembles your son?"

Rosalyn let out a sigh. "I came to Frederickport because I erroneously believed I would find a part of my son again. But then I came face-to-face with the man Traci Lind left Christopher with, and I realized I had been a fool. Bridget obviously named the child after his father. When I was shown Christopher's picture, I thought he looked just like his father. I was right; I was just wrong about who that father was."

The chief stared at Rosalyn. "Are you saying Christopher Singer is your grandson?"

Rosalyn frowned at the chief. "I probably didn't explain that clearly. But no, he is obviously Chris Johnson's son."

"I don't quite understand what you're saying. Perhaps you should go back to the beginning."

THIRTY-FIVE

I t took a few minutes for Rosalyn to gather her thoughts and ascertain what one might deem the beginning of the story.

"My son, Peter, died in a snowboarding accident about four years ago. Last year, my husband died from a heart attack. Peter was my only child; he's from my first marriage. I hadn't gotten over the death of my son when I lost my husband. Although I don't imagine a parent ever gets over the loss of a child."

"Kyle's your stepson?"

Rosalyn nodded. "Yes. Kyle and I have always had an amicable relationship, but he made it clear when his father and I first married that he didn't need me to be his mother. I respected that, and I suppose it's one reason it shocked me when he referred to me as his mother a little while ago. He's never called me that before. Yet he has become protective of me since his father's death. He's tried to take care of me. Which I find somewhat endearing."

"And how does Christopher fit into all this?"

Rosalyn let out a sigh. "When I met my second husband, he was living in Eureka, where his real estate business is located. At the time, Peter and I lived in the home I shared with my first husband, in San Clemente. After the marriage, Peter and I moved to Eureka, and I kept the San Clemente home. I always loved San Clemente. After Peter graduated from high school in Eureka, he moved back to Southern California and back into the San Clemente house. He lived there with some roommates during and after college. After he died, his roommates eventually moved out, and the house remained vacant. After my husband passed away, I started using the home again."

A knock came at the door. It opened, and a nurse walked in. "I just wanted to check on you. Is everything okay?"

"I'm fine. Can you leave us alone, please?" Rosalyn asked.

The nurse looked over to the chief and back to her patient. "Your son's out in the hallway. He's worried about you."

Rosalyn smiled. "I'm fine. Really. Please tell him to go back to the motel, and I'll call him when we're done."

The nurse gave a nod, glanced at the chief, flashed him a smile, and then left the room, closing the door behind her.

"Now, where was I?" Rosalyn let out a sigh. "I spent last week in San Clemente. One of my son's friends, Michelle Anderson, stopped by the house. She told me she had to talk to me. I hadn't seen Michelle for a couple of years. She showed me a picture of a little boy. It was Christopher. He looked just like Peter at that age. Michelle told me she suspected Christopher might be Peter's son."

"Because he looked like your son?"

"That and the fact Michelle had been at a party at my San Clemente house, where Peter lived at the time. Apparently, at the party, a girl named Bridget got inebriated, and according to Michelle, she was hanging all over Peter, and the two ended up going to his room. Michelle didn't see him again for the rest of the night. About two weeks later, Peter died in that snowboarding accident."

"Aside from seeing them together, what made Michelle wonder if he was the father?"

"That woman who was murdered in Frederickport, Traci Lind. I had never heard of her until a few days ago from Michelle. Michelle lives in San Clemente, where Traci Lind's brother lives. They have mutual friends, and the friend told her about the murder and about how Traci was the guardian of her friend's little boy. Michelle got curious, and I guess these days, you can find practically anything online."

"What did Michelle find?"

"A picture of the little boy and his mother. Michelle immediately recognized Bridget's picture, and while she noticed the strong resemblance between Christopher and Peter, it wasn't until she found Christopher's birth dates and started doing some math, back-tracking to the party."

"And she thought Christopher was Peter's?"

"She thought it was a good possibility and felt I should know. So she stopped by my house in San Clemente, told me what she knew, and gave me a picture of Christopher that she'd found online."

"But you no longer believe he's your grandson?"

Rosalyn shook her head. "Part of me always understood it was a long shot. From what Michelle told me, Bridget was barely scraping by when she moved in with Traci. Perhaps Peter was gone, but if Christopher was his, why hadn't Bridget come to me to get some financial support? I couldn't imagine a reason a young woman with a child to raise wouldn't try getting some help from the child's grandparent, especially when that grandparent can more than afford it."

"Even so, you thought there might be a chance he was your grandson?"

"More accurately, I wanted him to be Peter's son. I'm afraid I frustrated poor Kyle, not really explaining what I intended to do when I got up here. But I wanted to see Christopher first before I did anything. I suppose I wasn't being rational. And then I saw Chris Johnson, and well, I lost it."

"Why?"

"Because I realized in that moment the reason Bridget never came to me for help was because Christopher wasn't my grandson. Traci took him to his father. The father Bridget obviously named him after, and the father he looks like."

FRIDAY EVENING, the mediums of Beach Drive and their friends gathered at Marlow House to exchange information. Lily and Ian didn't come over, as Lily's parents were still visiting. The chief was also there with Eddy and Evan. MacDonald had already taken his sons aside and informed them of the ongoing investigation and the threats surrounding Christopher. While Evan saw spirits, and Eddy understood they existed, Christopher was oblivious to the ghost who had been looking over him.

The boys were in the parlor, playing video games, while Hunny and Max observed. The twins slept upstairs in the nursery, with the baby monitor on, and the adults and ghosts gathered in the living room. Should the babies make a sound, the monitor would alert them, and Marie would be in the nursery in an instant.

Before coming into the living room or setting up the video games for the boys in the parlor, they all had dinner in the dining room. Because Christopher was present, they didn't discuss the case and had waited to do that when the boys were in another room.

"I figured Joe might be here," Walt said after he handed Chris a scotch in the living room. "After all, he found the body."

"He didn't actually find her body," Heather said. "Just part of it."

"That is gross," Danielle told Heather. Heather gave a shrug in response.

"Joe and Kelly went out to dinner with Laura and her friend," the chief explained. "And we don't need Joe here if we want to discuss what information Marie and Eva might have."

"What do we have that's new?" Walt asked.

"They're keeping Rosalyn in the hospital one more night. Supposedly, they're releasing her tomorrow. I contacted the woman Rosalyn told the chief about," Brian said. "Michelle Anderson. She's the friend of Rosalyn's son, Peter, who told Rosalyn Christopher might be her grandson. And she confirmed everything Rosalyn said."

"Something else." Heather spoke up. "When Brian was telling me what he found out, he mentioned Rosalyn's son's name was Peter. And then I remembered. When talking to Traci's spirit, right before she vanished, I was explaining to her why Chris can't be the father. She said Peter, sorta like she had just remembered something. I asked her who Peter was, and she said it didn't matter, and that Christopher would be better off with Chris. And then she was gone."

"There must be a reason Bridget didn't want Peter's family to find out about Christopher," Danielle said.

"Considering the Tylers, who had intended to kill the boy, worked for Rosalyn's stepson, I have a few ideas," Chris said. "Follow the money." They all looked at Chris.

Chris looked back at his friends and shrugged. "We have all witnessed what it's like to have family members who want you dead so they can have your money. It's very possible Kyle inherits his step-mother's estate now that Peter is out of the way. While his father had a profitable business, Rosalyn was the one with the money. But if a grandson suddenly appears, that would probably nix his inheritance."

"I agree; sounds like a motive," Danielle said. "It's possible Kyle found out about Christopher before Rosalyn and decided to get rid of his competition."

"The irony, if the Tylers hadn't killed Traci, Rosalyn may never have found out about Christopher," Heather said.

"I'm not sure about that," Brian said. "Traci obviously knew something about Peter. All it would have taken was a DNA test to prove Chris wasn't the father to get Traci wondering who it might be."

Heather let out a sigh. "True."

"None of this really explains why Bridget didn't contact Peter's mother four years ago," Danielle said. "She could have used the financial support."

"There is one reason Bridget never contacted Peter's family," Walt said. "Perhaps he's not the father."

"Walt has a point. Maybe Bridget just had a type," Heather suggested. "There could be some other dude out there who looks like Chris and Peter."

"I'm feeling somewhat generic," Chris muttered. "But there is one way to find out. A DNA test. Get some of Rosalyn's DNA. I know where I can get the results rushed, and in twenty-four hours, we can find out if he's Rosalyn's grandson. If he's not, then I'll happily deliver the results to Rosalyn and the stepson, and while that might not help arrest the person behind Traci's death—especially if it's Kyle—at least the crosshairs will be off that little boy in the parlor."

"I'm not sure how safe Christopher will be if Kyle knows we're having his stepmother's DNA tested," Danielle said.

"I'm not suggesting we ask her for a DNA sample. I was thinking about going over to the hospital tonight, have a little visit with her. Apologize for making her so upset. Marie can come with me, and while there, she can help me get a sample without Rosalyn noticing."

"Visiting hours will be over," Brian said.

Heather chuckled. "You seriously think Chris can't sweet-talk the nurses at the nurses' station to let him visit her?"

"What about Kyle? He's family, and he could be there even if visiting hours are over," Brian reminded her.

"Eva's planning to monitor him after she leaves here, like she's been doing," Chris reminded them. "She can tell us if he's on his way over to the hospital."

"While we need to find out if Rosalyn is really Christopher's grandmother, I don't think we should tell her if she is. Especially if her stepson wants him dead," Heather said. "And what do we really know about her?"

"Perhaps you could talk to Laura's friend to find out more about Rosalyn," Eva suggested. The mediums all turned to Eva.

"Why do you say that, Eva?" Danielle asked.

"When I was over there checking on our suspects, Laura's friend came back to his room. I did a little snooping."

"He is attractive," Marie said with a snort.

Eva then told them what she had seen on Dane's computer. After she finished, Heather recounted what Eva had said for Brian and the chief.

"Are you saying the guy Laura met in London is connected to

one of our suspects? At least to the stepmother of our prime suspect?" Brian asked.

"Sounds that way," Heather said.

"Come on, from what Joe told me, not only is this the guy Laura met in London, the last time he was in the States, he was really young and doesn't even remember the trip. How would he know Rosalyn King?" Brian asked.

"I didn't say he did, just that he had a lot of her pictures on his computer," Eva said, yet Brian could not hear.

"It doesn't mean Rosalyn hasn't been to London," Danielle said.

"Or maybe he lied about previous visits to the US," Heather suggested.

THIRTY-SIX

B efore Chris left for the hospital with Marie, Eva checked on
Kyle. She had been looking in on him throughout the day. He
was still in his room, and by the empty pizza box sitting on the
dresser, she assumed he had already had dinner. He wore just boxers
as he lounged on his bed, watching television and drinking a beer.
By the empty beer cans scattered throughout the motel room, she
didn't imagine he would be in any shape to drive anywhere tonight.
Eva returned to Marlow House to update them before going back to
the motel, in case an inebriated Kyle left the motel.

The chief took his sons home, but Heather and Brian remained
at Marlow House with Christopher. They sat in the living room with
Walt, Danielle, and the twins, watching television.

"Now, exactly how are we going to do this?" Marie asked. She
sat in the passenger seat of Chris's car as they drove to the hospital.

"I talked to Fred and—"

"Who is Fred?" Marie interrupted.

"He owns the lab I'm going to use. He said he can use blood,
saliva, or hair. But with hair, it has to have roots attached."

"We obviously won't use blood. While she can't see me, she
might notice if I jam a needle in one of her veins."

Chris chuckled. "No. Not blood. I initially considered saliva. But even if we found some way to sneak the cup or straw she's using out of the hospital room, would it be enough saliva? Would it get contaminated before we got it to the lab?"

"Yes, a cup floating down the hall of the hospital might get some attention. It would be easier if you carried a purse." Marie chuckled. "You want to use her hair?"

"Yes. Unfortunately, you need to get ten strands. Five might work, but Fred said ten to be safe. And with roots attached."

"She won't notice if I start pulling out her hair?" Marie snarked.

"It's not like you'll be yanking out ten at a time. One strand will be a little pinch. And take it from the back of her head. That way, she won't notice hair floating around the room."

"Okay," Marie muttered, not sounding convinced.

MARIE GLANCED at the wall clock as they entered the hospital. "It's after eight. I'm pretty sure visiting hours are over unless you're family. I hope Heather is right."

It wasn't until they were in the elevator going up to the second floor and alone that Chris responded to Marie's comment. He didn't want to say anything while walking through the lobby of the hospital, considering those around him assumed he was alone. "You don't really need me in the room to get the strands of hair, and it shouldn't be that difficult to get them out of the hospital without someone noticing."

"Do you want to go back downstairs to the waiting area? I'll get the hair and meet you there."

Chris shook his head. "No. I want to talk to Rosalyn King. If she leaves tomorrow like the chief says she might, it could be my last chance. If she is Christopher's grandmother, which I suspect she is, I want to learn as much as I can about her. I understand I can't keep him away from his family forever. But I feel responsible. I want him safe and loved."

"You're a good man, Chris." Marie added in a less serious tone,

"Even though you're making me yank out some poor woman's hair."

When they arrived on the second floor, Chris walked to the nurses' station. He already had Rosalyn's room number, but he didn't feel comfortable going directly to her room, considering it was not only after hours, but he was a stranger to Rosalyn. Plus, seeing him had already caused the woman emotional stress. He hoped seeing him again didn't retrigger her.

As Heather predicted, Chris had no problem with the female staff of the hospital. At the nurses' station, they immediately recognized Chris, knowing him as the hot guy who worked for the Glandon Foundation. They also knew Rosalyn had had her emotional breakdown while on the foundation property, so they assumed Rosalyn knew Chris.

Before knocking on Rosalyn's hospital room door and entering, Marie peeked in to make sure the woman was alone and presentable for visitors. She found Rosalyn sitting up in her bed, her body from her waist down covered with a blanket. The television was off, and Rosalyn held a cellphone in her hands and appeared to be surfing.

Marie returned to the hallway and gave Chris the green light. He knocked on the door and walked into the hospital room. Rosalyn looked up from her phone, and by her expression, she hadn't expected this visitor.

Chris smiled at Rosalyn, who momentarily seemed incapable of speech. Now clutching the cellphone, no longer looking at it, Rosalyn stared wide-eyed at Chris.

"Hello, I was hoping I could have a few minutes of your time. I'm Chris Johnson. We met briefly yesterday."

Rosalyn's body relaxed. She smiled at Chris and set her cellphone on her lap. "Yes, right after I trespassed on your property, I made an absolute fool of myself."

Chris returned her smile and approached the bed. "I'm sorry we frightened you. I came to apologize."

Rosalyn frowned at Chris. "What do you have to apologize about? I was in the wrong."

Chris started to answer but was momentarily distracted when

Marie floated into the air, moving over the hospital bed. He told himself to focus, turned his attention back to Rosalyn, and said, "We normally aren't as aggressive when someone comes onto our property. But as you are aware, I'm currently responsible for a young boy whose guardian was recently murdered. And we're trying to keep him safe until the police learn more."

"I never considered Christopher might be in danger."

"We're just taking precautions. It's the reason my security guards pulled a gun on you. Which might have been extreme."

Rosalyn shook her head. "No. Not under the circumstances. By any chance, have you spoken to the police chief?"

Chris nodded. "Yes. Before I came over here."

"Did he explain why I…well…why I responded as I did?"

As Rosalyn asked the question, Chris's gaze wandered to the ghost hovering over her head, noting the way the top of Rosalyn's hair floated upwards as if reacting to static electricity. He hoped one of the medical staff didn't walk in. Chris started to answer her question, but paused when Rosalyn said, "Ouch."

"Are you okay?" Chris asked with a touch of guilt.

Frowning, Rosalyn scratched her head and then shrugged. "I'm fine. That was weird." She moved her right hand back to her lap and turned her attention to Chris.

"As for your question, yes. The chief explained. And I'm sorry my security guards scared you. I wanted to make sure you're okay."

"I'll be honest; my reaction probably surprised me more than anyone else. I thought I was doing better…and then I saw you."

"Do I really look that much like your son?" Chris asked softly.

Rosalyn motioned to the nearby chair. "Please, sit down."

Chris accepted her offer, pulling the chair closer to her bed. By the way she flinched the next moment he knew Marie had taken another strand of hair. She scratched her scalp again but said nothing about it.

"At first glance, yes. You could pass as brothers. You're taller than Peter. Any chance you have any Danes in your family?"

Chris frowned. "Danish?"

"No. Dane. It was my first husband's surname."

"Not that I'm aware. So how long are they keeping you here? I'm assuming there is nothing physically wrong with you."

"You mean as opposed to mentally?" She chuckled, then flinched and scratched her head again.

"I just meant—"

"No, that's okay. Actually, how I responded to seeing you wasn't much different from when I first heard my son had been killed. They had to sedate me that time, too."

"I'm sorry."

Rosalyn flinched again, scratched her head, and then said, "I had a long talk with the doctor early this evening. They're discharging me tomorrow."

Rosalyn flinched again, but this time she vigorously scratched her scalp with the fingernails of both of her hands. After a moment, she stopped scratching, looked at Chris, and then blushed. "I'm sorry. It must be a reaction to one of the sedatives they gave me. Almost like someone keeps pulling out strands of my hair."

"I'm sure it will stop."

"I'm close," Marie told Chris. "It will stop in a minute."

Rosalyn scratched her scalp again and said, "I spoke to Kyle. That's my stepson who came up here with me. I told him this had all been a mistake. Christopher isn't my grandson. I assume the police chief told you that part, too?"

"He did."

"There is obviously no reason for me to stay in Frederickport after they discharge me. We'll be heading home on Sunday. Kyle said it would be best if we didn't try leaving tomorrow. One never knows how long it will take them to discharge me."

They continued to chat while Marie diligently plucked single strands of hair from Rosalyn's head. When Marie finally had ten strands, she waved them in the air and said, "I have them."

AFTER GOING out to dinner with Joe and Kelly, Laura left with Dane, and the two drove over to his motel room so they could talk.

When they pulled up to his room, Laura asked, "Which room is theirs?"

Dane pointed to the room to the left of his. "That's her room." He pointed to the room on the other side of Rosalyn's, its blinds partially closed, but the lights on. "That's her stepson's room."

They got out of the car and walked up to Dane's motel room. When they were inside, Laura said, "I still can't believe she went over to the Glandon headquarters and then totally freaked out. I'm really glad you talked to the chief about her. If you hadn't, who knows what would have happened?" Laura took a seat in one of two chairs in the room.

"I don't think anything bad would have happened." Dane opened the small refrigerator in the room and turned to Laura. "Want a soft drink or some wine?"

"A little wine. And why don't you think anything bad would have happened?"

Dane removed a bottle of wine from the refrigerator and started pouring them each a glass, using the motel room's water glasses. "You heard what Joe told us. Your friend Chris looks just like her dead son." Dane walked over to Laura and handed her a glass of wine.

"I know Joe couldn't really talk about the case tonight. The only reason he said anything about her freaking out and going to the hospital is because this is such a small town, and considering all the responders who were there, it's not exactly a secret. But what he didn't mention, and just between you and me, I think the lady who freaked out is Christopher's grandmother."

Dane frowned. "How is she his grandmother?"

"Isn't it obvious? Her dead son is Christopher's father."

"I thought your friend Chris was the father?"

Laura shook her head. "No. According to my sister, Chris never hooked up with Christopher's mom. Sure, he knew her. And I guess she had a crush on him." Laura took a sip of her wine. "But Lily believes Chris. And what I know about him, I do too."

Christopher is Peter's son? Dane thought as he took a sip of wine.

THIRTY-SEVEN

E va followed Kyle into Rosalyn's motel room on Saturday morning. He carried a small plastic bag. Upon entering the room, he absently closed the door behind him, but as the door had done several times before, it failed to shut all the way. Once inside the room, Kyle grabbed some of Rosalyn's clothes and put them into the plastic bag. A few minutes later, he left the room carrying the bag of clothes. After stepping outside the motel room, he shut the door and tested the doorknob to make sure it had properly locked.

Kyle had tossed the bag of clothes on the passenger seat, so Eva sat in the back seat while they drove to the hospital. Two hours later, she again sat in the back seat of the car while Kyle drove his stepmother back to the motel.

"First thing I want to do when we get to the motel room, I need to take a shower," Rosalyn said.

"After your shower, you can get into something comfortable and rest. You've been through a lot."

"I'm sorry I put you through all this."

Kyle glanced briefly over to the passenger seat and said, "We'll go home, and you can put all this behind you."

Rosalyn let out a long sigh, leaned back in the seat, and looked out the side window, watching the scenery move by. "Yesterday when we talked about that, I hoped it was possible, but now I'm not so sure."

Frowning, Kyle looked over at Rosalyn and then back to the street. "What do you mean?"

"While you were right when you said I shouldn't come, this isn't over. When we go home, I'm going to do what I should have done in the first place."

"And what's that?"

"I'm calling my attorney and asking him to arrange a DNA test for Christopher."

"I don't understand. Why? You told me yesterday you no longer believe he's Peter's son. What is the point?"

"I'm not so sure Christopher is Chris Johnson's son after all."

"Oh my," Eva muttered from the back seat.

"Why do you say that?"

"I didn't tell you, but Chris Johnson visited me last night. He said he wanted to make sure I was okay. He apologized for his men being so aggressive when approaching me. But he never once said Christopher was his son."

"Did he say he wasn't the boy's father?"

"No."

"I'm not sure how him not announcing he's the boy's father means he isn't. He doesn't know you. I can understand him stopping in to make sure you were okay. But him not mentioning the boy's paternity means nothing."

Rosalyn turned to Kyle. "Did you know Derrick and Kevin were in Frederickport when Traci Lind was murdered?"

"I didn't until yesterday when I talked to the police."

"Why didn't you tell me?"

Kyle shrugged. "Why would I? Especially considering you were in the hospital, dealing with your own issues. I told you they had been in Oregon looking for investment property. It's only a strange coincidence they came to Frederickport. But considering they were looking for beach property, I suppose we shouldn't be surprised.

239

And we both know they had nothing to do with Traci Lind's death. They didn't even know her."

Rosalyn let out a sigh and looked back out the window again. "You're right. I just thought it was so strange."

"Are you hungry? You didn't have lunch yet."

"A little, I suppose."

"How about a burger and chocolate milkshake? There's a drive-through up ahead."

Rosalyn laughed. "When would I ever turn down a chocolate milkshake?"

When they got to the Seahorse Motel, Eva followed the pair into Rosalyn's motel room, with Kyle carrying the food they had purchased. "I'm putting your milkshake in the refrigerator, and you go take your shower. When you get out, we can have lunch together." He set the bag of food on the table in the room before setting Rosalyn's milkshake and his soda in the room's small motel refrigerator.

"Thank you, Kyle. But don't you want to eat now while your burger is warm? I can wait for my shower."

"No. Take a shower. Wash off the hospital. You'll be more comfortable, and we can both enjoy our lunch. But can I use your bathroom first?"

"Certainly." As Kyle left for the bathroom, Rosalyn glanced at the door and noticed it had not closed all the way. It had done that when they had first checked in. Letting out a sigh, she walked to the door, shut it securely, turned back to the room, and began gathering up the clothes she intended to wear after her shower.

Eva didn't follow Kyle into the bathroom. If she had, she would have seen him grab a clean washcloth and use it to help him keep fingerprints off the bottle of prescription sleeping pills he removed from Rosalyn's makeup bag sitting on the bathroom counter. He opened the bottle, and after pouring the pills onto the counter, he used the bottom of a water glass to smash the pills into powder while holding the glass with the washcloth so as not to leave fingerprints on the glass. After carefully returning the crushed sleeping pills back into their bottle, he rinsed off the bottom of the glass and set it back on the counter. Kyle secured the lid on the pulverized sleeping pills, wrapped the bottle with a tissue, and shoved the bottle into one of his pockets. Before leaving the bathroom, he pulled off some toilet paper, and after dampening it, he wiped down the bathroom counter, tossed the toilet paper into the toilet and flushed.

When Kyle stepped out of the bathroom, he found Rosalyn standing near the door, clean clothes in hand. She told him she would hurry, to which he responded, "Take your time. We're in no hurry. I'll watch a little TV while you're in the shower." She thanked him and stepped into the bathroom, leaving Eva and Kyle now alone in the room.

"I really don't want to watch television. I've seen your taste in movies," Eva said before disappearing. She intended to come back shortly, but she wanted to give Chris and the others an update on Kyle and Rosalyn and tell them Rosalyn hadn't abandoned the idea that Christopher might be her grandson.

Now alone in the motel bedroom, Kyle flipped on the television, walked to the motel refrigerator, and retrieved the pill bottle from his pocket. After removing its lid, he set the lid, bottle, and tissue on top of the refrigerator. He removed the chocolate milkshake from the refrigerator. Grateful they had already inserted a straw in the milkshake's lid, he gently removed the lid, leaving the straw intact. After dumping the powdered sleeping pills into the cup, he used the straw to stir the powder into the milkshake without removing the straw from the lid. When satisfied it was sufficiently blended, he reattached the lid to the cup and then set the milkshake back into the refrigerator.

EVA HAD FOUND Chris and Heather at Marlow House with Walt and Danielle, sitting outside watching Christopher play ball with Hunny. Marie was upstairs in the nursery with the twins. Eva had just finished telling them about Rosalyn's decision to ask for a DNA test.

When Eva finished her update, Danielle said, "I talked to the chief right before you got here. One cop the chief talked to from Eureka was familiar with the King family. Peter left town and attended college in Southern California. But Kyle, who is a few years older than his stepbrother, joined the military. When he came back, he got his real estate license and started working for his dad. The Tyler brothers were high school friends of Kyle's, and for a while, right after Kyle came home from the service, they were all roommates."

"Had there been any sign they were cold-blooded killers?" Eva asked.

"According to whoever the chief talked to, nothing unusual stood out regarding the Tyler brothers. They didn't terrorize the town as teenagers or anything. He remembered them doing typical stupid teenage stuff."

BACK AT THE MOTEL ROOM, Rosalyn sat at the small table with Kyle, eating her lunch, the television now turned off. While she had been taking a shower, Kyle had opened the blinds, letting in the afternoon sunlight. Unbeknownst to Rosalyn or Kyle, Eva had popped in briefly. They were eating lunch, and Rosalyn wore a robe. Eva doubted either was going anywhere for a while, so she left again.

"I'm rather tired," Rosalyn said as Kyle gathered up the trash from the table after they had finished their burgers and fries.

"Lie down. Take a nap." He put the trash in the nearby trash can.

"That's all I've been doing since I got here." She rubbed her eyes and frowned. "I feel...odd."

"You just need to rest. You had an emotional week."

Rosalyn started to stand but then stumbled; Kyle grabbed her by the arm. "You need to lie down," he said before guiding her to the bed.

"I'm not sure what's wrong with me." Rosalyn sat on the side of the bed. With Kyle's help, she removed her slippers and put her feet on the bed.

"You've just been through a lot." He moved the almost empty milkshake cup to the side table next to the bed and then closed the blinds. When closing the blinds, he failed to notice the window they had opened after checking in was still partially open.

"So weird," Rosalyn muttered from the bed. "Last night I felt like someone was pulling my hair out, strand by strand, and now I feel like I've just had three martinis."

Leaving his stepmother confused on the bed, Kyle walked to the bathroom, where he disposed of the now empty sleeping pill bottle, along with its lid. Instead of throwing the tissue in the trash can, he flushed it down the toilet.

"I think something is wrong with me," Rosalyn said when Kyle returned to the bedroom. She tried to sit up but kept falling back.

"You're fine," he told her while glancing around the room, looking for her cellphone. He spied it sitting on the dresser. Walking to the dresser, he looked over to Rosalyn, who was not looking his way, but continued to struggle to get up. Using his elbow, not wanting to leave fingerprints on her cellphone, he nudged the phone off the dresser. It fell on the floor, out of sight, and out of Rosalyn's reach.

Kyle returned to the bedside. He stood over Rosalyn, her eyes glassy as she looked round the room. Kyle smiled and then glanced over to the motel phone on the nightstand on the other side of the bed. He walked around the bed, unplugged the phone, and then wiped his prints off the cord with the cuff of his shirt.

"Why did you do that?" Rosalyn asked, her head on the pillow, but her face turned toward him.

Kyle walked back around the queen-size bed and smiled down to his stepmother. "You don't need the phone tonight. You need to rest."

Rosalyn shook her head. It rocked back and forth on the pillow. "I feel funny. I think you should call someone," she whispered.

Kyle leaned down closer to Rosalyn, his face inches from hers. "You think you can get up?"

Rosalyn tried, but she couldn't even lift her head off the pillow. Blinking her eyes, she looked up at Kyle. "What's wrong with me?"

"It's been rough the last few years. I don't think anyone will be surprised. First you lost Peter. And then your husband. And everyone saw how upset you were when you found out that there was no grandson who might replace that void. So you did the only thing you could do. I'll see you in the morning, dear stepmother."

Kyle dropped a kiss on her forehead before turning from the bed. As he walked toward the door, he heard her faint, barely audible cries calling out to him.

THIRTY-EIGHT

Not long after Kyle left his stepmother's room did Eva return to the Seahorse Motel. Eva popped into Rosalyn's room first. They had obviously finished lunch, and Eva assumed Rosalyn had lain down to take a nap since she was in bed. Eva failed to look closely at the woman, being more concerned about Kyle's whereabouts than Rosalyn's. Eva and the mediums didn't feel Rosalyn was a danger to Christopher, but they all agreed Kyle was the prime suspect, and they wanted to keep him under observation.

Eva left Rosalyn's room and checked in on Kyle. She found him lounging on his bed, drinking a beer, and watching a movie on the television. Unlike Kyle's previous viewing choices, Eva actually liked the movie he was watching, so she didn't bother making an excuse to pop out every ten minutes. Eva took a seat in a chair and started watching the movie.

DANE PULLED into the Seahorse motel parking lot early on Saturday afternoon. He had just dropped Laura off at her sister's house, but he needed to get back to his motel room and answer some business emails on his laptop computer.

Dane stood at the door to his motel room, preparing to enter, when what sounded like someone vomiting in the room next door caught his attention. He stepped closer to Rosalyn's open window and heard more vomiting, followed by a faint cry for help.

Dane rushed to the door of Rosalyn's motel room and was surprised to find it partially open. Without thought, he pushed the door, and it swung open wider. Sounds of moaning and soft cries for help greeted him. He stepped into the motel room and found Rosalyn sprawled atop the bed; her head hung over the mattress.

"DAMN, I didn't check the lock when I left Rosalyn's room," Kyle blurted in the middle of a commercial. He jumped out of bed, slipped on his shoes, and started for the door.

"Where are you going?" Eva asked as she followed Kyle.

A moment later, Kyle stepped out of his motel room, glanced next door, and then let out a curse when he spied the partially open door to his stepmother's motel room. Eva followed him next door.

When they entered the motel room, both Kyle and Eva were surprised to find Rosalyn was not alone. A man was at her bedside, his back to them as he blocked a clear view of Rosalyn. The next moment, Kyle grabbed a bronze statue from the dresser and slammed it on the back of the man's head.

"Why did you do that?" Eva shrieked. She looked down at the man now unconscious on the floor. It was Dane. Kyle turned and ran through Eva's apparition to the open door. After closing the door and locking it, Kyle ran back toward the bed. Eva stepped to the side as he rushed past her. The next moment, she vanished.

Eva reappeared at Marlow House. She found Chris and the others still outside on the side patio.

"Quick, call the police; tell them to go to Rosalyn's room at the Seahorse motel. Tell them Kyle has attacked a man in her room." Eva vanished.

When Eva returned to the motel room a few minutes later, she found Kyle pacing the room as his right hand erratically combed through his hair. Rosalyn appeared to be passed out on the bed, her hair matted in what looked like vomit. Moans came from Dane, who remained on the floor, his eyes closed and the top of his head bloody.

Kyle stopped pacing and looked down at the man. "What the hell am I supposed to do about you? Crap, this was supposed to be easy." He started pacing again. "It was perfect. I would come to get Rosalyn in the morning. She would be dead from an overdose. The empty bottle of sleeping pills, her own prescription, in her bathroom. A half a dozen or more cops saw her freak out; who would not believe it was a suicide? And with her dead, it didn't matter if the brat was her grandkid. She already left me everything. This should not be happening!" Kyle stomped a foot like a child having a tantrum and for a moment, Eva thought he was going to kick Dane.

"What's going on?" Marie asked when she appeared a moment later. Before Eva responded, Marie noticed the bloodied man on the floor and the woman in the bed. "Oh my. Heather told me I needed to get over here. They've called Brian and Edward." Marie leaned closer to the man on the floor. "Is that Laura's friend?"

They heard sirens in the distance. The sound grew closer and louder. Kyle rushed to the window and peeked out through the blinds. A few minutes later, he saw the police car pull up. He rushed back over to the door and made sure it was locked.

A moment later, Brian knocked on the door of the room and called out, "Police!"

"No reason for Brian to find Sam to open the door. Let's hurry this up," Marie said as she unlocked the motel room door and pulled it open.

BRIAN HENDERSON SAT on one side of the table in the interrogation room while Kyle King sat on the other. In the adjacent office, Chief MacDonald, Eva, Marie, and Heather watched through the one-way mirror. Heather had gone down to the station to play interpreter for Eva and Marie. Fortunately, Joe had the day off, so there was no reason to make up an excuse about why she was there.

Both Dane and Rosalyn had been taken to the hospital, and so far, there was no word on either one's condition. While neither Eva nor Marie could talk to Brian back at the motel room, that didn't stop the spirits from letting him know Rosalyn had been drugged. After the other officers arrived on the scene, Marie had grabbed Brian's hand and led him to the bathroom. When he saw the empty pill bottle rise out of the trash can, he understood what she was trying to say.

"Yes, I hit him," Kyle admitted. "When I checked on Rosalyn, I found a strange man standing over her bed. I grabbed the first thing I could find and hit him over the head. I would do it again."

"You didn't think to ask him why he was there?" Brian asked.

Kyle frowned at Brian. "Why would I do that? A strange man is standing over her bed in a motel room. You expect me to have small talk? I didn't know if he had a gun on him. Now, can I go? You have my information. I want to check on my mother."

Brian glanced at the one-way mirror. He knew the chief was in the next room with Heather, Eva, and Marie. His cellphone rang.

"Excuse me." Brian reached for his phone.

"Can I leave?" Kyle started to stand.

Brian answered his phone while motioning for Kyle to sit back down. Kyle begrudgingly complied.

"I like how he calls her his mother," the chief told Brian.

"I noticed that."

"When I talked to her at the hospital yesterday, he did the same thing. Rosalyn said it was the first time he had ever called her that."

"I wonder why," Brian snarked, his eyes never leaving Kyle. "What do you want me to do?"

"We know from Eva he tried to kill her. But I need to talk to her. I just got a message from the hospital. They pumped her stomach. The doctors said it was a good thing she had just eaten. I guess a bottle of sleeping pills doesn't mix well with a burger and fries. She told the doctors she didn't take any sleeping pills."

"You going over there now?"

"Yes. Arrest him and put him in lockup."

Brian ended his phone call, stood up, slipped his phone in a pocket, and pulled handcuffs from his belt and said, "Kyle King, you are under the arrest for the attempted murder of Rosalyn King—"

"What?" Kyle stood.

Brian started reading Kyle his Miranda rights as the door to the interrogation room opened, and two more officers walked into the room.

AT THE HOSPITAL, Chief MacDonald found Rosalyn sitting up in bed, once again wearing a hospital gown. Her hair was damp, as if someone had just washed it.

"I guess we need to stop meeting this way," Rosalyn said in a half-hearted attempt at humor. The chief flashed her a smile and approached her bed. As he did, her eyes filled with tears, and she said, "I didn't take any sleeping pills. I promise."

Grabbing a tissue from a nearby box, the chief handed it to Rosalyn and said, "I believe you."

Wiping away the tears, Rosalyn gave a sniffle and looked up at the chief. She frowned. "You do?"

The chief nodded.

"But the doctors, they pumped my stomach. They said the police found an empty bottle of sleeping pills in my bathroom. I picked up some sleeping pills at the pharmacy before leaving San Clemente, before coming here. I never opened the bottle. But the doctor said there were traces of the sleeping pills in my milkshake, and my bottle of pills was empty. But I didn't take them. I don't know how they could have gotten into my milkshake."

With a sigh, the chief pulled a chair over to the side of the bed and sat down. "You didn't put the sleeping pills in your milkshake.

But that's what was in your stomach. If you didn't do it, who else could have?"

Rosalyn's frown deepened. "Kyle wouldn't have," she whispered.

"When did you get the milkshake?"

"After Kyle picked me up from the hospital, we went through a drive-through. We brought them back to the motel."

"Was Kyle ever alone with the milkshake before you drank it?"

Rosalyn nodded. Tears filled her eyes.

"Who inherits your estate if you die?"

Rosalyn looked up to the chief, tears slipping down her cheeks. "Kyle."

"And if Christopher is your grandson, who would inherit?"

BEFORE LEAVING THE HOSPITAL, the chief had one more patient to visit, Dane Carslaw. When he arrived at Dane's room, he found the patient not alone. Laura Miller sat by Dane's bedside, holding his hand.

"Chief!" Laura blurted as she stood up.

"Hello, Laura." He looked at Dane and said, "Nice to see you again. But I'm sorry it's at a hospital. How is your head?"

"The doctor says I'm going to be alright, but they want to keep me overnight in case of a concussion."

"That crazy man tried to kill Dane, and all he was trying to do was help!"

"I would like to speak to Dane alone for a few minutes, Laura."

Laura frowned at the chief. "Is there something wrong?"

"No. I would just like to talk to him alone, please. Wait in the lobby. It shouldn't be too long."

Begrudgingly, Laura left the room. When she did, the chief turned from the bed, walked to the door, closed it, and then turned back to the bedside. "I'd like you to tell me everything that happened at the motel until the police arrived."

Dane nodded, gave a sigh, and then said, "I had just dropped Laura off at her sister's. Right as I was going into my room, I heard someone throwing up and then calling for help. I walked to the door. It was already open. After walking into the room, I saw Rosalyn trying to sit up in bed while partially hanging over the mattress, throwing up on the floor. I thought she was going to fall off. I went to the bed, and, well, it felt like my head exploded."

"I just spoke to Rosalyn—"

"Is she okay?"

The chief nodded. "Yes. The doctors say she will be fine. Your version matches hers. I just have one more question."

"What is that?"

"What is your connection to Rosalyn King?"

Dane stared at the chief. "Connection?"

"There is a connection between you and Rosalyn. I know there is one, but I can't tell you how I know. If it comes out later, I'm afraid it might muck up the case we're trying to build against Rosalyn's stepson."

"Kyle? What case?"

"We've charged Kyle with the attempted murder of his step-mom. He's also the prime suspect in the murder of Traci Lind."

Dane shook his head. "I have nothing to do with any of that."

"I don't think you do. But I just don't like surprises when we're trying to put a killer behind bars. Please tell me. Who is she to you?"

Dane let out another sigh and leaned back in the bed. He looked up at the ceiling. "It's nothing nefarious. More of a coincidence."

"Coincidence?"

Dane looked over to the chief. "Yeah. Coincidence. I never imagined I would run into Rosalyn King in Frederickport. Or anywhere, for that matter. Her first husband was my father. Her son, Peter, was my half-brother. And I guess that makes Christopher my nephew. Is he my nephew?"

THIRTY-NINE

A member of the hospital staff brought Dane his breakfast. They were discharging him this morning, but apparently not before breakfast. He had already gotten dressed to leave. The night before, Laura had gone over to his motel room with her friend Kelly and picked up some clean clothes so he would have something to wear this morning.

Dane ate his breakfast, and instead of waiting in his room for them to bring in the discharge papers, he decided to visit another patient—Rosalyn King. Last night, Laura got Rosalyn's hospital room number for him. This was after the chief had left the hospital and after Dane had disclosed to Laura his connection to Rosalyn.

Five minutes later, Dane stood at the open doorway of Rosalyn's hospital room. He found her sitting up in her bed, eating her breakfast, and it appeared she was still wearing a hospital gown. He knocked and called out, "Can I come in?"

Rosalyn stopped eating and looked at Dane. She stared at him a moment before saying, "Yes." Dane walked toward her bed, and when he was a few feet away, she said, "You were in line when we checked into our motel room."

Dane nodded. "Yes."

She looked at the bandage on Dane's head and frowned. "You're the one Kyle attacked. You heard me crying for help."

"Are you feeling any better?"

She nodded and asked, "Have we met before? When we were checking in, I thought you looked familiar."

He shook his head. "No, we've never met."

"You're from the UK, aren't you? The accent."

"I live in London. My name is Dane Carslaw."

Rosalyn dropped the spoon she had been holding. It rattled the tray. Her eyes now wide, she stared at Dane. "You look just like your father. Why...why are you here?"

"I wanted to see if you were okay."

"No, I mean, why are you here in Frederickport; does this have something to do with Christopher?" Rosalyn's tone shifted from friendly to fear.

Dane let out a sigh. "No. This is what they call a bizarre coincidence. This is my first time in the States—since I moved when I was an infant. I'm here visiting a friend. A friend who happens to be a friend of the local police chief."

Rosalyn released a breath she had been holding. While she looked less fearful, she remained wary.

"I recognized you at the motel," Dane said. "I'm sorry, by the way, about Peter. Over the years, I admit I stalked you on the internet, yet mostly Peter. I never had any siblings, just a half-brother I had never met. I was curious."

"Does your mother know you're here?"

"My mother died years ago, right before I started college."

"Oh...I'm sorry. And she never married?"

"No."

"I...I never met your mother. I learned about you...about her... after Charles died."

Dane shrugged. "That's all behind us. I imagine you plan to seek custody of your grandson. I met him, by the way. He seems like a good kid."

"I don't know if he's my grandson. He might be Chris Johnson's son."

"From what Laura says—that's my friend—Chris Johnson is not Christopher's father."

"Did he take a DNA test?"

"He claims he was never with Christopher's mother. They were only friends when he lived in California. Nothing more."

Rosalyn let out a little hopeful gasp. "You've met him?"

DANIELLE STOOD in the doorway of Walt's attic office and surveyed the room. Since moving their bedroom furniture to the second floor, the attic looked enormous with all the extra floor space.

Next to his desk, Walt had spread a blanket, and on it were the twins, along with an assortment of baby toys and Max, his black tail twitching as he watched Addison and Jack. At the moment, Max was using one paw to push a small ball to Addison, whose little right hand swatted said ball, sending it back toward the cat.

Walt sat at his desk, his computer on, yet he faced his wife.

"You going to be okay, you and the babies, with no Marie?" Danielle asked.

"Max and I have it all under control," Walt said. "He's going to keep them entertained, and if I get too engrossed in my writing, Max promises to alert me if Addison or Jack needs my attention; he'll meow."

Danielle chuckled. "Our cat nanny."

Walt glanced over to the blanket and back to Danielle. "He's gotten rather fond of those two."

"I suspect the feeling is mutual. June said something to Lily about how she needed to keep Sadie and Max away from Emily Ann until she's older. But Ian stepped in and told his mother there were studies that show children who have early exposure to dogs and cats are less likely to develop allergies later on."

"I suspect June wasn't worried about allergies. Scratches from cats can lead to nasty infections, as we've seen from some of Max's victims."

Danielle chuckled. "True. But they deserved it."

"WORKING ON A SUNDAY, CHIEF?" asked a familiar voice from the open doorway.

Edward MacDonald glanced up from his desk and saw Danielle standing inside his office doorway.

"Morning, Danielle." He looked at the time on his computer monitor. "Or should I say early afternoon?"

"Well, it's not quite noon yet." Danielle stepped into the office. "I understand Eddy and Evan are spending the day over at the foundation headquarters, enjoying their beachfront."

"Evan doesn't mind helping keep Christopher occupied, and Eddy just enjoys hanging out with Heather."

Danielle sat down in one chair facing the desk and flashed the chief a smile. "Chris mentioned Eddy seems to have something of a crush on Heather."

The chief leaned back in his chair. "I'll have to admit, when we told Eddy about his brother's gift, I didn't expect how he would react."

Danielle arched her brows. "How so?"

"For one thing, he doesn't mind hanging out with his little brother. He sees Evan as...well, cool. Although, I don't think he would use that word."

Danielle laughed. "Probably not. And you didn't expect the crush on Heather?"

"As for that, I think Eddy always had a little crush on Heather, but knowing she's a medium, well, it just makes her—"

"Cooler?"

The chief laughed. "Something like that. So to what do I owe this visit?"

"Walt and I are having a barbecue tonight, and since I was out running errands, I thought I'd stop by and invite you in person. To make it easy for you, you can come straight over from work to our house. Chris and Heather can bring the boys over when they come."

"Thanks. Sounds better than what I had planned for dinner."

"What was that?"

The chief shrugged. "I have no idea."

Danielle grinned and then asked, "I understand Chris already told you about the DNA results."

"Yes. It looks like Christopher is Rosalyn's grandson."

Danielle nodded. "So has your prisoner spoken to his attorney yet?"

"Yes. And the judge is not setting bail."

"Anything new on the case?" Danielle asked.

The chief leaned forward, placing his elbows on his desk as he looked at Danielle. "To begin with, the Tyler brothers were not Bridget's cousins. Which didn't surprise me, considering everything else. We found the cousins. And they were sorry to hear about Traci but can't take care of Christopher."

"No surprise."

"They got a search warrant for Kyle's house, and they found some items used to make the bomb, and we know from Kyle's military history, he had the expertise to build one. He didn't do a terrific job of covering his tracks, and I'm not just talking about what they found at his house."

"What do you mean?" Danielle asked.

"Kyle drove up from Eureka to put that bomb on their car. He obviously knew where they were staying. They found some video footage of Kyle at a gas station. Unfortunately for him, he wasn't able to make that round trip on one tank of gas. I imagine he assumed no one would suspect him."

"I have a theory on this case," Danielle began. "From what the Tyler brothers told Heather, I figure Kyle hired his old high school buddies who happened to work for him and, from what I understand, didn't sell a lot of real estate and could use the money, to remove the threat to his inheritance. At first, I thought he killed them because they'd screwed up the job, and he needed to get rid of them because if they were caught, they would likely throw him under the bus for a lesser sentence. But then I realized, I don't think he just happened to have everything to make a bomb sitting around his garage. I bet he intended to kill them all along when the job was over. Unfortunately for him, they didn't finish the job. "

The chief nodded. "That's pretty much what I believe happened."

"But how did he learn about Christopher in the first place? The woman who told Rosalyn only pieced it together after Traci was murdered."

MacDonald leaned back in his chair. "The weekend of the party when Christopher's parents got together, it seems Kyle was in San Clemente at the time and staying with Peter. Kyle probably knew about the hookup, and it's possible he didn't piece it together until after Bridget was killed and Traci became Christopher's guardian. From what I understand, there was a lot of news coverage in California after her death, especially so soon after her mother's sensationalized death just months before, which also put the court judgment against the family's business back in the spotlight."

"Was Bridget's death an accident or—"

"You are wondering if Kyle had something to do with Bridget's death?"

Danielle nodded.

"I talked to authorities in San Clemente, and they're convinced it was simply an unfortunate accident. Plus, Kyle, along with the Tyler brothers, were at a real estate conference in Las Vegas at the time, and there are plenty of witnesses who can verify they were there, along with postings on social media."

POLICE CHIEF MACDONALD arrived at Marlow House before the other guests, late Sunday afternoon. Danielle greeted him at the front door and then led him to the kitchen, where she had left Walt minutes earlier, preparing the chicken for the barbecue while the twins each sat in a swing, happily kicking their feet, waving their hands and making gurgling sounds.

"Hey, Edward," Walt greeted when the chief and Danielle walked into the kitchen.

"I see I'm the first to arrive."

"Heather and Marie are on their way here with the boys," Danielle said while opening the refrigerator to grab a drink for the chief. "They should be here pretty soon."

"I suppose Chris told you he went to talk to Rosalyn at the hospital?" Walt asked while washing his hands.

"Yes. And he told her she's Christopher's grandmother." The chief sat down at the table with his drink. "I wasn't sure how he was going to explain how he got her DNA sample, but apparently she bought his story that he took something from her room when visiting her." The chief chuckled and took a sip of his drink.

"Which is actually true." Danielle took a seat at the table. "Rosalyn is coming to the barbecue. Chris is picking her up."

"It was nice of him to drive her back to the motel from the hospital. I was going to arrange something, but he offered," the chief said.

Walt joined them at the table. "It will be interesting tonight. Laura is bringing Dane."

"I will have some good news for all of them. Although, I'm not sure how Rosalyn will feel. She didn't want to believe Kyle was behind all this." The chief took another sip of his drink.

"Good news is always nice. What is it?" Danielle asked.

"Kyle has taken a plea deal to take the death penalty off the table."

Danielle frowned. "Isn't there still a moratorium on the death penalty in Oregon?"

"True, but they have sound evidence for the double murder of the Tyler brothers and the attempted murder of Rosalyn. Plus, with Mrs. Brown's testimony regarding seeing the Tyler brothers in San Clemente before they came up here, and some evidence found in the brothers' home, Kyle would likely face additional charges of attempted murder of a child, which is a capital offense in Oregon. A moratorium won't necessarily save him from the death penalty, but a plea deal will."

FORTY

Laura sat with Dane on the back patio of her sister's house. They looked out at the ocean. Inside, her family prepared to go across the street to Marlow House for the barbecue.

"So he's really my nephew?" Dane asked as he absorbed what Laura had just told him.

"According to Lily, Chris sent Rosalyn's and Christopher's DNA in to be tested, and it confirms it. She's his grandmother."

"When did he do that?" Dane asked.

"Chris visited her on Friday, when she was in the hospital the first time. While he was there, he took something from the room with her DNA on it. Not sure if it was strands of hair from her brush or used tissues or her water glass. Lily didn't say. I guess he did it on the sly; Rosalyn didn't realize he had taken anything. At least, that's what Lily told me."

"I can't believe they got the results that fast."

"Well, with Chris, umm…he sort of knows people and how to fast-track things. So how are you handling all this?" Laura studied Dane's expression. Since she had told him Christopher was Rosalyn's grandson, he had been staring out at the ocean and not looking at her.

"I guess this means…I have family." Dane turned to Laura, no longer looking out to sea. He smiled.

"I remember when you told me both of your parents were gone, but I never thought that meant you didn't have family. There aren't any aunts, uncles, cousins?"

Dane looked back out at the ocean. "I never met my father, and from what I found online, he was an only child. I never mentioned Peter to you before because I'd never met him. It doesn't mean I wasn't curious. Mom's parents disowned her when she came back from the States pregnant. I actually think the fact my father paid her off to leave—a generous amount—bothered them more than if she had come home pregnant and destitute."

"So there was never a relationship with them?"

Dane shook his head. "I never met them, and they passed away when I was a teenager. Mom had two brothers, much younger than her. They were never close. I imagine my grandparents were responsible for that. I've never met my uncles. They didn't come to Mom's funeral. Although to be fair, I'm not sure if they heard she died. I had no idea how to contact them. While I don't know if they married and had any kids, they probably did. I imagine there are some cousins out there."

"You were never tempted to search online and see what happened to your uncles?"

"No. I had no desire to meet them after they shunned their sister. Peter hadn't rejected me like Mom's family did her. I figured he was probably never told about me. I was ten before I learned about him. Growing up, all I was told was that my father died when I was a baby. I fantasized about someday meeting my brother. But I never got the courage. Instead, I just stalked him online."

"You never mentioned you had been born in the States. That means you're a US citizen."

Dane looked up at Laura and smiled. "Yes. I have dual citizenship. Does it make a difference?"

Laura frowned. "What do you mean?"

"If I'm a US citizen, would falling in love with me still be such a horrible thing?"

"It was never about your citizenship. After being away from the States that long, away from my family, I just realized I couldn't live in another country, so far away from them."

"You could have asked me what I wanted."

CHRIS PULLED his car up in front of Marlow House and parked behind Adam and Melony's car. He looked over to the passenger seat where Rosalyn sat. She had barely spoken since he had picked her up at the motel. While she looked better than she had when he had talked to her earlier that day, when visiting her at the hospital, telling her about the DNA results, and then offering to drive her back to the motel, she now looked uncertain, if not uncomfortable.

"Are you sure it's okay that I'm here?" Rosalyn made no attempt to remove her seatbelt. "I feel like I'm barging in on someone's party."

"It's just a barbecue with friends. And you've already met the chief."

"Yes, when he arrested me." Rosalyn reluctantly smiled.

"I don't remember it as an arrest exactly. Anyway, Christopher is here. And you want to meet him."

Rosalyn looked at Chris. "What do I say to him?"

"The truth. I'd start there. He's a smart boy." Chris unfastened his seatbelt.

Rosalyn let out a sigh, unbuckled her seatbelt, and said, "Okay. Let's do this."

Chris and Rosalyn entered through the front door. It was already unlocked. Chris found Evan and Christopher in the parlor, playing video games. Hunny sat between them. Chris walked into the parlor and said, "Where is everyone?"

Upon hearing Chris, Hunny, tail wagging, jumped off the sofa, went to greet him, but then promptly returned to where she had been sitting between the two boys.

"In the kitchen or outside. Lily and her family aren't here yet."

Evan glanced over Chris's shoulder and saw Rosalyn standing quietly. His father had already told him who she was.

"Can I talk to Christopher alone?" Chris asked.

Evan flashed Chris a smile, gave him a nod, and then set the game controller on the coffee table. "Hey, Christopher, we can finish the game later."

A few minutes later Christopher sat on the sofa, Hunny by his side, and watched as Chris walked into the room with a woman. He recognized her from the picture police chief MacDonald had shown him.

Now standing a few feet from the sofa, Rosalyn by his side, Chris said, "Christopher, I would like you to meet someone. Her name is Rosalyn King."

Christopher looked at the woman and smiled. "Should I call her Mrs. King?" He called Heather and Danielle by their first names, but some adults, like Mrs. Brown, were called by their last names.

Chris stepped closer to the boy, knelt on a knee so he could be eye level with him, and then placed his right hand on his left shoulder, looking the boy in his eyes. "I know Traci wanted to find your father. But what she didn't realize, your father died months before you were even born."

Christopher blinked several times, resisting tears. "Everyone dies."

Chris nodded. "Eventually. It's all part of life. Some people die sooner than we would like. But while we couldn't bring you your father, we found your grandmother. Rosalyn here, she's your father's mom. And until a few days ago, she didn't know about you. And now that she does, she is very excited to meet you."

Christopher's eyes widened as he looked up at the woman standing behind Chris.

"I have a grandma?"

Chris nodded. "Yes. And she would like to talk to you. Would it be okay if I left you two alone so you can talk in private? Or would you rather I stay in here with you while you two visit?"

Christopher looked from Chris to Rosalyn, back to Chris. "Can Hunny stay with me?"

Chris nodded. "Sure."

CHRISTOPHER SAT on the sofa between Rosalyn and Hunny, his right hand absently stroking Hunny's back.

"Are you really my grandma?" Christopher asked after Chris left the parlor, leaving the door slightly ajar.

"Yes, I am. I would love for you to call me Grandma. But if that doesn't feel comfortable for you, you can call me Rosalyn."

Christopher peeked shyly at Rosalyn. "Grandma, what was my dad like?"

Rosalyn's smile broadened. "Oh my. Well, when he was a little boy, he looked just like you."

"Really? Do you have any pictures?"

"Yes. At my house in San Clemente, I have lots of pictures of Peter when he was a little boy. Peter was your father's name."

"I wish I could see them." Christopher turned his head, now looking straight ahead while he continued to pet Hunny.

"You can. Christopher, I would like you to come live with me. We are family, me and you. Your friend Chris told me about Mrs. Brown and how you liked to play with her grandchildren. My house isn't that far from where Mrs. Brown lives. We can ask her to come over for lunch some weekend and maybe bring her grandchildren."

Christopher looked at Rosalyn. "Do you have any dogs? A cat?"

Rosalyn smiled at the boy. "No, not at the moment. But Chris told me how good you are with animals. I think every little boy should have their own dog. We could get you your own puppy. You can pick it out."

Marie, who had come into the parlor to eavesdrop right after Chris left, chuckled. "Smart move. Win him over with a promise of a puppy. But from what I've learned about this child, it won't just be a puppy. He'll be talking you into a cat, too."

Rosalyn and Christopher had been chatting for a while when they heard voices coming from the front entry. They looked up to the now open doorway when a male voice said, "Hello."

Rosalyn recognized the man. It was Peter's half-brother. Chris had already told her he would be coming tonight.

"Hi, Dane!" Christopher greeted. "Do you know my grandma?"

Dane smiled and stepped into the parlor. "Why, yes, I do."

"I forgot you two have met before," Rosalyn said.

"Yes, when I first arrived in town, across the street at the Bartleys'. Of course, I didn't know who he was at the time." Dane then added, "And I'm not sure he knows who I am now."

"Aren't you Dane?" Christopher asked with a frown.

Rosalyn put out a hand to Dane and said, "Come, I think we should properly introduce you two."

Dane stepped closer, and Christopher looked from his grandmother to Dane. By his expression, he was clearly confused.

"Christopher, Dane is your uncle."

"He's your son too?" Christopher asked.

Rosalyn shook her head. "No, but he was your father's half-brother. They had the same father."

Christopher frowned up to Dane. "Does that make him my half uncle?"

"I'd rather be just your uncle Dane. And uncles are famous for spoiling their nephews."

DANIELLE STOOD ON THE GRASS, under a tree, beyond the outdoor kitchen, watching the boys kick a soccer ball around the side yard while Hunny and Sadie tried catching it, and Max lounged on a branch overhead, watching his canine friends. She held Jack, who was wide awake and squirming, while the chief was on the other side of the patio, holding a sleeping Addison, her chin resting on his shoulder, while he chatted with Brian and Joe.

Next to Danielle stood Eva and Heather, while the rest of their friends were scattered around the patio, in the kitchen, or standing by the grill, watching Chris and Walt cook the chicken.

Danielle, Eva, and Heather were far enough away from the rest of the party so as not to be overheard.

"I still can't believe Dane is Christopher's uncle. I mean seriously, what kind of wild coincidence is that?" Heather asked. "What are the chances he would be at the Seahorse Motel at the same time as Rosalyn?"

Eva laughed. "Heather, you aren't seriously asking that question, are you?"

Heather and Danielle turned to Eva.

"There are no coincidences?" Danielle asked, more a question than a statement.

Eva smiled. "I suppose, in some circumstances, yet not in this one."

"They were supposed to meet?" Heather asked.

Eva looked over at Dane, who stood next to Laura, his arm draped over her shoulders, while they talked to Melony and Rosalyn. "Definitely."

"Does that mean the Universe arranged for Traci's murder?" Heather asked.

Eva shook her head. "Certainly not. It doesn't work that way. Had the Tyler brothers not killed Traci, she would still have left Christopher with Chris, and Dane would still have come to Frederickport, and Chris would have had Christopher's DNA tested, and it would have eventually led to Rosalyn. And don't forget, we still have free will. The Universe gives us nudges—and sometimes we ignore them. Had that been the case with Dane, he might have stayed in London and not followed Laura. While it wasn't a coincidence he came to Frederickport, it was also never a guaranteed outcome."

"According to what Laura told Lily, Dane is moving to the States so he and Laura can give their relationship a chance, and he wants to be in his nephew's life," Danielle said.

Heather let out a sigh before saying, "Well, I'm going to miss Christopher when he leaves. And pretty soon, Evan and Eddy will be back in school."

"And then things can get back to normal." The moment the words left Danielle's mouth, both she and Heather looked at each other and burst into laughter.

FORTY-ONE

A fter returning home from Marlow House on Sunday evening, Christopher had a bath, changed into a pair of clean pajamas, and climbed into bed. When Chris came into the room to say goodnight and tuck him in, the bedroom light was still on. Christopher sat up in bed with his stuffed Snoopy on his lap, and Hunny lay on the end of the mattress.

Chris noticed the boy's pensive expression. Christopher stared down at Snoopy, fiddling with his black nose while deep in thought. "Are you okay, bud?"

Christopher looked up in surprise. He hadn't heard Chris walk into the room. In response to the question, he gave a shrug.

Chris walked to the bed and sat on the side of the mattress. His eyes on the boy, he absently reached back and petted Hunny while asking, "How are you doing? It was a lot to take in today. You have a grandma and an uncle."

His eyes now on Chris, the boy asked, "Am I really going to live with her?"

"Do you want to?"

Christopher shrugged. "I have to live somewhere."

Chris let out a sigh, stopped petting Hunny, and focused his attention on Christopher. "You don't sound as enthused about the idea as you did earlier."

"It's just sort of scary. Can I ask a favor?"

"Sure, what?"

Christopher glanced briefly at the stuffed animal on his lap and then back at Chris. "Can I maybe take Snoopy with me? It's okay if I can't."

"Snoopy is yours. Of course you can take him. Just like you can take all the toys Heather bought you."

"Heather said you bought them for me."

Chris smiled. "Heather did the fun part; she got to go with you when you picked out all that stuff. I did the boring part. But why did you think you would have to leave him?"

Christopher shrugged. "When we lived with grandma, I had lots of toys to play with. But Mom said I could only take my stuffed animal with me when we moved in with Traci. So I figured it would be the same now, and maybe I could take my stuffed animal this time, too."

Chris let out a sigh. "Yes, you can take Snoopy. Along with everything Heather bought for you. They're yours to keep."

Christopher smiled weakly at Chris. "I'm going to miss my friends here. I'm going to miss you."

"When you leave Frederickport, we aren't saying goodbye forever. I promise to visit you. And I bet I could get Evan and Eddy to come with me. And when Connor is older, maybe him too."

"And Heather?"

Chris chuckled. "Yes, definitely Heather. I have a feeling she would be mad at me if I didn't take her to see you. And I'm sure your grandmother will bring you back up to Frederickport for visits. You guys can stay with me when you come. This bedroom will be here for you, and I have another one for your grandma to stay in."

"When will I go?"

Chris shrugged. "I'm not sure. Your grandma will be talking to an attorney tomorrow. There are grown-up things we need to work out. But in the meantime, you will stay here with me, and when we have an actual date, Heather will help pack up your stuff."

"I'd sorta like to leave some toys here."

Chris arched his brows. "You would? Why?"

"Well, when I come for a visit, there will be some stuff I can play with. And when I'm not here, Connor and Evan can play with them."

Chris chuckled. "Okay. I'll leave that to you and Heather to figure out what you want to take and what to leave here. But I think we should both get to sleep; it's been a long day."

CHRIS OPENED his eyes and found himself sitting on the porch swing in front of Marlow House, a full moon lighting the night sky. The swing moved back and forth in a steady rhythm.

"Hello, Chris," a woman's voice said.

Chris turned to the right and found Bridget Singer sitting on the other side of the swing. She smiled at him.

"Bridget?" Chris looked around quickly and back at Bridget. "This is a dream hop."

Bridget smiled. "I heard that's what your friend calls it. I wanted to thank you for taking such good care of Christopher."

"He's a good kid."

Bridget gave a nod. "Yes, he is. Better than I deserved. I made a lot of mistakes. I realize that now."

"Can I ask you a question?"

Bridget shrugged. "Sure. I imagine you will have more than one. Ask away."

"Was your death really an accident?"

Bridget laughed. "It was not only an accident; it was a stupid accident. Those shoes weren't meant for narrow stairs, and certainly not while texting."

Chris cringed. "I've heard of fatal car accidents while texting."

Bridget shrugged. "It's just as lethal while wearing four-inch heels and rushing downstairs."

"Next question, why did you tell everyone I was Christopher's father? Why did you make that sworn affidavit? Obviously, a DNA test could disprove it."

"Your friend Walt wasn't wrong when he suggested why I wrote that affidavit."

"You know about that?" Chris asked.

"Yes, there are a lot of things we observe from the other side." Bridget's right hand held onto the chain rope of the swing as her feet pumped back and forth, keeping the swing in motion. "I made that for my father's sake. I knew he would never contact you. He believed you were an out-of-work slacker, and if he discovered who Christopher's father really was, I knew he would contact the family. I never worried about him discovering who you really were because I never knew. Not until after I died."

Chris stared at Bridget. "Why would you want your parents not to know who the real father of your child was? He was dead, and I'm certain his mother would have been willing to help you financially."

Bridget let out a sigh and leaned back in the swing. "There were a lot of reasons. To be honest, I was a little ashamed. The only reason I was with Peter, I had too much to drink, and I thought he looked like you."

"You weren't really in love with me, were you?"

Bridget looked at Chris and smiled. "At once I thought I was. But no. It was a schoolgirl crush, and you were a more than decent guy, who never once took advantage of the situation. Other men would have. As for Peter, he was closer to my age. Traci and I met him at a concert. He invited me to a party at his house the next week. Traci and I talked about how much he looked like you. I ended up going to the party. Traci didn't. I never told her what happened that night. Peter and I had too much to drink. I'm not sure what would have happened had Peter not gotten killed in that accident. Maybe I would have told him."

"Why not later, after your parents were gone, and you could have used the financial help?"

Bridget shrugged. "I couldn't tell Traci the truth. I'd told that lie so long. And like I said, I was embarrassed. I know I behaved poorly around you, and you may not believe this, but I didn't go around hooking up with random guys. Yes, I went clubbing after Christopher was born, but I didn't know how else to meet men. And I wanted to find someone. I never went home with any of them."

"I have another question. Why didn't you let Christopher take any of his toys with him? Surely the bank would have let you take Christopher's personal things. They let you take your jewelry."

"Another thing I handled poorly. I didn't leave Christopher's personal belongings behind—or mine. At least not permanently. Before moving into Traci's apartment—a very small apartment—I packed up everything and put it in storage. I paid a year in advance, and it should still be there, along with all the family pictures and keepsakes. I told Christopher he could take one thing to Traci's apartment. He misunderstood me and must have thought that meant everything else was given away."

"And where is this storage unit?"

Bridget told Chris where he could find the storage unit, along with the combination to the lock, which was easy to remember, since it was Christopher's birthdate.

"Do you have anything else you want to ask?"

Chris considered her question for a moment and then said, "No." He was about to say something more, but was interrupted when Christopher suddenly appeared, sitting on the swing between him and Bridget. It was a tight fit with the three of them.

"Where am I?" Christopher asked. He looked to the right and saw his mother. "Mom!"

"Oh, Christopher!" The swing came to a stop, and Bridget threw her arms around her son. The two hugged. She looked over the top of the child's head and said, "I need to talk to my son now. I think you're about to fall out of bed." The next minute, Chris disappeared.

CHRIS WOKE up on the floor in his bedroom. Moonlight slipped through the window blinds. The room was quiet, and he was alone.

"Dang, I really fell out of bed," Chris grumbled as he picked himself up off the floor and climbed back into his bed. He resisted the temptation to check on Christopher. He didn't want to wake him up and interrupt the conversation between him and his mother.

The next morning, Hunny woke Chris. Before taking Hunny outside, Chris peeked into the boy's room. He was still sleeping. After taking Hunny outside and bringing her back in again, Chris went into the kitchen and started making coffee.

"Mom visited me last night!" Christopher said a few minutes later as he ran into the kitchen while hugging Snoopy.

Chris turned from the counter and faced the smiling child. "Did you have a nice visit with your mom?"

"It was real, wasn't it? Just like you said."

"If it's the dream where I fell out of my bed while on the swing in front of Marlow House, then I would say yes."

Christopher's grin broadened. "I knew it!"

"So tell me, what did your mom have to say?" Chris led Christopher to the living room while his coffee brewed. The two sat down on the sofa.

"Mom said she loves me and is looking over me. And even if she can't visit me all the time, I have to remember she's always with me. Oh, and she told me not to be afraid to move in with my grandma. She said she's a really nice lady who just wants to love me."

"Wow, sounds like you had a pretty nice visit."

Christopher smiled up at Chris. "I'm glad Mom named me after you. I'm glad you're my friend. And you know what else?"

"What?"

"I'm not afraid anymore."

Chris wrapped one arm around Christopher's shoulders, pulled him to his side, and kissed the top of his head while saying, "I'm glad you're my friend, too." Hunny, who had followed them into the living room, leapt onto the sofa, her tail wagging, as she pushed herself between Chris and Christopher, demanding her share of attention. The three rolled off the sofa. Laughter and barking ensued.

THE GHOST AND CHRISTMAS MAGIC

RETURN TO MARLOW HOUSE IN

The Ghost and Christmas Magic

HAUNTING DANIELLE, BOOK 37

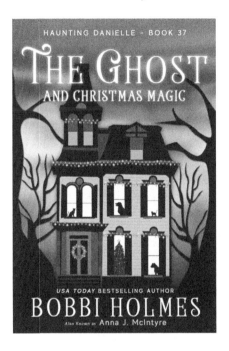

It's Christmastime in Frederickport, and the twins and Emily Ann's first Christmas. What magic is in store for the mediums of Beach Drive? It will be a Christmas they won't forget. And neither will the rest of Frederickport.

BOOKS BY ANNA J. MCINTYRE

COULSON FAMILY SAGA

COULSON'S WIFE

COULSON'S CRUCIBLE

COULSON'S LESSONS

COULSON'S SECRET

COULSON'S RECKONING

Now available in Audiobook Format

UNLOCKED ♥ HEARTS

SUNDERED HEARTS

AFTER SUNDOWN

WHILE SNOWBOUND

SUGAR RUSH

NON-FICTION BY
BOBBI ANN JOHNSON HOLMES

Havasu Palms, A Hostile Takeover

Where the Road Ends, Recipes & Remembrances

Motherhood, a book of poetry

The Story of the Christmas Village